Demon Princess

REIGN CHECK

MICHELLE ROWEN

Walker & Company
New York

First published in the United States of America in June 2010
by Walker Publishing Company, Inc., a division of Bloomsbury Publishing, Inc.
www.bloomsburyteens.com

For information about permission to reproduce selections from this book, write to
Permissions, Walker BFYR, 175 Fifth Avenue, New York, New York 10010

Library of Congress Cataloging-in-Publication Data
Rowen, Michelle.
Demon princess : reign check / by Michelle Rowen.
p.   cm.   — (Demon princess ; 2)
Summary: Sixteen-year-old Nikki is again summoned to the Underworld to appear before
the Demon Council, the king of the faerie realm enrolls at her small-town Canada high
school to experience human life, and her mother begins dating one of her teachers.
ISBN 978-0-8027-9549-6 (paperback) • ISBN 978-0-8027-2093-1 (hardcover)
[1. Demonology—Fiction. 2. Fairies—Fiction. 3. High schools—Fiction. 4. Schools—
Fiction. 5. Best friends—Fiction. 6. Friendship—Fiction. 7. Canada—Fiction.] I. Title.
II. Title: Reign check.
PZ7.R7963Dej 2010   [Fic]—dc22   2009028796

Book design by Nicole Gastonguay
Typeset by Westchester Book Composition
Printed in the U.S.A. by Worldcolor Fairfield, Pennsylvania
2 4 6 8 10 9 7 5 3 1 (paperback)
2 4 6 8 10 9 7 5 3 1 (hardcover)

This one's for my dad!
xoxo

Demon Princess

REIGN CHECK

1

Act normal, I told myself as I pushed through the front doors of Erin Heights High School. *Everything's going to be just fine.*

That thought lasted exactly thirty seconds. Then I saw Melinda, my best friend, waiting for me by our lockers. The look on her face immediately made me nervous. She looked way too excited about something.

It was eight thirty on a Monday morning and freezing cold outside. The roads were sheets of ice that only looked like roads. Everything else was blanketed in thick snow. Christmas break was still a whole week away. Obviously, in my opinion, there was nothing for Melinda to get all that excited about.

It was probably nothing. But I couldn't help being on edge. After all, I now had a secret that had to be kept from everyone, including Melinda.

A week ago, I was a normal, boring teenager.

Then I met my father for the first time and found out he was a demon. And not just any demon: he was also the king of another dimension, called the Shadowlands.

Which made me a princess—a *demon* princess.

So very *not* normal.

That was the secret I now had to keep from everybody. After all, I didn't live in the Shadowlands. I lived here, in the real world. With homework, crabby teachers, and a curfew.

Not that anyone would believe me if I actually told them the truth. It sounded all kinds of crazy, didn't it?

I approached Melinda warily. I hadn't spoken to her since Saturday morning—during a quick ten-minute phone call in which I pretended I was sick to get out of going to the mall with her. I'd been recovering from my near-death experience in the Shadowlands, when my demonic aunt Elizabeth had tried unsuccessfully to kill me and my father so she could take over the throne. That I wasn't up for a few hours of shopping the next day didn't make me a bad friend—just one who needed to sleep in as long as possible.

This morning the blonde, model-pretty Melinda looked as perfect as she always did. She was the queen of the "Royal Party," which is what a group of the most popular kids at Erin Heights were called.

"Nikki!" Melinda greeted me enthusiastically.

"Hey, what's going on? You look like you're ready to explode."

"There's a new guy starting today in our grade," she said. "Wait till you see him. He's *gorgeous*."

"New guy?" I repeated. "That's why you look like you just won the lottery? There's a new student. Big deal."

She had a serious perma-grin thing going on. "I think I'm in love."

I relaxed a bit. Happily, this seemed to be an issue that had nothing to do with me. I could deal with any new student Melinda thought was hot.

Not a problem.

I shifted my heavy backpack to my other shoulder. "I thought you only liked older guys."

She shrugged. "I'm making an exception to my over-sixteen rule. Rumor has it he's a foreign exchange student, but he doesn't have an accent."

"You've talked to him?"

"Not yet. But Larissa bumped into him and he said 'Excuse me' and asked for directions to the principal's office. She's so lucky."

I tried to refrain from rolling my eyes. Larissa and I didn't get along that well. "That's definitely one of the words *I'd* use to describe her."

Melinda worked on the combination to her locker and swung it open.

"Nice crown." I nodded at the top shelf inside.

"Thanks. I want to keep it close. It makes me happy." She ran her fingers over the shiny silver plastic headpiece tipped with snowflakes. She'd been crowned Winter Queen last Friday night at the school's formal dance. "I'm still dying to know how everything went with you and Chris. You guys left so early and I haven't seen you since."

With that, she gave me a huge grin, as if she thought Chris Sanders and I were soul mates and she was taking the credit for setting us up in the first place. Which, admittedly, she kind of did.

"There's not too much to say," I began, trying to think of a way to change the subject as quickly as possible.

Melinda looked over my shoulder. "Oh, here he comes now. Hey, Chris!"

My face froze and I slowly turned around.

Chris Sanders stopped walking, right in the middle of the hallway, and his eyes widened a little when he saw me. He was just as good-looking now as the first time I'd seen him when my mom and I moved here two months ago—all tall, broad-shouldered, and blue-eyed. I'd developed an immediate crush on him. I had been so thrilled when he'd asked me to Winter Formal, you have no idea.

Funny how things changed.

"H-hey, uh, Melinda." Chris stuttered the greeting in an awkward manner that majorly conflicted with his usual confidence. "And . . . Nikki . . . um, good to see you."

I pasted a smile on my face. "Yeah . . . you, too."

Melinda looked at us each in turn, confused.

Then again, she didn't know what happened between Chris and me when we left the dance early. He'd had too much to drink and cornered me in the back of an empty limousine. I freaked out and tapped into my demon side. We're talking black leathery wings, horns, talons, extra strength, the works. A teenage she-demon who could kick butt.

I'd . . . sort of kicked Chris's butt.

Well, he totally deserved it.

Unfortunately, he now knew my secret. I was really, really hoping that he'd convinced himself he'd imagined it all. I mean, he *was* pretty drunk.

"You're coming to my party on Saturday night, right?" Melinda asked after a long, uncomfortable moment of silence passed among us in the busy hallway.

Chris nodded stiffly. "Wouldn't miss it."

"You have to choose a name for the gift exchange. So do you, Nikki."

The frozen smile on my face was starting to cramp. "Sounds like fun."

"Yeah," Chris agreed halfheartedly. For just a moment I thought he was going to leave without another word, but instead he looked directly at me. "Nikki, I . . . I want to talk to you."

"Now?" I squeaked.

I really hated it when I squeaked.

"No, but soon. Really soon. It's important." He gave me a significant look and then walked away.

He wanted to talk to me. About what?

Like I had to ask.

I could deal with him. *Sure.* I'd just convince him that he'd seen things. Spiral-horned, black-winged, red-eyed things that threw balls of energy in self-defense. While wearing a fancy dress and high heels.

No problem.

Melinda looked perplexed by this exchange. "He's acting strange. What was that all about?"

"I have absolutely no idea," I lied.

"Aren't you two together anymore?"

"*Anymore?* Were we together in the first place?"

"You went to the dance together."

"So?" I tried to look innocent. It was difficult. "Does that mean I have to marry him or something?"

She finally smiled again. "Yeah, you have to marry him. Didn't you know that? Going to Winter Formal means you're automatically engaged."

I couldn't help but snort a little at that. "Then we're in serious trouble."

She sighed. "It's too bad. I thought you and Chris would be perfect together. Are you interested in somebody else?"

I looked at her cautiously. "Why? Are you going to play Cupid again?"

"Depends on who you pick."

"Nobody comes to mind."

Yet another secret I couldn't share with Melinda—or anyone else—was that I did have a boyfriend.

Michael didn't go to school here. He also wasn't exactly what you'd call a normal boyfriend. In fact, he was about as nonnormal as you could get. He wasn't a human. Or a demon. He was a Shadow, and he lived in my father's castle. Shadows were enslaved to demons and had been practically forever. It was ridiculous and outdated. From what I'd seen, the Shadowlands were seriously like something out of Medieval Times dinner theater. Only no jousting. Or turkey drumsticks.

Demons and Shadows were forbidden to be together as anything other than master and servant. *Also* ridiculous.

And get this: my father had originally assigned Michael to be *my* personal servant. But I didn't think of him that way at all. Plus, since Michael put his life on the line to help defeat my aunt late last Friday night, I'd made my father promise Michael wouldn't have to be a servant anymore. That was the last time I'd seen either of them.

It was all complicated enough to give me a big fat headache when I thought about it for too long. I rubbed my temples and finally opened my locker so I could unload my backpack and grab my books for the first class of the day—biology. I had it on fairly good authority that today was dissect-a-frog day. I was looking forward to that disgusting prospect only a little more than my now-inevitable conversation with Chris.

"So your party's definitely on, huh?" I asked, trying to concentrate on something else.

Melinda nodded as she stuck her head back into her locker. "Saturday night starting at eight." She hesitated. "Chris is coming. Is that going to be a problem?"

"A problem? No, of course not."

Sure it was.

I was finding it difficult not to obsess about Chris. He was going to be a big problem. Would he tell anyone what he'd seen? Would anyone believe him? And if so, what would happen then? Would I be able to deal with it?

Yes, of course I would. I'd battled my evil aunt, who wanted to kill me. I could deal with Chris knowing my secret.

Still, my head began to throb even worse.

I knew I had to keep on top of my emotions. Since I was a Darkling—half human, half demon—all this power had built up inside me since I turned sixteen, just waiting for a chance to burst free. And when your inner demon wants to burst free, it's not a pretty sight. Trust me on that.

I looked at the little mirror on my locker door and gasped.

Thanks to my stress about Chris, my eyes had turned red—full red with black slits for pupils, like a cat's eyes. And they were glowing.

No. Not here.

I couldn't change into my Darkling form right here in the middle of the school hallway. I suddenly pictured screaming, panicked students running in every direction trying to escape from me. Yelling and pointing at the monster with the big leather wings wearing jeans and a hot pink V-neck sweater.

Relax, I told myself. *Everything's okay.*

"Can you come over earlier on Saturday and help me set things up?" Melinda's voice echoed inside her locker.

"Yeah . . . sure. No biggie." I squeezed my eyes shut and attempted to breathe normally. I tried to think happy thoughts.

I thought about Michael.

Dark hair, green eyes, a rarely seen but amazing smile.

Michael's lips. Michael *kissing me.*

Okay, I started to feel calmer. Happier.

I opened my eyes and looked in the mirror again, relieved to see they had returned to their usual hazel color. I pulled my long blonde hair back and tucked it behind my ears. After quickly applying a little lip gloss from the zippered pocket of my backpack, I was all ready to go to my first class.

I could do this. Everything was fine.

I repeated it over and over in my head.

Everything is going to be fine. Chris is my only problem this week, and I can totally deal with him.

"I guess I'll see you at lunch," I said.

"Oh my God." Melinda grabbed my arm. "Nikki, there he is."

"There who is?"

"The exchange student." She bit her bottom lip, her attention focused behind me. "So hot. I could die."

I turned to look and my mouth dropped open.

Melinda was right—the new guy *was* really good-looking.

He was tall and cute with short chestnut brown hair. He had dark brown eyes. I wasn't close enough to see the color at the moment, but I knew they were dark brown.

How did I know? Because I'd already met the new student Melinda was excited about.

His name was Rhys. He was sixteen years old. But like me, he wasn't all that normal.

Believe it or not, he was the king of the faery realm. The forest that bordered the Shadowlands led directly into his kingdom.

And he knew I was a demon princess.

Had I thought Chris was my only problem at the moment? Um . . . wrong. So very wrong.

The last time I'd seen Rhys, only a couple of days ago, he'd mentioned a fascination with visiting the human world some-day. He'd never been here before. He brought it up during the same conversation when he'd threatened to kill me with a very sharp sword.

Out of the corner of my eye I could see Melinda's smile fade. "That's weird. Do you already know him, Nikki?"

"I . . . uh . . ." I clamped my mouth shut before I said

anything that might get me into more trouble than I was already in.

Despite his death threat the last time we'd been face-to-face, the sixteen-year-old faery king was currently waving at me.

"Weird" didn't even begin to cover it.

2

"Never seen him before in my life," I said to Melinda after I found my voice. "Maybe he's waving at *you*."

"Oooh, you think?" Surprisingly, this hadn't occurred to her.

"Absolutely." My throat felt dry.

"We'll definitely talk later," she said with a grin. "Gotta go. See you at lunch."

"Okay."

I stood there in place as Melinda walked away, books held tightly in her arms. I tried to breathe normally.

I'd be brave. I'd march right up to him and demand to know what he was doing here. I wouldn't let the faery king intimidate me.

But when I'd summoned up enough courage and turned to look at him again, Rhys was gone.

Maybe I'd been wrong. Maybe it wasn't even Rhys. After all, I'd last seen him in a dimly lit forest, where he'd accused me of being evil. But just because I was half demon didn't mean I was evil. At the time, he hadn't seemed to understand that.

Thus the unfriendly sword pointing and the whole "get out of my forest" thing.

If it was Rhys, why was he here? Maybe he was just sightseeing or something. Half an hour of wandering around in the middle of December . . .

Of all the places in the human world he could have picked to visit, he chose snow-covered Erin Heights?

Yeah. That made sense.

I exhaled shakily and, turning left to head to my biology class, came face-to-face with Rhys.

"Hi there," he said. "Remember me?"

My mouth gaped open. "You . . ."

He ran a hand through his cropped brown hair as he waited for me to say something else. When I didn't, he continued. "We met in my forest. You were harassing a unicorn."

"I . . . I remember. And I . . . I wasn't harassing it." My body tensed, but I stayed as still as possible as I waited to see what he'd do next.

"If you say so."

"What are you doing here?" I managed.

He shrugged. "I'm on vacation."

"Right."

"You don't seem that happy to see me."

"Last time I saw you, you tried to kill me." My voice was so low that even I could barely hear it.

Rhys raised an eyebrow at me. "I didn't *try* to do anything. I simply gave you a warning that you were trespassing on my territory. And you *were*."

"And now you're trespassing on *my* territory. Don't tell me you're on vacation because I don't think anyone in his right mind would want to come here in the middle of the winter."

"You don't know me very well, then."

"I need to get to class." I walked away from him without saying another word. It only took a moment before I realized he was following me. I tried to ignore him, not knowing any other way of dealing with him at the moment.

Rhys trailed after me into my biology classroom. I glared at him over my shoulder and saw him hand Mr. Crane a piece of paper. The teacher adjusted his oddly fashionable glasses (fashionable for a teacher, anyway). Some girls had a major crush on him. I wasn't one of those girls.

He nodded. "Yes, Rhys Oberon. I was told to expect a new student today. Welcome to Erin Heights."

"Thank you. I wonder if it would be possible to sit with Nikki. She's a new friend of mine."

"I'm sure that can be arranged." Mr. Crane looked at me. "Nikki, thanks for making Rhys feel so welcome on his first day here. Of course, I'm not surprised. It wasn't that long ago that you were the newcomer, right?"

"I . . ." How was I supposed to react? Words were failing me along with the higher-functioning parts of my brain.

But then Mr. Crane was distracted by several other students asking him questions as a steady flow of kids entered the room.

My gaze narrowed and moved to the faery king. "What do you think you're doing here?"

He shrugged. "Learning about high school biology. It's on my schedule. After this I have algebra. Sounds fascinating."

I went to my desk and sat down with a thud.

Rhys sat down to my left. No sharp sword was currently visible, which was vaguely encouraging. Then again, it was only quarter to nine. He had until ten o'clock if he wanted to kill me during this class.

I clenched my right fist on my lap under the desk, feeling a surge of power flow into it. I wasn't helpless. I would certainly be more than able to protect myself if I had to. But still, my heart was beating three times faster than normal.

"That desk belongs to someone else," I informed him.

"The student who normally sits here has left for an all-expenses-paid vacation to Hawaii with his parents. They won it on the radio over the weekend. What amazing luck, don't you think?"

From what I could see, the class had silent but mixed reactions to the new student now seated next to me. Half weren't paying any attention at all. The other half looked at the young faery king with varying degrees of curiosity. They had no idea who he really was—or *what* he was.

"Okay, everyone. We're going to start in just a moment," Mr. Crane announced. "I'll be around to hand out your samples."

I looked at Rhys. "You need to go back to your home."

He smiled. "I thought the teacher wanted you to make me feel welcome, Princess Nikki."

"Don't call me that here." My eyes darted around the classroom.

"Don't worry. No one can hear what we're saying right now."

"They can't?"

"No. I've used magic to shield our conversation." He looked incredibly sure of himself. Cocky, actually.

Now that he mentioned it, I suddenly realized I could barely hear anyone else around us. The chatter in the classroom had become muffled and specific words indiscernible.

I swallowed hard. "You've put us into an invisible magic muffle bubble?"

"That's one way to put it. Thought we could use a little privacy in the center of this human chaos."

My palms were sweating, but I fought to remain calm. "I'll ask you again, Rhys. Why are you here?"

He watched me closely for a long, uncomfortable moment. "It's my job to protect my kingdom from harm and investigate anything that might hurt us now or in the future. So I'm here to investigate you."

"Investigate *me*? I'm not planning on hurting your . . . your *kingdom*." Even knowing he was magically shielding this conversation, I nervously glanced around at the class of oblivious students.

"But how do I know that for sure?"

"Because I'm telling you." I gritted my teeth and glared at him.

The faery king was wearing black jeans and a green button-down shirt—both looked brand-new. The last time I'd seen Rhys, he had pointed tips to his ears and graceful, iridescent wings.

At the moment, however, there were no tips and no wings. He looked entirely human.

As if he'd read my mind, or at least had followed the direction of my eyes, he touched his ears. "It's called a glamour. Much like I'm able to hide our conversation right now, I can hide certain things about myself I don't want just anyone to see.

That way I can more easily fit in around here. It's quite simple, really."

"Magic," I said quietly. Even after everything I'd seen with my own two eyes, it was still hard to accept.

"Yes. And you . . ." He took a moment to examine me in greater detail. "I believe you literally shift form rather than using a glamour, yes? I've heard of demons changing forms before. It's"—he made a sour face—"disturbing."

"You need to leave right now." My head had started to throb with frustration and growing anger, and that wasn't a good sign. I had to remain calm or my own, very *non*-graceful, *non*-faery black wings might pop out of my back. I was quite sure their presence would disturb more than just Rhys.

He leaned back in his chair. "Your unwelcoming attitude only helps to confirm my suspicions about you."

"What suspicions?"

"That despite your innocent appearance, you're actually a dangerous and deadly creature of darkness. Just as I suspected."

That earned him a full-on glare. It sounded like he was being flippant, yet the expression on his face was anything but.

"I'm not dangerous *or* deadly," I said. "Or particularly dark."

His eyes narrowed. "Well, that's what I'm here to find out."

"At my high school using a glamour."

"Consider me undercover."

"And there's nothing I can do about this?"

"Less than nothing." He was close enough now that I saw his brown eyes also contained gold flecks.

"And what happens if you mistakenly decide you're right about me?" I had to ask.

All feigned friendliness vanished from his expression. "Then I'll do what I have to in order to protect my kingdom."

A shiver raced down my spine as I got another flashback of that sharp sword nearly touching my throat. If he decided he was right—that I was evil—was he seriously going to kill me?

I really didn't like this guy.

While I tried to figure out what to say next to make him leave me alone, I noticed Mr. Crane standing directly in front of us. He was saying something, but I couldn't hear what it was for a moment.

". . . it's like you're not even listening to me." His words suddenly became loud and clear. "I don't want to have to repeat myself again."

"What?" I said. "Sorry, uh, I was focusing on something else."

"Yes, I see that, Nikki." Mr. Crane looked at me sternly. "But you'll have lots of time to get to know Rhys better *after* class. Okay?"

He thought I was so taken with the new student that I was oblivious to everything else going on. How embarrassing.

A small frog, smelling of formaldehyde, was plunked down between us. Belly up. Greenish gray, dead and slimy.

"Rhys, I'm not sure if they already covered this in your previous school," Mr. Crane said. "Let me know if you have any questions. Otherwise, I'm sure Nikki will be happy to help you out." He then moved on to the next pairing.

"Happy" definitely wouldn't be the word I'd use when it came to the undercover faery king.

Deadly, dark, and dangerous. That's really what he thought I was? How could I prove I wasn't anything like that?

I'd been told there hadn't been any other human-demon offspring in a millennium. That's a thousand years Darkling free until I was born. It was forbidden for humans and demons to have children together due to the whole "Darklings are dangerous" thing. Also, it was very rare for a demon even to be allowed to enter the human world, to prevent their meeting any humans to mate with.

Obviously my father had totally broken the rules to be with my mom. It was kind of romantic, really. My mother, on the other hand, never knew he was a demon. She knew him only as a college student who'd abandoned her when she was eighteen, alone, and pregnant, and I'd promised my father I wouldn't tell her any differently. For now, at least.

I forced myself to look at Rhys again, surprised to see that his face had paled, his jaw had tightened, and his attention had now shifted from me to the frog.

"The frog is dead," he stated.

"You're so observant." I picked up the X-Acto knife—better to have control of a potential weapon than to let him grab it first—and realized my sweaty hand made it difficult to get a good grip.

His lips thinned. "It's *barbaric*."

"It's fairly disgusting, sure, but we have to do it."

"Why?"

I shrugged. "We just have to."

Anger flickered in his eyes and the gold flecks there appeared to swirl. "You agree with this disgusting human practice of murdering innocent animals for meaningless experiments?"

Okay. Overreacting much? "If I don't, I'll get a failing grade on this assignment. If it grosses you out, I think you can do a simulated dissection on the computer instead."

Without another word, he brought his hand down on top of the frog.

I cringed. "What are you doing?"

"Be quiet, I'm concentrating." His hand began to glow with a strange, dim light and his brows drew together. After a moment, he shook his head. "It's too late. I can't save it."

Before I could say anything else, he swore under his breath, got up from the desk so quickly that his chair skittered backward, and stormed out of the room, casting a very dark look at the teacher.

"Nikki," Mr. Crane said when Rhys was gone. "What happened? Where's he going?"

"He, um, wasn't feeling very well."

Mr. Crane nodded with understanding. "Not uncommon during this particular experiment, I've found." He watched as a girl, covering her mouth with her hand and gagging, ran out of the room next.

I felt off balance. First from having to talk to Rhys at all, and second from his furious reaction to the dead frog (may it rest in peace). And what had he meant by saying it was too late to save it? Was he trying to bring it back to life? Could he really do something like that?

Apparently not, since the frog was still majorly dead on arrival.

I didn't know all that much about faeries, other than they were territorial and dangerous and had wings and pointy ears that could be covered up with a glamour.

Now I knew they might be card-carrying members of PETA.

At least Rhys was gone. But I didn't feel relieved. Not yet.

"Check it out," a guy named Pete two rows up from me said. "I totally slayed the slimy beast."

He'd cut the frog's head off and had mounted it on the top of his knife like a frog lollipop.

The sight of it made my oatmeal breakfast suddenly decide it wanted to make a reappearance. I clamped my hand over my mouth before I hurled right then and there. Thankfully, I didn't. But it was hard to breathe. My eyes burned and my back and temples itched. Worried equally about vomiting in public and turning into a horned, winged Darkling, I got up from the desk, grabbed my things, and ran out of the classroom.

"There goes another one," Mr. Crane said, and sighed to himself as I whizzed past him.

Luckily, he didn't try to stop me.

3

After a few deep breaths in the hall outside the classroom, I began to feel better. I didn't see the girl who'd run out, but I did see Rhys sitting halfway down the hallway with his back against the lockers.

I'd hoped he'd taken the dead frog as a bad omen and gone back to the faery realm.

My first instinct was to return to class, but instead I marched over to where Rhys sat. He glared up at me, anger at my biology class's mistreatment of innocent amphibians still apparent in his expression. I also saw something else there, something a bit more raw. Sadness and . . . *grief*? That's what it was. But why would a dead frog affect him so much?

It surprised me a little and I lost some of my determination.

"You need to go back home," I said simply.

He got to his feet and I took an automatic step back from him, suddenly reminded how tall he was. Before I'd met him, I'd always thought faeries were small and delicate. And, well, *not real*. But Rhys was very real. And not small or the least bit delicate.

"I'm not going anywhere until I accomplish what I came

here to do," he said firmly, despite that strange grief-filled look in his eyes.

It wasn't just the frog. Something else must have happened to Rhys. Something bad.

"And what was that again?" I asked, then held up my hand. "Oh, right. The 'Is Nikki Donovan a threat to faery life' thing. Well, trust me, I don't have any deep, dark secrets." I paused. "Except for the one you already know, of course."

He studied me for a moment. "Have you told anyone else what you are?"

"No."

Chris didn't count. I hadn't technically *told* him anything. He'd seen it with his own two eyes.

"So you think you can still fit in here"—he glanced around—"pretending you're a normal sixteen-year-old girl?"

"That is the general idea. And since I *was* a normal sixteen-year-old girl until last week, I'm surprisingly good at it. Feels very natural, actually."

Confusion now clouded his expression. "But . . . why would you want to do that? You're royalty—a *princess*—and yet you'd choose a life like this?"

"Didn't realize I had a choice. Besides, this is what I know, and believe me, I'm perfectly fine not living in a castle all the time. It's not like I'm just going to give it up for a tiara and . . . uh, whatever else demon princesses get."

Still he looked confused. "Aren't you afraid?"

"Of you?"

"No, not me. Of . . . of the prophecy."

Hadn't expected that answer. "What prophecy?"

"The one about you."

I blinked at him. "What are you talking about?"

That earned me a skeptical look. "You seriously don't know about it?"

"There's a prophecy about *me*?"

He seemed genuinely shocked I didn't know. "Yes. It's what prompted me to come here in the first place. What made me believe there was no time to waste."

The only thing I knew about prophecies was that they were predictions of the future. I had my very own prophecy? That was a surprise. I mean, I didn't even have a blog or a Facebook page, although I was getting to those eventually.

"What does it say?" I asked, unable to help my curiosity.

"All I know is it's a new one. And it's raised some immediate and considerable . . . *concerns*. Otherwise the news of it never would have reached as far as my kingdom as quickly as it did."

A strange shiver went down my arms. "What do you mean, it's raised some concerns?"

"That you're the first Darkling in a thousand years has already put everyone on edge," he said. "Enough for me personally to come and find out as much as I can about you. The prophecy only adds fuel to the fire."

"I can't believe this."

He seemed unsure what to make of my reaction. I could see it wasn't what he'd been expecting. Maybe he wanted me to deny it or get angry?

He turned away from me. "Perhaps I shouldn't have said anything."

I grabbed his arm. "No, I need to know everything you know about this, Rhys. You're making it sound serious."

"I don't know any more about it. My advisers learned of it only the day before yesterday from a source in the Underworld, which means it is spreading throughout the rest of the dark worlds as we speak. Not only the news that the prophecy exists, but that the rumors of King Desmond having a half-human daughter are true."

A wave of anxiety went through me, and I released my tight hold on his arm. I was about to ask him a dozen more questions but stopped at the pale look on his face. He watched me warily, as if waiting for my scary demon-girl reaction.

"Are you afraid of me?" I asked. It sounded stupid as soon as I said it.

He hesitated. "No. Of course not."

My eyes widened. "You're lying. You're afraid!"

"I'm a king," he said, scowling at me. "I'm not afraid of anything."

"Yeah, you're a king, but you're also only sixteen. I'm sixteen and I'm afraid of lots of things. I have a list."

"We're different."

"You're right about that." I knew he wasn't going to help me. I hissed out a frustrated sigh. "Do me a favor and don't follow me, okay?"

Without waiting for a reply, I went into the nearest bathroom and splashed cold water on my face, staring at my reflection and trying not to think. Unfortunately, not thinking wasn't something I could control that easily.

My face was now flushed, which brought out the freckles

on my nose that I hated. I pushed my hair back behind my ears and rubbed my lips together. At the moment, I looked fairly normal, all things considered.

Maybe Rhys had only been trying to get a reaction out of me—trying to get me to sprout my wings so I wouldn't be able to show my face in school ever again. Getting all emotional was one way to bring out my demon side. Then I'd be just as much of a freak as he was.

I mean, who had to be a king when they were so young? I'd almost become queen of the Shadowlands—even now, if my father died, I'd automatically have to take the throne—but it wasn't something I'd ever choose for myself. And why would Rhys, as king, leave his world to come to mine just so he could poke at me like I was his own personal dead frog to dissect? He could have simply sent one of his advisers in his place if he was oh-so-concerned.

If there was a prophecy about me, my father would have told me about it by now, right?

And it's not like I wasn't safe. The Shadowlands were surrounded by a magic-infused barrier, controlled by my father, that protected the faery and human worlds from the demon ones—the "dark worlds," as they were called. Since he was king, my father couldn't leave the castle because maintaining the barrier was his prime responsibility.

I closed my eyes and concentrated.

Michael, where are you? I need to see you.

Since Michael had been my officially designated "servant" the first time I'd met him, we had this telepathy thing between us. However, it didn't work long distance. I had no idea where he was at the moment. Probably at my father's castle. In other words, nowhere close to me.

I desperately wanted to see him again. He'd know what to do. Also, I just really missed him. He was someone who accepted me exactly as I was—horns and all—and I felt totally safe when I was with him, unlike how I felt around Rhys.

I stayed in the bathroom trying in vain to contact Michael for so long that, by the time I emerged, biology was over. Of all my teachers, Mr. Crane was probably the coolest and most easygoing, so I hoped I could make up the assignment another day.

After scanning the hall for Rhys, who was nowhere to be seen, I went to my other morning classes and formulated my plan for how to deal with the faery king. Even though he'd tried to hide it, I'd definitely seen a flicker of fear in his eyes. He didn't know what I was capable of. I'd use that to my advantage and scare him back to Faeryville. It was worth a try.

It felt like forever before lunch arrived, but when it did I entered the cafeteria, grabbed a sandwich and a piece of fruit— an apple a day keeps nasty prophecies away—and started walking over to the center table that the Royal Party called home.

Despite my recent friendship with Melinda, I was still considered an outsider. At least, that's the impression I always got from Melinda's, well . . . *ladies-in-waiting* was probably the best way to describe the brunette Larissa and redheaded Brittany. The three of them had been closer friends before I'd arrived. Now Melinda either spent time hanging out with me or going to her after-school dance lessons—her latest obsession.

I didn't get the usual fiery glares from them when I

approached the table. They were too busy gawking at the cute guy seated next to Melinda.

It was Rhys, of course. Melinda had obviously swooped in at her first opportunity and snagged him. For a moment I tried to look at him the way she probably did. He was inarguably good-looking and had an effortless confidence about him that helped him stand out in a crowd. However, the moment his gaze shifted to me I could see the gold flecks in his eyes appear to swirl, as if I bothered him on some deeper level he couldn't hide—at least not from me.

"There she is," Rhys said with a nod in my direction.

I tensed. Had he been talking about me? And saying what?

Instead of shock or horror at whatever they'd been discussing regarding yours truly, Melinda looked at me with confusion in her blue eyes.

"I thought you said you didn't know Rhys," she said.

Caught in a lie. Not good.

I cleared my throat. "I'd forgotten that we do kind of know each other already."

"Kind of?"

Rhys smiled, but it looked forced. "It's a family thing."

"You two are related?" Brittany asked with interest, twisting a long piece of red hair around her manicured index finger. "That's so cool!"

Rhys let out a genuine laugh at that, and his face shifted into something much more pleasant. It wasn't hard to see why Melinda thought he was megahot. "Not even slightly related, trust me. No, our families . . . well, they've never really seen eye to eye on most things, have they, Nikki?"

I didn't know much about faery-demon relations, but I imagined they weren't particularly pleasant. After all, faeries wouldn't need the Shadowlands' barrier to protect them from the Underworld and Hell if everyone was good buddies with each other, would they?

But my father . . . well, he was a demon, but he also ruled the Shadowlands, which kept faeries and humans safe from the *bad* demons. And yet, Rhys wanted to lump him in with the others. Figures.

"You could say that," I replied stiffly.

Rhys hadn't taken his eyes off me for a moment since I'd approached the table. "No offense intended, of course, but I'd even go so far as to call Nikki's family . . . *demonic*."

He wasn't pulling any punches today, was he?

Melinda's eyebrows raised. "Wow, that's harsh. I've met Nikki's mom. She's really nice."

"Just my opinion, I guess." Rhys shrugged.

Not sure why it hadn't occurred to me yet, but I suddenly realized, crystal clear, that Rhys didn't just dislike me, he completely hated my guts. Because I was half demon? Or just because I was *me*?

I cleared my throat, feeling the now-familiar irritation toward him bubbling up to replace my uncertainty. I wanted to hate him in return. It really was the least I could do.

He glowered at me, his irises swirling their strange mix of molten gold and chocolate brown. Was I the only one who could see that very inhuman trait of his? Melinda was looking right at him and wasn't reacting as if anything was strange, so it had to be true. Maybe he didn't currently have wings and pointy ears, but he was so not human that I could sense it from ten feet away.

Stress began to mix with frustration as we stared at each other and I clutched my sandwich a bit too tightly, my nails popping right through the plastic container. I looked down to see that my regularly short polished fingernails had turned long, red, and razor sharp. I dropped the sandwich in surprise and whipped my hands behind me to hide them.

Relax, Nikki, I told myself. *Right now.*

I really didn't like the way Rhys was affecting me. I had everything totally under control until he arrived unannounced and messed up my concentration.

"Nikki . . . ," Melinda began, uneasily eyeing both me and Rhys in turn. Luckily, I didn't think she noticed my unwelcome demon talons make their first high school appearance. "Why don't you sit down and have some lunch with us?"

I cleared my throat. "I . . . I have to do something first. I'll be right back."

Sidestepping my fallen egg-salad sandwich, I retreated from the cafeteria to the hallway, cursing myself. I was the one who was supposed to scare *him* away, not the other way around. So much for me being all in charge of the situation. I couldn't even stay in charge of myself for more than five minutes.

I touched the bracelet my father had given me. It was a simple gold chain with a clear crystal charm in the shape of a teardrop. He'd told me it was an actual dragon's tear.

Yes, a fire-breathing dragon. They existed—and, apparently, were quite emotional.

It was supposed to help keep my so-called Darkling powers

under control. Since it didn't come with an instruction manual, I kept my hand on it and just tried to concentrate really hard.

Slowly, with a small twinge of pain, my fingernails receded to their short pink-polished versions. I let out a shaky sigh of relief.

"Hey, Nikki, everything okay with you?" A voice made me turn around. Larissa leaned against the wall by the cafeteria entrance, her long dark hair swept over her right shoulder.

I was surprised to see her. Out of the entire Royal Party, she'd be the last person I'd expect to check on my well-being.

"I'm fine," I said.

She thrust her chin in the general direction of the lunch table past the closed doors. "I think I know what happened in there."

That was unlikely. I hoped. "Oh yeah?"

"You and Rhys used to date, right? Maybe at your last school?"

The thought was almost humorous. "No, we didn't. Me and Rhys, we were . . . uh, acquaintances only. And it was so long ago that I'd practically forgotten about him."

Her eyebrows went up. "How could you forget a hot guy like him?"

I shrugged. "I guess his hotness faded substantially in my memory. I barely remember him, actually."

She didn't look convinced. She slowly approached me and, without speaking, scanned me from top to bottom.

"What?" I prompted after a moment, concerned that some other demon appendage had appeared without my knowledge.

"Nothing." She pressed her lips together. "I'm just trying to figure it out, that's all."

"Figure what out?"

"Why you feel like you have to lie so much."

This time *my* eyebrows went up in surprise. "Excuse me?"

"It's the only way you could have wedged yourself into Melinda's life so quickly and easily—by lying about everything. You think you can have whatever you want, whenever you want. But I've waited a long time for her and me to be best friends, and just when we were getting closer, *boom*, you show up and ruin everything."

I thought I could have anything I wanted? She was so wrong.

"You and Melinda *are* friends," I reasoned.

"It's not the same as *best* friends." She shook her head. "I can't figure out why she even wants to be your friend. I mean, you're a total nobody."

"Luckily, I don't care what you think." Even though I said it, my throat felt thick and my eyes now stung with gathering tears. It was one thing to get a generic evil glare from Larissa, but another thing to hear exactly how she felt about me. Sharp words cut deep. I wasn't invulnerable.

"Now Melinda's always with you. Or she's going to her stupid ballet lessons. She never has time to hang out with me."

I wasn't going to let her see she had any effect on me. "Sorry to hear you're so needy, Larissa. But that doesn't have anything to do with me."

"And now with this Rhys thing—"

"What Rhys thing?"

"Melinda really likes him. I've never seen her like any guy so fast. You told her that you didn't know him, but you lied. You *do* know him. It's obvious you want to steal him away."

Oh, this was just getting better and better. But now I was more angry than hurt. "You don't know how wrong you are. And frankly, I think Melinda could do a lot better."

Yeah. *Human* would be good for starters. No faery kings need apply.

I wasn't winning Larissa over. She thought I was a big liar who believed I could get whatever I wanted. Then again, she wasn't the smartest girl at school.

Her expression soured further. "Good thing Melinda has me around to watch her back. It won't be long before she realizes once and for all who her true friends are and who's just trying to weasel themselves in."

"Weasel?" I repeated.

"Yeah. *Weasel.*" Her eyes narrowed into little eye-shadowed slits.

So did mine. I tried very hard not to let the annoyance prickling at my skin spread any further. "Gee, Larissa. I think you have a way higher opinion of yourself than you should have. Normally your opinion would mean nothing to me, but since I'm having a bad day already, it means *less* than nothing. If that's even mathematically possible."

"You don't fit in here and you never will. It's only a matter of time before Melinda figures that out."

Okay, that one stung. I winced, as if she'd slapped me.

"Why don't you go back to Melinda and keep kissing her

butt?" I suggested. "Maybe you can date her next ex-boyfriend if you're lucky."

"Go to hell."

"I'll send you a postcard." Irritation swelled inside me, pushing through my hurt feelings. "You said that I always get what I want. You know what I want right now?"

"What?"

"For you to get out of my face."

"Gladly." She turned and went back into the cafeteria.

I was now seething—my anger had built gradually until it was nearly overwhelming. My temples started to itch, a warning that my demon horns were planning to appear. That would be bad. It would be harder to hide a set of horns at the moment than a handful of talons.

"I'm seriously going to lose it," I said to myself. "Right here, right now."

::No, you're not. Don't let her get to you, Princess. Just breathe.::

Yeah, *breathe*. I'd breathe fire out of my nostrils, just like the dragon who sobbed out the tear on my bracelet. And then I'd sneeze all over Larissa and her stupid opinions about friendship and loyalty and Rhys and . . .

Wait a minute. I stopped thinking about revenge for a moment.

Did I just hear what I thought I did?

A breath caught in my throat.

I scanned the hallway until I stopped on a tall, very good-looking guy watching me intently while leaning against the lockers about twenty feet away. He had dark hair that was a bit too long and shaggy—it nearly touched his shoulders and partially covered his vivid green eyes and high cheekbones. A dark blue hooded sweatshirt and baggy faded jeans hid the fact he had a leanly muscled athletic frame that any jock at school would envy.

Michael.

My heart leaped. All anger forgotten, including any potential fire-breathing directed at stupid girls named Larissa, I made a beeline toward him.

I couldn't believe it had been less than a week since Michael had first been sent here with the instruction to bring me back to the Shadowlands so I could meet my father for the first time. To say I'd resisted everything Michael told me would be putting it mildly. At the time, how was I supposed to know he was telling the truth?

Yeah, Michael and I had started off a bit shakily, but he'd more than made up for it since then.

We weren't alone in the hallway. Other students moved past us steadily, heading in and out of the swinging cafeteria doors, which was the only factor that made me refrain from throwing my arms around him. I couldn't remember being happier to see anyone before. I couldn't keep the grin off my face, my troubles with Larissa (almost) forgotten.

"You were fighting with your friend." Michael's voice was very serious and filled with concern.

"I wouldn't exactly call her my friend. And it was more of a loud disagreement than an outright fight."

He glanced warily toward the cafeteria doors. "If she'd made any attempt to harm you, I would have intervened immediately. If she had any idea who you are—"

"But she doesn't and she won't," I said firmly. "Don't worry. I can handle Larissa."

He still looked troubled. "As long as you're okay."

"I'm fine now." I decided I didn't care about the potential audience of students. I went up on my tiptoes and kissed him quickly.

"Princess, you really shouldn't do that here," he said cautiously, but the glimmer of a smile was struggling to appear on his lips.

I glanced around to see a passing guy looking at us strangely and my face reddened. Michael called me "Princess." I'd asked him repeatedly to call me Nikki, but he almost always refused, instead insisting on addressing me by my official royal title.

Grabbing Michael's hand, I led him over to the doors at the end of the hallway, where we could talk more privately.

"You think we shouldn't kiss in public?" I asked.

"Yes." He swallowed and looked down at the ground. Then he raised his eyes and met mine. "I mean, don't get me wrong. It's fine with me. More than fine, really. But if anyone sees us . . ."

Right. The stupid, pointless rule that forbade demons and Shadows from openly dating. "Forget about that. I honestly don't care what anyone thinks. I thought you already knew that."

"I do." His hands were now clasped behind his back, his amulet, a bright green stone that looked like a large flat emerald, visible on top of his zippered sweatshirt.

Because Michael was a Shadow, the magic amulet the exact color as his eyes helped him keep a solid form. Without it, he became as disembodied as a ghost—or an actual *shadow*—one that would quickly fade away to nothingness. A common punishment for Shadows who refused to do what they were told was to temporarily (or worse, *permanently*) take away their amulet.

Like I said before, Michael wasn't exactly a normal boyfriend. Also, if I wasn't mistaken, he was blushing a little bit from me kissing him in front of everybody. It only made me want to do it again as soon as possible.

"What are you doing here?" I asked.

"Your father ordered me to bring you to the Shadowlands immediately. He wants to talk to you."

I frowned at that. "He *ordered* you?"

"Yes."

I would have preferred he use the word "asked" or "requested," which would have fit much better with Michael's new nonservant status. Unless . . .

"Hold on," I said. "You spoke to me telepathically a moment ago. Can we still communicate that way even though you're officially not my servant anymore?"

He met my eyes. "About that . . ."

I shook my head, a feeling of dread twisting in my stomach. "Don't even try to tell me nothing's changed. My father promised me."

"Princess, please. It doesn't matter."

"I can't believe this. Why would he lie to me?"

"King Desmond didn't lie. I do believe he meant what he said at the time he said it."

"So you're still a . . . a *servant*?"

"I am what I've always been." He held up a hand when I was about to say something, I didn't know what. He must have seen the outrage on my face. "Please, don't overreact, Princess. I didn't expect things to change overnight. In fact, it's very possible things will never change."

Quite honestly, ever since my father had made the promise, I hadn't given it much more thought. I'd just assumed things would change immediately.

"Why aren't you fighting this?" I asked. "Why do you seem to accept this so easily?"

"Because it's not the time. Your father has been very good to me over the years. You really have no idea."

"How? By ordering you around?"

"He allows me to come here through the gateway and see you. Otherwise I wouldn't be able to at all."

"Allows you," I repeated, disliking the sound of those two words used together.

"Shadows are servants to demonkind. That's how it's always been. He told you what you wanted to hear because he loves you and wants you to be happy. Please, Princess, don't make a big deal over this."

"I don't know if that's possible. It is a big deal."

He hesitated. "Does it change anything . . . between *us*?"

"No, of course not."

"Good." He nodded, and that smile I found so completely devastating (in a good way, that is) touched his very kissable lips again.

I took his hand in mine. His skin was warm but coarse, as if he did manual labor. When we first met, Michael had kept his servant status from me because he'd been under the impression that I would think him less worthy. He'd been dead wrong. I didn't care who he was—rich, poor, a servant, a Shadow, or whatever.

I set aside my annoyance for now, but my father and I would be having a talk about this issue very soon. "You said my father wants to see me? About what?"

He shook his head. "I don't know."

"Didn't he tell you?"

"No. He only said it was important that you come back with me immediately."

"I wonder if it has to do with the prophecy," I mused.

His dark brows drew together. "What prophecy?"

"Apparently there's some prophecy about me that was just uncovered." I shivered, thinking about it.

"Who would have told you something like that?"

I glanced over my shoulder and a distinct feeling of unease flowed through me when I saw the bearer of my prophecy news exit the cafeteria and scan his surroundings before spotting me.

"I really wish he'd just go away," I grumbled, and let go of Michael's hand.

"Who?"

I gestured in the direction of the approaching faery king. "Him."

"Nikki," Rhys said drily as he reached us, his eyes flicking to Michael for a moment. "There you are. Trying to avoid me doesn't change anything, you know."

"Who are you?" Michael asked.

Rhys stared at him. "Who are *you*?"

"You didn't answer my question."

I cleared my throat. "Rhys is the king of the faery realm."

It took a moment for this to register with Michael. "What are you doing in the human world?"

Rhys pursed his lips. "I thought that was going to be our little secret, Nikki. Or maybe you want me to spread your little secret around as well?"

I glared at him. "Michael lives in my father's castle. He's not a student here." I looked at Michael. "Rhys came here to investigate me. Thinks I'm some sort of threat to his fellow iridescent-winged friends. He's the one who told me there's a prophecy."

Michael took this information in, his expression steadily darkening. "Did he threaten you, Princess?" he asked quietly.

The implied threat in biology was still at the forefront of my mind. "A little. But I—"

Before I could say another word, Michael grabbed Rhys by the front of his shirt and slammed him against a nearby locker.

"Leave the princess alone," Michael growled, sounding as dangerous and protective as I'd ever heard him. "Or you'll have to deal with me."

My eyes widened. "Michael . . ."

"Let go of me," Rhys snapped.

It took several seconds, but Michael finally released him. He held his arm out to block me from Rhys, who was leisurely brushing off the front of his shirt.

"I'll forgive that behavior only once," Rhys said calmly,

although his brown eyes swirled, a sign I now took to mean he was more worked up inside than he cared to show on the surface. His gaze dropped to Michael's amulet. "I wasn't aware Shadows were allowed to leave the dark worlds."

"I guess you were wrong," Michael replied tightly.

"I guess I was. Still. It doesn't seem appropriate for a Shadow to enter the human world."

"It doesn't seem appropriate for a faery king to go to a human high school, either," Michael said, standing protectively between me and Rhys. "Don't you have a kingdom to run, Your Majesty?"

"The safety of my people comes first, no matter how I need to ensure it."

"The princess isn't a threat to your people."

"We'll see." Rhys looked at me. "I think you need to keep a tighter rein on your servant, Nikki."

"Michael's not really—," I began.

Rhys cut me off. "So, Shadow, are you here because of the prophecy?"

Michael continued to glare with unfriendliness at the faery king. "You shouldn't be filling the princess's head with lies that will only worry her."

"It's not a lie," Rhys said firmly. "Besides, you're in no position to tell me what I should or shouldn't do."

Michael ignored him. "Princess, we need to leave. Your father's waiting."

There was no question whether or not I'd go. I'd ditch my afternoon classes; not a problem. My father wouldn't summon me if it wasn't something important. And besides, I really wanted to talk to him about Michael's continuing servant status. I needed answers and I needed them now.

I looked at Rhys. "I'll make sure to tell my father that you've decided to harass me."

Rhys's eyes stayed on Michael. "By the looks of the company you keep, Nikki, I'd say I'm the least of your problems."

I frowned at that. "Thanks so much for your opinion."

I expected him to walk away, but he stood there, his arms crossed, watching Michael carefully before his attention returned to me.

"Just be careful with this one," he said distastefully.

"With who? Michael?"

"Yes."

I snorted. "You're really telling *me* to be careful? What do you care one way or the other?"

His eyes swirled. "Fine. Forget I said anything, then."

Without another word, he turned and walked back into the cafeteria.

Um, what was that? The dude who was thinking about killing me if he decided I was evil suddenly wanted me to be careful?

Sure. That made sense.

4

"I don't know what his problem is," I said as Michael and I left the school. "Why would he tell me to be careful if he hates my guts?"

"Because he doesn't hate your guts. I think he likes you." Michael was walking so fast I had to jog to keep up with him. "Isn't it obvious?"

I gaped at him. "You're not serious."

"I am." He stopped walking and turned to me to show he actually looked a little amused now.

"You think this is funny?" I asked.

"When I got here and you said he'd threatened you, I was worried you'd been in danger and I'd had no clue."

"Kind of difficult for you to know what's going on from the Shadowlands."

"I know." His amusement faded. "It's disturbing to me."

"He doesn't like me. I saw it in his beady little faery eyes. He can't stand me, actually. And he's a little bit afraid of me. It's a whole mix of unpleasantness."

"Why would he be afraid of you?"

"He's scared of my Darkling side. He thinks I'm all nasty and evil underneath my shiny, happy exterior."

"Then for a king he's a bit of a fool, isn't he?"

"I totally agree. Do all faery royals have to take the throne so young? Maybe the power's gone to his head."

"The king and queen of the faery realm died recently. Rhys was their only son and heir to the throne."

"Oh." It hadn't even occurred to me that he'd become king so young because his parents were dead. Then again, that was what would happen to me if my father died. It wouldn't matter how old I was—I'd be queen of the Shadowlands.

I felt a sudden surge of sympathy for Rhys having to take on so much responsibility at his age. I didn't want to feel it, but there it was. Had he been close with his parents? Did he miss them? Was this the reason for that grief I'd seen in his eyes earlier?

"How did they die?" I asked.

"I don't know." Michael shoved his hands into the pockets of his jeans, looking suddenly uncomfortable talking about death with me in the middle of a cold but bright Erin Heights street. "It doesn't excuse him from bothering you in any way, shape, or form. He needs to go back to his kingdom and keep his nose out of issues that have nothing to do with him."

"Hopefully he'll take the hint."

Michael looked at me intensely for a moment. "Whether he likes you or not, I swear, if he lays one finger on you, I don't know if I'll be able to stop myself from hurting him. I don't care if he's a king."

I gave him a slow grin. "And I appreciate that."

He pulled me to him and kissed me quickly, then backed away a few steps, looking a bit guilty about what he'd done. "Can't do that when we're around your father."

"What would he do if he found out?" I challenged. "And do we really care?"

"Princess, please. Let's keep it a secret."

I let out a sigh of frustration. "How can you be so accepting of everything? Dumb rules and lame behavior."

"They might seem dumb to you, but they're still rules that govern the behavior of everyone inhabiting the dark worlds. It's how it's always been."

"Then it needs to change."

That earned me an actual laugh from him. "Just because you don't like a few things, everything has to change?"

That sounded about right to me. "Sure. Why not?"

He shook his head. "Let's not argue. Let's just go see your father. I don't want to keep him waiting too much longer. I'm trying to detect the gateway. I know we're close."

"Fine, we'll go see him," I said. "But this discussion definitely isn't over. Understood?"

His lips curled into a half smile. "Understood."

"While you're doing your gateway detecting, I have to call my mom quickly." I fished into my backpack and pulled out my cell phone, pressing the speed dial to call home.

"Hey, Mom," I said when she picked up on the third ring. "I just wanted you to know that after school I'm going out with Melinda for a bit."

It was amazing how easily the lie spilled forth. I felt guilt swirl inside me, but I couldn't tell her where I was really going, could I? And if I wasn't home right after school, I knew she'd worry. I'd rather come up with a nice little white lie that didn't hurt anybody.

"Oh, really?" Mom said, and I could hear disappointment in her voice. "I was hoping you'd be home right after school."

"Why?"

"I finished my book today and wanted to celebrate with dinner out and a chick flick."

My mom was a paranormal romance novelist. When she got into a new project, she lived and breathed the vampires or werewolves or whatever her characters were for months. When it was all done, she suddenly had a lot of time on her hands and liked to cram in a whole bunch of mother-daughter events and excursions before she started on her next book.

"I'll be home later, I promise."

"What time?"

"Uh . . . *later?*" I felt bad about being so vague, but it couldn't be helped.

"Okay, well, instead of dinner out, maybe I'll order Chinese food delivery. Will you be here by six?"

"Sure. I promise." I glanced at Michael. "No later than six. And Chinese sounds great."

"All right, then. Say hi to Melinda for me."

"I will. Bye, Mom." I hung up and let out a long, shaky exhale.

My father was under the impression Mom was newly married and happy without him all these years. The truth was, she'd been married *four times* in her ongoing search for Mr. Right and had just got rid of the most recent Mr. Wrong a couple days ago.

What would she say if she found out my father hadn't really abandoned us on purpose? Would she consider giving him another chance?

The idea filled me with a strange sense of hope.

I pulled myself out of thoughts of playing matchmaker with my mom and dad and looked at Michael.

"Have you found the gateway?" I asked.

"Not yet." His face looked strained from how much he'd been concentrating.

"Is there a problem?"

He scanned the street. "No. I just need another minute."

"Really?" I was surprised. He hadn't had any problem finding the shifting gateway that would lead us directly into the Shadowlands the other times he'd taken me there.

"After what happened with Elizabeth, I . . . I'm still recovering my strength," he admitted.

My aunt Elizabeth had taken Michael's amulet away from him, and he'd almost faded away to nothing before we got it back just in time. He'd regained his form quickly, but I guess it wasn't something he could snap back from like a moment of wooziness.

"You're okay, though?" I asked with concern.

He nodded. "I'm fine. Although, it might take me a few more days to completely regain my strength."

"Can I help find the gateway? I do have a dragon's tear, after all." I extended my arm to show him my bracelet. "My father said it could help me get to the Shadowlands, but he didn't tell me exactly how to do it. It's like he automatically assumes I just know all this demon-related stuff. And, well, I don't."

Michael took my hand and turned it over so he could look closer at the crystal. "Do you wear this all the time?"

I nodded. "I haven't taken it off once. Mom asked about it, so I told her I got it at the mall for five bucks."

"It's very valuable. *Priceless*, as a matter of fact."

"You mean it's not the latest trendy dark-world accessory?"

"Definitely not. I've never actually seen one before, only heard of them." He ran his thumb over the thin gold chain and his touch made my skin tingle. "But, yes, I think we can use it to help us find the gateway, if you're willing to give it a try."

"Cool. Just tell me what to do. You can be my tutor."

He laughed a little at that. "Never been anyone's tutor before. But it's really just a matter of concentrating on what you want—focusing your thoughts toward your goal. In this case, it's finding the gateway, which is pretty simple. I've heard a dragon tear's magic can do much more than that. But we'll start with baby steps."

"Baby steps are good."

"Be careful. Magic sometimes comes with a price."

"That sounds ominous. But I used it before and nothing bad happened. Of course, it wasn't for this sort of thing."

He shook his head. "I'm sure it'll be fine, then. You're not tapping too deeply into its magic. Besides, your father would never give you a gift that could potentially hurt you."

"Let's hope not."

"Just concentrate. See the gateway in your mind. Focus on it."

"And then what?"

"And then"—he shrugged—"you'll either know where it is or you won't."

"Not an exact science, is it?"

"Afraid not."

"Okay, here it goes." I closed my eyes.

Concentrate on the gateway. I knew what it would look like. A translucent rectangle the size of a door, with glowing edges around a swirling kaleidoscope of color. Barely there, hanging in midair or against a wall. I focused all my thoughts on that image. *Show me where it is.*

After a few seconds I felt a sensation like fingers squeezing a sponge in my head. Hadn't felt that the last time I'd tried to focus on the magic in my crystal. But maybe I hadn't been concentrating quite this much. I felt the crystal heat up against my wrist. It was normally cold and had never warmed to my body temperature before.

Then, suddenly, I sensed where the gateway was. As if a GPS device had clicked on in the center of my brain, directing me to the right place, I knew where it was. Michael had been right—we were close.

I opened my eyes and felt a twinge of pain. I grimaced and brought my hand to my head. "Ouch."

"What?"

"Headache."

His hand was on my forehead. "Is it bad?"

"No, not really."

He brushed his lips against my temple.

"Probably shouldn't let my father see that, either, huh?" I grinned at him.

"Definitely not."

The headache had faded to nothing as quickly as it had arrived. "Come on. I know where it is."

I led him around a corner up ahead. We were only three blocks from the school and at the edge of the downtown business area. The gateway to the Shadowlands was near the back of a Starbucks and down an alley.

I felt suddenly nervous at seeing my father again, but I tried to be brave. "Okay, let's go."

"Princesses first."

"Such a gentleman." I turned from him toward the swirling gateway.

He grabbed my hand before I went through. "Princess, I just wanted to say thank you."

"For what?"

"For wanting to ignore the rules when it comes to me. You don't know how much that means."

I smiled at him. "I guess I'm a rebel."

"You're so completely different from how I expected you to be. I still can't get over it. You're not a spoiled brat who thinks she can get whatever she wants whenever she wants it."

"Maybe if I'd been born a princess, I'd be more like that."

"Somehow, I doubt it."

"I only want a few very specific things," I said pointedly. "But I do get cranky if I can't have them."

I really didn't care about any rules, especially those that told me who I was and wasn't allowed to like. And I'd make that very clear to my father.

Michael was my boyfriend. And if my father didn't like it . . . well, that was just too bad, wasn't it?

I stepped through the gateway feeling a new surge of purpose. I could change things. I *knew* I could. Just because it had been one way for thousands of years didn't mean it always had to be that way, did it? Shadows shouldn't be forced to be servants. And they should be able to date whoever they wanted, whenever they wanted, without anyone telling them they couldn't.

How difficult could it possibly be to change some stupid and outdated rules?

5

The moment after I stepped through the gateway there was a familiar feeling of vertigo, where I couldn't see or hear anything. But before there was a chance to get scared or think about anything at all, I'd already arrived on the other side.

The gateway from the human world opened up at a beautiful pastoral clearing between the Shadowlands and the faery realm. Green grass replaced snow-covered pavement. The scent of spring flowers hung in the air. It was warm enough for me to remove my winter jacket immediately.

A second later, Michael appeared next to me—just like magic. He pushed his dark hair back from his face. "So are you ready to see your father again?"

I looked toward the line of tall thick trees—the forest that bordered Rhys's land. So beautiful and lush and strangely welcoming. Then I turned to look at the field of flowers where we stood. Slowly it changed from soft green grass to sharp gray rock, leading to a black, windowless fortress with massive spires reaching up into the stormy, lightning-etched skies above.

The Shadowlands castle—the nasty-looking, scary place

my father called home and that filled me with a healthy dose of dread whenever I saw it.

Despite how uneasy the castle made me instinctively feel, I finally nodded. "Let's go."

The walk took ten minutes, after which we reached the twenty-foot-tall front door of the castle. We stood on the threshold, and the door slowly began to creak open enough to let us inside. It did that automatically for me—apparently the castle itself could sense that I was the princess and therefore allowed inside.

Michael led me through the cavernous foyer toward a spiral staircase at the center that seemed to extend right up to a ceiling so high I could barely even see it. I'd been here before, of course, but this time I took a moment to look around at the darkness that surrounded me. This wasn't a happy place. It was cold and unwelcoming, and it sent a shiver of fear down my spine.

The very stone this castle was made from helped keep unwanted elements from the dark worlds—including any demons who would like to find a way into the human and faery worlds for malevolent reasons. Supposedly it worked well—and had for a long time. I guess it didn't have to look like Disneyworld, did it?

Still. A few colorful cushions or wall hangings might be a nice, friendly touch.

"I can't believe you've lived here all your life," I said to Michael in a hushed voice.

"Since I was a baby," he said. "It's really not that bad. You'd get used to it if you had to."

"I wouldn't count on it."

Out of the corner of my eye I saw someone walk by. I jumped. The gray-haired man glanced at us, then disappeared into a room up ahead without saying a word.

"It's okay," Michael said. "The servants have all returned to take care of the castle and the king."

"More Shadows like you?" I asked.

He shook his head. "No, I'm the only Shadow here. The other servants are all demons. There aren't that many, really, but you'll see them here and there. They won't bother you unless you need something from them."

"Oh, uh . . . okay."

The last time I'd been here, my aunt had sent the servants away while my father was dying, so they wouldn't see him in such a weakened, pain-filled condition. It was out of respect for the king's image. Of course, it turned out that he was only dying because she was slowly poisoning him. Any servants she allowed to stay around might have been witness to that.

Michael led me upstairs, and I found that my usual feeling of anxiety was now mixed with something more like anticipation. I honestly looked forward to seeing my father again, even though I was really mad at him for keeping Michael a servant.

My father was waiting for us in his large stone-walled meeting room. He sat alone at the head of a long black table surrounded by heavy high-backed chairs. A huge fireplace blazed across from the archway leading into the room. It seemed to be the only source of light, casting the room in flickering shadows. He stood up and walked over to us when we entered.

"Nikki," he said, greeting me warmly. "Thank you for coming on such short notice."

Even though I didn't want to, I couldn't help but smile, still shocked by how much I looked like him. My whole life, I'd never really wondered if I did, but now I could clearly see that I resembled my father.

He had blond hair, a few shades darker than mine, and hazel eyes. He was dressed in black clothes—a shirt and pants that looked surprisingly human, given the medieval ambience.

Yes, in his human form, my father looked like he would fit in just fine in my world. No one would ever guess for a moment, at least not at first glance, that he was a demon king. However, I knew his demon form was very different from that of the handsome man who currently stood before me.

"Glad to be here," I said. "Because we need to talk."

"Oh?" He looked taken aback. "About what?"

"About . . . a promise you made." I looked at Michael. He'd already backed away from me, putting some distance between us. What did he think I was going to do? Grab him and start making out with him in front of my father to prove a point?

Not likely. I might be a rebel, but I wasn't a stupid one. At least, I certainly hoped not.

My father glanced at the two of us warily. "There is a more pressing issue to discuss today, Nikki. Can you hold off on anything else until we've handled that?"

"Handled what?"

"I have a guest who wishes to speak with both of us. That's why I asked for you to come here today. He promises to be brief."

Something caught my eye. Someone else was in the room with us. I hadn't even noticed him standing over in a corner of the room unlit by the fireplace. It was a man, tall, with jet-black hair. He looked familiar, but it took me a moment to put my finger on who he was.

"Hello, Princess Nikki," the man said as he drew closer. "It's a pleasure to finally meet you in person."

I drew in a ragged breath. I'd seen him once before. His name was Kieran. *Prince* Kieran, from the Underworld. He was my aunt Elizabeth's boyfriend. The one who'd helped her poison my father in an attempt to take over the throne of the Shadowlands and gain control of the barrier protecting the human and faery worlds.

"What is he doing here?" I asked my father, taking an immediate step back from Kieran.

I felt my father's hand on my shoulder. "Nikki, it's fine."

"Fine?" My voice sounded pitchy. "How can you say this is fine?" I looked at Michael. "Did you know about this?"

He shook his head, his jaw tight. "No. I promise I didn't."

My father crossed his arms. "I didn't tell Michael anything other than that I wanted him to fetch you."

Fetch me? Did he even realize how demeaning that sounded? But at the moment, I couldn't think about it. I was too freaked by seeing Kieran up close and personal.

My gaze shot to my father. "How could you even let him in the castle? What if he tries to kill you?"

"Prince Kieran denies any allegations that he was assisting Elizabeth with her plans."

"And you believe him?"

His lips pressed together and I could see the tension he'd been trying to hide. "What I believe is inconsequential at the moment. All I can tell you is that if, by chance, anything

unexpected happens while the prince is here in my kingdom"—
his eyes turned from hazel like mine to demon red in a split
second—"it would be highly unacceptable."

He sounded civil, but I could hear the underlying threat in
his words. If Kieran tried something funny, then he'd seriously
regret it . . . but only for a short, painful moment.

The thought was oddly comforting.

Kieran's expression didn't change from neutrally pleasant.
"To ease your mind, Princess, let me explain that, while any
member of demon royalty visits the Shadowlands, it's a rule
that they must voluntarily give up their powers for as long as
they stay. I'm as helpless as a human at the moment."

"Elizabeth wasn't helpless," I said.

"No," my father replied. "She was an exception, since she
was family. But she can't return again."

Elizabeth had been banished to the Underworld as punishment for her crimes. Not much of a punishment as far as I was
concerned, but at least it meant she was far away from here
with no chance of ever returning.

I glared at Kieran. "Speaking of my aunt, how is she?"

"She's understandably shaken," Kieran replied coolly. "She's
very sorry for any pain or distress she caused you both and wishes
she could take back the unfortunate events that occurred."

Yeah, sure. She was only sorry that she got caught. But I
held my tongue and didn't say that out loud.

As my heart rate slowly returned to normal, I took a moment
to study the prince. I remembered my first impression of him
when I'd seen him through my aunt's gazer—a means of
communicating between the demon worlds by looking into a

shallow pool of water. He looked unnaturally attractive, sort of like the airbrushed male models on the covers of my mom's romance novels, with piercing ice blue eyes under slashing black brows. There were no flaws I could see on Kieran's perfect face. I could almost understand why Elizabeth had been ready to kill her own brother to do whatever this guy wanted her to do. *Almost.*

I suddenly realized I was clutching Michael's hand for support. I didn't actually remember grabbing onto it or when he'd come to stand next to me again.

His green-eyed gaze captured mine. ::It's okay, Princess. I'm here and I swear I won't let anything bad happen to you.::

Thank you was the simple thought I projected back to him. I squeezed his hand before letting it go.

The action and unspoken connection between us was observed by Kieran. "You and your Shadow servant are very close, aren't you, Princess Nikki?"

My shoulders stiffened at the sound of his deep voice. "Michael's not my servant. He's my . . . my *friend.*"

I looked at my father, who stood next to me, his attention on the prince. I could have sworn I saw him bristle slightly at my wording.

"How very forward thinking of you, Princess. But . . . *only* friends?" Kieran asked, then glanced at my father. "Your Majesty, the way your daughter looks at the Shadow worries me. I can't help but wonder if there might be something else between them. But of course, that would be against the laws of our worlds, wouldn't it?"

The smug bluntness of the statement made my stomach

coil, and I suddenly felt extremely self-conscious and wary about every move I made.

"Kieran," my father said impatiently. "Why don't you get to the point of your visit and what it has to do with my daughter so we don't have to take up any more of her valuable time. Her life is not here, after all, and I expect she'd like to get back to the human world as soon as possible."

"Actually, the point of my visit *is* your daughter," Kieran said.

"What about me?" I asked.

"I am a member of the demon council—"

"Demon council?"

He nodded. "Yes, it's a five-member, specially chosen tribunal that regularly meets in the Underworld and is in charge of passing rules and regulations in the dark worlds. We have been discussing you in great detail over the past couple of days."

"You've been discussing *me?*" I glanced at Michael, whose brows were raised with confusion at this statement.

"Yes," Kieran said. "Your existence wasn't known to any of us until last week. But now that it is . . . and for you to be the first half human, half demon born in a thousand years . . . Well, it has obviously sparked some significant discussion about the problem this creates."

Before I could speak, my father cut in. "My daughter is not a problem. As you can see, she isn't anyone the council could possibly consider a threat. She's a sixteen-year-old girl raised entirely in the human world."

Kieran took a moment to study me. "Appearances can be deceiving, Your Majesty. The last Darkling was also reported to be fair of face and slight in stature, but she was also highly dangerous, a volatile creature who left a great deal of destruction in her wake."

"I have looked into this," my father said, sounding less and less cordial with each passing moment, "and I could find no official record of what specific damage the last Darkling caused. In fact, even her name was impossible to find, as well as where she made her home."

"Those records are not for everyone's eyes," Kieran said. "It's top secret, highly sensitive information that my mother, the queen, keeps under lock and key."

"Okay," I said. "So the last Darkling had a bit of an itchy trigger finger, or whatever. That was a long time ago, and it doesn't have anything to do with me. Honestly, I don't want to cause any trouble or hurt anyone, like, ever."

"Of course you don't." My father nodded. "So, as you can see, Kieran, your visit here was a waste of your time and ours. There's no indication that my daughter is any danger to you or your precious demon council now or any time in the future, and basing your facts on something that allegedly happened a millennium ago is ludicrous. I realize Queen Sephina has always kept a tight rein on her kingdom and her concern is not completely incomprehensible, but I assure you, worrying about Nikki in any way, shape, or form is wholly unnecessary."

"I would normally agree with you one hundred percent, Your Majesty." Kieran crossed his arms as he continued to study me. I swear, during this entire conversation, he hadn't taken his attention away from me for more than a second. I felt as if I was being inspected like a blonde slab of beef.

"Normally?" I said. "So what's the problem now?"

"The problem now, Princess Nikki, is not that there are rumors or legends about a past Darkling being troublesome—though this is, after all, what brought about the law forbidding humans and demons from procreating. It was in order to avoid creating a hybrid of the two species. Isn't that right, Your Majesty?" He glanced meaningfully at my father.

"Kieran, stop mincing words and tell us what the issue really is," my father said impatiently, ignoring the jab.

Before Kieran spoke another word I suddenly got a chill, a dark sense of foreboding. I looked at Michael and saw the same realization in his widening eyes.

::Princess, do you think this has to do with what King Rhys told you earlier?::

I inhaled sharply.

"There is a prophecy," Kieran said, confirming what Michael and I were thinking. "It was revealed last week, on the very day Princess Nikki turned sixteen. At the time, it wasn't known what it meant or who specifically it pertained to, but now it's very clear to the council."

"And what does this prophecy say?" my father asked sharply.

Kieran's blue eyes tracked back to me. "That your daughter, the first Darkling born in a thousand years, will single-handedly destroy us all."

6

Rhys had been right, after all. He wasn't lying. There was a prophecy about me.

And it was a really sucky one.

"That's completely crazy," was the first thing I said after I found my voice again. "I'm going to destroy everyone? That doesn't even make sense."

Kieran's intense gaze didn't waver. "That is what the prophecy says."

"I don't care what it says. It's the most ridiculous thing I've ever heard."

"I agree," my father said.

I stared at him. "You do?"

He nodded, and looked at Kieran. "Who related this prophecy?"

"The official palace oracle. One who has relayed prophecies for a hundred years to my mother and to her mother before her. He has never been wrong before and certainly never about something so specific or catastrophic."

"Well, your oracle is wrong now." My father dismissed him without missing a beat. "It's clear to me this must be a false prophecy based on a thousand years of rumors and lies about Darklings."

"Your opinion is noted, of course, Your Majesty," Kieran said thinly. "But I'm afraid your objectivity in this matter is at question."

My father ignored him and placed his hand gently against the side of my flushed face. "There is no part of you that is destructive, Nikki. I know that. You are so much like your mother, and she is a beautiful and truly good woman. She'd never hurt a fly."

I nodded in full agreement. "She takes spiders outside in glass jars so she doesn't have to kill them."

He smiled and rested his hand protectively on my arm. "I don't doubt it for a moment."

I relaxed ever so slightly. He didn't believe the prophecy, so of course I didn't have to freak out about it. This was a major relief.

"Prophecies are taken very seriously by the council," Kieran said. He leaned casually against the edge of the large black table.

"And what does the council propose to do about this?" my father asked evenly.

"That remains to be seen, based on my report," he said. "It's likely the next step will be for the princess to be presented to the council in person, and a decision will then be made regarding what to do about her."

"That's not going to happen." My father kept his hand on my arm, as if shielding me from the prince. "You insisted you tell us this news in person. I now see that wasn't entirely necessary, was it?"

"There are procedures to be followed," Kieran said. "It's a rule that information of this level must be given face-to-face."

My father hissed out a breath, betraying the annoyance he'd been trying to hide until now. "You have delivered this news. I respectfully request that you leave my kingdom."

"But there's much more to discuss," Kieran protested. "This is a highly volatile situation and one that needs to be handled immediately. A prophecy like this can't simply be ignored. I need to ask the princess more questions about her intentions."

"No. You've had your say. You've gauged our reactions. Now it's time for you to leave. If there is anything else you wish to discuss, you may contact me by gazer."

His hand began to glow with red light and he waved it toward the door, which turned from a normal entrance to a swirling gateway.

"You may return to the Underworld now, Prince Kieran," he said.

Kieran's gaze flicked to me and his head cocked slightly to the side. "Your daughter means a great deal to you, doesn't she, King Desmond?"

"She does, indeed."

"I understand why you'd wish to protect her, no matter the cost." The prince's eyes moved to Michael, who stood silently at an arm's reach from me.

I glowered at the prince. How could a statement that sounded so friendly, so matter-of-fact, be so filled with malice?

Kieran gave us a forced smile. "This matter will be resolved. Denying the validity of the prophecy will only complicate things."

"Please give my regards to Queen Sephina and Princess Kassandra." My father's words were clipped. There wasn't any friendliness in his voice. In fact, I'd describe it as ice-cold.

"I'll do that." Kieran dipped his head in my direction. "Princess Nikki, I look forward to the next time we meet."

Without another word, he walked through the gateway. It disappeared in a quick flash of light a moment after he did.

"I *really* don't like that guy," I said.

"Kieran is only a messenger," my father said, walking past the table and toward the fireplace. "He has no real authority, here or anywhere else. That's what makes him the way he is—desperate to please his mother and to show his existence actually matters."

"Does it work?"

"I doubt it," he said. "I'm sorry you had to experience that. It must have been a shock to you to hear what he had to say."

"Not as shocking as you might think. I already knew there was a prophecy."

His eyebrows went up. "How?"

I quickly told him about Rhys—his enrollment in the high school, his presence in my biology class, and finally his reason for being there—to find out more about the threat of Nikki Donovan, sixteen-year-old Darkling-o'-danger.

"Faeries are naturally curious and extremely protective of their own kind," he replied after he'd processed it all. "And King Rhys, since the death of his parents, has been attempting to prove himself to his advisers and the rest of his kingdom."

"He threatened the princess," Michael said.

My father's eyes clouded with anger. "He did?"

"Well . . . not in so many words," I said quickly. "Seriously, I'm sure he'll go away eventually. Especially when he realizes the prophecy about me is a false one. My main worry with him is that he'll tell everyone at school my secret."

I didn't exactly know why I was defending Rhys, even in the slightest, but I guess I was. Did I feel sorry for him now that I knew he'd been forced to become king after his parents' deaths? I did. How was I supposed to know whether that was hard for him? It was an assumption. I didn't care who you were—human, demon, or faery—losing both your parents at any age would be a terrible thing. I couldn't imagine how I'd feel if I lost my mom. And, since finding my father after all these years, I didn't want to think about never seeing him again. The thought made a hard lump form in my throat.

There was silence in the meeting room for a moment. I finally looked up to see my father and Michael exchanging a glance.

"You said the prophecy is false, right?" I asked.

My father nodded. "I did say that."

"So . . . why aren't we celebrating?"

"Nikki, please sit down."

The panicky feeling I'd had earlier began creeping back up on me. "You said it was *false*."

He spread his hands. "And it probably is."

"*Probably?*" My mouth felt dry. "You sounded so certain when you were talking to Kieran."

"I feared what he might do otherwise."

"So you think there's a chance there's some truth to it?" Michael asked.

My father took in a deep breath, his brow creased. "I honestly don't know."

That wasn't very reassuring. "It's not true. I don't care what this crazy oracle guy says, there's no way that I could ever destroy anything or anyone."

"I know." His eyes flashed. "Still, it is worrisome. Dragon oracles are rarely wrong when it comes to a prophecy this specific to an individual. And that Kieran said it was related on your birthday, the day you would have begun to manifest your half-demon powers, worries me even more."

It couldn't be true. That my father had just been lying to Kieran—faking him out—so he wouldn't put me under arrest or something and drag me to some Underworld prison, and—

Wait a minute.

"Did you just say *dragon* oracle?" I asked.

He nodded. "Yes, of course. All oracles are dragons."

"But not all dragons are oracles," Michael added.

I pointed at my dragon's tear bracelet. "Big, scaly, fire-breathing dragons."

"Much like demons," my father explained, "dragons are capable of shifting form when it suits them. But yes, they can be big, scaly, and fire-breathing if they choose to be."

Brain exploding now. "*Okay.* And they can make prophecies."

"They see glimpses of the future and interpret them, then pass this information along to those whom the prophecy affects. They communicate when they have something . . . *prophetic* . . . to share that will affect demonkind, but they live wherever they please, be it the dark worlds or elsewhere. I know there are several living in the human world as we speak."

"But . . ." I licked my dry lips, a thousand questions swirling around in my head. "How can they be in the human world? How can they get through the barrier here?"

"Dragons are the only creatures capable of easily moving between the worlds without using gateways. However, they took an oath of peace centuries ago and are very rarely, if ever, dangerous unless provoked."

I tried to wrap my head around all of this. I finally sat down in the closest high-backed chair and gripped the edge of the table as if trying to anchor myself. "So that's why one of their tears works to help me focus my power?"

"A dragon is a very powerful and magical creature. It'll cry only one tear in its entire existence—at the very moment of its death—a tear filled with all the power it had during its lifetime." His expression turned grim. "Since dragons are naturally immortal, their death must come at the hands of someone else."

"You mean when someone kills them?"

"Yes."

"So the dragon that cried the tear on my bracelet is dead?"

There was a heavy pause before he replied. "That's correct."

I shuddered. "This place is so violent—all this talk of killing and death and destruction."

My father sat down across the table from me. "Is the human world that much more peaceful?"

"It's different."

"Yes, I agree with you. But along with all that is light in the human world, there is still much that is dark."

"Like me?" I looked up at him.

He shook his head. "Don't even think that."

"But that's what you're saying, isn't it? That there's a possibility the prophecy's true? That I might be like the last Darkling and go postal on everyone?"

He studied me for a moment, a quizzical look on his face. Maybe he'd never heard that particular expression before. "I'm only saying that we must be very careful in future dealings with Kieran and the demon council. They're the dangerous ones in this scenario."

I didn't want to believe it, but now that I knew my father wasn't entirely confident in the prophecy being a total lie, how was I supposed to be so sure, myself? After all, I'd seen myself in action in total Darkling mode a couple of times now. I'd felt that violence deep inside me that came from using my power. I'd blasted Chris out of the limo at Winter Formal, and only when Michael arrived and helped calm me down did I know I wouldn't do more damage. The same happened when I'd used my power to stop my aunt. I'd wanted to destroy her, not just protect myself from harm.

What if I really lost control someday?

What if Rhys was right in thinking I was dangerous and deadly?

"Michael, would you be so kind as to fetch us something to drink?" my father asked, studying my stricken expression.

It snapped me out of my thoughts. There was that *fetch* word again. Michael wasn't a trained dog.

"Of course, Your Majesty," Michael said.

::I'll be back as soon as I can, Princess.::

I could hear his concern etched into the telepathic message. I watched him leave the room.

My father watched me watch him leave the room.

"Nikki," he began, "about Michael—"

"You said he wasn't going to be a servant anymore," I said, surprised at how sharply and forcefully I'd spoken the sentence.

I could tell I'd surprised him. "I know. But I shouldn't have said that to you or him. I was weakened and not thinking straight at the time."

"That's not a good excuse."

He folded his hands in front of him. "Shadows are servants," he said firmly.

"I get that."

"No, I don't think you do. I don't think you *get that* at all, in fact." His jaw tightened. "It was very dangerous to say what you did in front of Kieran."

"What did I say?"

"About Michael being your friend and not your servant."

"He is my friend."

"Maybe so. But . . . how do I put this so you'll understand? Kieran and the inhabitants of the dark worlds in general will not understand this manner of thinking. I know that our ways are different from yours, Nikki. But humans also have servants."

"Not ones that serve against their will."

"Michael isn't being imprisoned here against his will."

"No, but he doesn't exactly have much of a choice, does he?" When he didn't answer that, I continued. "Are you trying to tell me I'm not allowed to be his friend? Because then I think we have a problem."

"Yes, it's clear to me we have a problem." My father stood up from the table so quickly and suddenly that his chair squeaked backward. The sound made me jump. I hadn't realized how tense I was. He paced to the fireplace, and when he came back I realized something. My father was angry, but trying very hard to control it.

"What?" I asked, now uncertain.

"It's against the rules, Nikki."

"What is?"

"I assigned Michael specifically as your servant because I thought you'd feel more comfortable with him. He's the only servant here who's around your age." He rubbed his forehead. "I wasn't thinking. It was foolish of me, I see that now."

"I don't understand."

"That's the problem, but unfortunately not one that can be solved today." He let out a strained breath. "I think you should go home now. Try to forget about the prophecy. Try to have a normal life. Take care of your mother and keep her safe."

I stood up. "My mother should know about this, you know. About *you*. She has a right."

His expression darkened. "No, Nikki."

"No?" I'd gone from uncertain to frustrated to angry in no time flat. "Just like that? No discussion necessary?"

"That's right."

"She isn't with anyone right now, you know. She broke up with the last guy because he was a jerk. And I also saw him hit her once."

His eyes flashed red at that particular mental image. "Nikki . . ."

"She keeps meeting these creeps and hopes they'll be the right guy for her, but it never works out. I know she still thinks of you. She was madly in love with you once, and I'm positive she still feels that way, even after everything that happened. And I think that you—"

"Nikki, stop!" He slammed his fist down on the table so hard that I heard a loud crack as it splintered down the middle.

I jumped back, and regarded him with wide eyes. He'd been so quiet, harboring more of a simmering anger, that I hadn't realized it had grown to destructive levels—but, he was a demon, wasn't he? I feared for a moment that he was furious with me, that I'd crossed some invisible line, said too much, pushed him too hard. I'd been upset and wanted to lash out.

So I lashed out at a really sore spot for him. Obviously I'd hit the mark.

"Let me try to put this in terms you'll understand," he said, his voice already quiet and controlled again. He blinked and his eyes returned to their usual hazel shade which matched my own. "What happened with your mother and myself was a mistake."

I flinched.

He shook his head. "No, not because of you. Back then, I was young and foolish and willing to break the rules I'd grown up with simply out of rebellion. Because I hated my father and wanted to prove that he had no control over me. I was fully aware that I was forbidden to fall in love with a human. I just didn't know what the consequences would be."

I knew this already. "You had to come back here and take the throne. You were told my mom was dead so you never tried to contact her again."

He waved a hand. "Yes, but that wasn't the penalty for breaking the law. I didn't realize it at the time, but being with Susan and ignoring the very strict and specific rules of the dark worlds meant that I was putting your mother's life at risk."

"Her life?"

"Yes. She never knew what I really was, and that was in her best interest. If she found out I was a demon, if I told her then or now out of some selfish need to be with her, she would be in grave peril. The most common punishment for breaking a law like this is death. Since I am royal, I might be pardoned. But your mother is not royal, and she would certainly be punished—the council would see to it."

"They'd kill her?" It was barely a whisper.

"Yes." His expression was stony.

This was why he didn't want her to know about him. Because he was afraid she'd get hurt.

"But you're king here," I breathed. "Can't you do something? Can't you change things?"

"I am king, but the Shadowlands are only a small part of the dark worlds. They serve one solitary purpose—maintaining the barrier. In fact, my title holds very little weight with the council. Perhaps if I were to become more lax in my duties and let those who wish to pass through to the faery and human worlds at will, like Kieran, have their way, then my opinion might be more valued. But I know I can't do that. My sense of duty makes me an outsider to them. I have no doubt that if they learned I had told your mother everything and drawn her into a world she never knew existed, I would be signing her death warrant. And I will never do that."

I was trying to process everything. Make sense of it. Trying to find another answer. There had to be one, right?

"You need to know, Nikki," he continued, "that the decisions I make regarding your mother, as well as those I make about Michael, are not to hurt them but to protect them. Even when those decisions may seem harsh or difficult to understand." He looked at me very intensely. "You are my daughter. And even though I only had the privilege of meeting you very recently, I know you will make the right decisions. I don't think you'd ever put anyone you care about at great risk if you knew you could protect them."

He was being purposely vague, I thought, but there was no mistaking his meaning. Just by liking Michael as more than a servant, I was putting his life at risk because of the laws in the dark worlds.

Indignation rose inside me but quickly settled into a strange, sick feeling in the pit of my stomach.

"It's not fair," I said quietly.

"I know."

The next moment, Michael entered the room carrying a metal tray with a pitcher and two silver goblets on it.

"Thank you, Michael," my father said. "But I think it's time for you to take my daughter back to the gateway so she can return to her normal life."

Michael put the tray down on the table. "Yes, Your Majesty."

Then my father looked at me, his eyes, so similar to mine, holding a shadow of the pain he felt inside. That he'd felt for nearly seventeen years since he'd been forced to leave my mother without a word of explanation. "I'll send Michael to you when I have more news from the Underworld."

I nodded. "Okay."

"And please, Nikki, remember what I said."

"I will."

"Try not to worry about the prophecy. I don't believe you're capable of anything like that. There has to be another explanation, and I assure you I'll find it."

He said it with such conviction, such belief, I couldn't feel anything but grateful to him. He was in a difficult position as king of the desolate and disrespected Shadowlands, someone who'd had to make tough decisions and sacrifices all his life. I wished I'd known him longer, instead of thinking my real father was some kind of jerk who'd simply abandoned my mother and never looked back. He'd quickly become one of the most important people in my life.

With a last glance at him standing in the meeting room all alone, I left with Michael and descended the massive staircase. My brain was working overtime and it ached—not because my horns were about to appear but from all the information I'd had to take in.

Rhys had been right. There was a prophecy about me. I felt bad about accusing him of being a big fat liar.

My father thought it wasn't true, but he had doubts. Could

it be true? Was I capable of destroying everyone? What did that even mean?

I could barely crush a soda can when I was done with it, let alone anything bigger.

Then again, I hadn't tried to crush any cans since I came into my Darkling powers. I was willing to bet I could crush a lot more than that now.

I nervously twisted my bracelet as Michael led me outside. He'd been giving me concerned looks ever since we'd left my father.

"It's going to be okay," he said.

I laughed suddenly at that, and it came out a bit hysterical. "You think?"

He nodded. "Yes. Don't give the prophecy another thought."

"I'll try my hardest."

He took a step closer to me when we reached the swirling gateway. "Although, if you need to destroy anything, I think you should start with Kieran."

"Are you kidding?"

"Half kidding." He smiled, but it faded when I didn't return it. He reached down to take my hand. His skin felt warm against mine.

"You're really worried about this," he said.

"It's not just the prophecy." I looked at him. "It's the servant thing, too. My father made you a promise, and now he's backing out of it."

He sighed. "Don't worry about me, Princess. I'm used to how things are here. Your father actually does treat me very well.

Your attitude, your ability to see things as they could be, is so amazing to me. It's made me think, just maybe, things could be different some day."

I looked at the ground but felt his hand come under my chin, tilting my head back so I could look into his green eyes. Then he leaned toward me and brushed his lips against mine. When he moved back, he looked a bit confused. I hadn't kissed him back. I guessed there was a first time for everything.

I tried to find the words, but they escaped me. How could I tell him that I couldn't be his girlfriend? Not that I didn't want to be, not that it was because I cared what his social status was. No, because I didn't want him to get hurt because of me.

"Michael," I began, and my voice cracked.

And just like that, he *knew*. I could see it in his eyes.

He blinked hard. "I think I understand why your father wanted me to go get drinks. Did he talk some sense into you? Remind you of what I am?"

"He reminded me of the rules."

"The rules that you didn't care about only an hour ago? The rules that you thought were stupid?"

"They *are* stupid. This whole place is stupid. But . . ." My throat felt thick. "But that doesn't mean we can break them. Not if we don't want to get in trouble. Do you know what the penalty is?"

"Yes." He said it with such certainty that it surprised me. "Of course I know. It's the penalty for breaking just about any major rule in the dark worlds. And they're even more strict when it's a Shadow that breaks the rules." He smiled, but there was no humor there. "Some demons are afraid of Shadows."

"Afraid? Why?"

He shrugged. "I don't know. But I'm sure it's why the rule that forbids Shadows and demons . . . or demon *princesses* . . . from being together exists in the first place."

"Why? To protect the *demon?*" It didn't make any sense to me.

"That's what I've heard from some of the other demon servants. But I've never met any more of my kind to get the real story." His lips thinned. "I guess Shadows tend to break a lot of rules. Gives demons an excuse to get rid of us one by one so there's no risk at all, right?"

"Don't say that."

"But it's true." He exhaled. "It's fine, Princess. Honestly. But I guess I thought . . ." He shook his head, his expression tight. "It doesn't matter now. You're making the right decision, of course. Go home. It's where you belong. I won't bother you until your father sends me to you again, I promise."

He didn't sound angry or upset or even sad about this. He sounded accepting and matter-of-fact, as if he'd been expecting me to break up with him for a while. It made my heart ache.

He turned away.

"Michael . . ." I grabbed his hands and pulled him closer to me so I could look deeply into his eyes.

His face was tense. It betrayed the major emotions he was trying to hide.

"This is stupid," I said. "I know it is."

"I agree completely." His green eyes were stormy now. "I wish there was another way, but I won't risk your safety, especially with Kieran poking around in everyone's business right now."

I almost laughed at that. He wouldn't risk *my* safety? And here I was doing this because I didn't want *him* to get hurt.

"Kiss me," I said.

"One more time before we go back to being only princess and servant?"

I nodded.

He gave me a half smile. "I think I can manage that."

He put his hands on either side of my face before pressing his lips against mine. I kissed him back this time, feeling an ache in my chest, knowing that this might be the last time. It was too dangerous for him to be my boyfriend—for *him*—and I didn't want anyone I cared about to get hurt. Just like my father was protecting my mother, I would protect Michael.

My mind was elsewhere, swept away by the crazy, conflicting emotions I was feeling. I should have remembered why it was a very bad idea to let my mind wander while kissing Michael.

The moment his amulet pressed against me, I felt a bone-jarring *zzzaaappp!* that nearly knocked me out of my winter boots. As well as giving a Shadow solid form, his green stone amulet worked as a shield, a layer of protection against demons. Or *half* demons.

"*Ouch!*" I touched my chest where the shock had made contact and staggered back a few feet. "That really hurt."

"I'm sorry." His expression grew pained.

I swallowed hard. "Me, too."

And I wasn't just talking about the amulet.

"I'll contact you the moment your father has more information. I know this is for the best, Princess." His voice sounded thick. "But I do wish it could be different."

"So do I." Tears pricked at my eyelids, but I commanded myself not to cry as I turned toward the gateway.

I liked Michael more than any guy I'd ever known in my life, and he liked me in return—but he couldn't be my boyfriend, not even a secret one. And that just completely and totally sucked.

"Good-bye, Michael," I said.

"Good-bye, Princess."

I walked through the gateway that led me back to my semi-normal life.

Michael didn't follow me.

7

I stomped against the snow-covered sidewalk, feeling more upset about what happened with every step I took. My winter coat hung open, but I didn't even feel the cold.

Had I been wrong to break up with Michael? Should I have been braver and continued my—up until now—silent revolution against stupid and ridiculous rules?

I sighed. If I was only risking myself, then *maybe*. But my decision affected Michael as well. I'd already seen firsthand what the punishment for a Shadow could be. When my aunt Elizabeth took away Michael's amulet, he'd nearly died, nearly faded away to nothing. I knew it hurt him badly, too. I didn't want to cause him any pain, now or in the future. Not because of me.

This still hurt. Just in a different way.

Stupid rules.

And I was at the mercy of some demon council I'd never met before. I didn't ever want to meet them. They sounded horrible.

But they hadn't met me, either. So how were they supposed to know what to make of this prophecy? They didn't know I was the kind of girl who read the directions when I microwaved popcorn. I followed the recipe exactly to make chocolate-chip cookies. I didn't do anything at school to get sent to the principal's office—not counting the classes I'd skipped today. At my last school I was so well behaved that other students called me a goody-goody.

Now this goody-goody was prophesied to destroy . . . destroy what, exactly? The prophecy sounded pretty vague to me. Destroy everything? Everyone? And how exactly was I supposed to do that?

I mean, the dark worlds were the Shadowlands, the Underworld, and, *hello?* Hell itself. I'd seen lots of movies about Hell, and it was full of brimstone and fire and—

I shuddered.

Destroy that. *Me.*

The whole thing, including what had happened with Michael, made me feel sick to my stomach.

I needed to buy something, maybe. Possibly something made of chocolate. It might help me feel better. More normal. More human.

From the gateway, by the Starbucks where it had been earlier, I walked fifteen minutes to get to the Erin Heights Town Center, a big shopping mall. By a glance at the big clock tower in the middle of it, I knew school was officially out for the day. I didn't have much money—only about five dollars—so I window-shopped to try to take my mind off things for a while, although it didn't really work. I used my money at the convenience store to buy a Diet Coke and a Snickers bar, which sat heavily in my stomach after I ate it.

Then I walked home. It was past seven o'clock by then,

and I didn't feel any better than I had when I'd left the Shadowlands. It wasn't until I saw my house, though, that I remembered with a sinking feeling that Mom had wanted to celebrate finishing her book. The smell of Chinese food hit me the moment I stepped through the front door.

Several open containers of the delivery food were in the kitchen.

"Mom?" I called.

"In here," she replied from the family room.

I padded through the kitchen and along the hallway. Mom was curled up on the sofa with a half-eaten plate of fried rice and stir-fried veggies on her lap.

"I started the movie already." She nodded at the television. "*Sleepless in Seattle.*"

"One of my favorites."

"That's why I rented it," she said pointedly.

I cringed. "I'm sorry I'm later than I thought I'd be."

There was silence for a moment. "Is there anything you want to tell me, Nikki?"

There was tons, actually. I wanted to tell her that I'd seen my father and he still loved her but couldn't say anything or he'd be putting her life at risk because of stupid demon-world rules. That I had just had to break up with my boyfriend for pretty much the same reason. Oh, and that, by the way, I was half demon and sometimes sported horns and wings, and had destructive prophecies about me delivered by soothsaying dragons.

"Congrats on finishing the book," I said instead.

"Thanks."

"This is the vampire one?"

"Most of my books are about vampires lately. Love and fangs just seem to go together these days."

"Oh, right."

Maybe it would be easier if I were a vampire.

She leaned against the sofa cushions. "So how's Melinda?"

I dug my toe into the carpet. Right, my lie about who I was with after school. Had to keep things like that straight in my head. "She's . . . she's great. Yeah, we went to the mall and looked around for a bit. She needed a new leotard for her dance lessons."

"Did she find one?"

I continued to force the lie out even though it made me feel increasingly horrible. "She did. Hooray. Mission accomplished."

Mom nodded. "You know, it's really funny you say that."

"What's funny?"

"About you and Melinda going to the mall after school."

"Oh?" I tensed.

She placed her plate of food in front of her on the coffee table. "Because Melinda called here two hours ago looking for you. She was concerned because you left school early and she couldn't reach you on your cell phone. She had to wait until her ballet lesson was over, but she wanted to check on you as soon as she could."

I gulped. *Uh-oh.*

"So I'm not exactly sure who you were with at the mall looking for a new dance leotard, but it wasn't Melinda. She wasn't even aware of these plans to go out after school with you." She crossed her arms and looked up at me sternly. "Now do you want to tell me the truth about where you really were, or what?"

"I . . . I . . ." I searched for something to say. Why hadn't I thought of this possibility? Well, the truth was I hadn't been thinking too clearly earlier. If I had been, I would have remembered that Melinda *always* called me. And of course she would have wondered where I'd taken off to at lunch and gotten worried.

I was such a lousy friend.

"I . . . I *was* at the mall." This was true, at least. Partially, anyway.

"With whom?"

"Myself."

Her forehead creased, and she pulled her long dark hair around so it draped over her left shoulder. "Why did you tell me you were going out with Melinda if you weren't?"

"I don't know." It sounded so weak, but I was too tired to come up with a better excuse. My brain wasn't working, and I just didn't want to heap on any more lies at the moment.

"You don't know," she repeated. "Okay. Well, I have to say I'm disappointed that you felt you needed to lie to me, Nikki. Of course you have a right to go to the mall by yourself or with a friend. But I really wanted to celebrate tonight. I was in such a great mood when I finished my book. The fact that you'd rather go to the mall by yourself than come home and spend time with me makes me feel pretty lousy."

All of a sudden, the emotions I'd been feeling for the past several hours bubbled over and I started to cry.

"I'm sorry," I blubbered, wiping my face. "It doesn't have

anything to do with you, really. It's me. I'm going through some stuff right now and I can't . . . I had to deal with it by myself. I'm sorry I wasn't here for you, with the food and the movie and all."

I wished I could tell her everything, but I knew I couldn't tell her or anyone else here what I was going through. The thought made me feel very alone.

She stood up and came over to stand in front of me, looking shocked at my impromptu sob fest. "Honey, what is going on with you?"

"Nothing."

"This isn't nothing." She stroked the hair back from my face and then hugged me. "I think I know what's really happening here."

I leaned back. "You do?"

She nodded gravely. "This is about a boy, isn't it?"

"A . . . a boy?"

"Is it that Chris fellow? The one you went to the dance with? Are you having troubles with him?"

I almost laughed, but of course I didn't. Troubles with Chris. The least of my worries at this very moment.

"No, it's not Chris."

"Someone else?"

My bottom lip wobbled. It was enough to confirm her suspicions.

"I see." She sighed. "Nikki, honey, if you're having troubles with boys, you can tell me. Maybe I can help."

"Not with this."

"I'm here for you if you need to tell me something." Her

expression grew concerned. "*Whatever* you need to tell me. I can handle it. If you want to go to the doctor and get started on birth control, then we need to make an appointment as soon as—"

"Mom!" I exclaimed, horrified.

"It's important. When I was your age—"

"No, no. It's nothing like that." I cringed. "I'm . . . well, I *was* seeing somebody but we broke up. I'm having a hard time with it, that's all."

I didn't want to continue lying to her—were partial truths still considered lies?—but I had to move my mother away from any talk about birth control or doctor's visits. It was responsible and totally cool of her to be the understanding mom. But, come on. *Mortifying* much?

"Who is he?" she asked.

"His name's Michael and he . . . he . . . it doesn't matter anymore." I knew I shouldn't be saying anything at all.

Her expression grew more concerned. "Was this Michael mean to you?"

"Mean? No, he was . . . he was great."

"Then what was the problem?"

I tried to figure out the best way to put it. "We're really different. And that got in the way. We're going to stay friends, but . . . we can't be more than that."

I didn't think I could get any more vague and still be sort of telling her the truth. But I owed her that. As much as I'd have liked to tell her everything from A to Z, I couldn't. It was better—and *safer*—this way.

"You're so young," my mom said, wiping my tears with her thumb. "There are so many boys out there who'd love to date you. You'll find somebody else."

I shook my head. "I don't want anybody else."

"Then you should find a way to fix things, if you feel that strongly about it."

"I don't think I can." I dried my face with the sleeve of my shirt. "It's okay. I'll be fine."

"I know you will be."

"And I'm sorry for lying to you. I didn't mean to hurt your feelings."

She nodded, but there was still tightness around her mouth. It would take more than an apology to regain her trust. "Remember, all we can really depend on in this crazy world is each other. Just like always."

"Right." I sniffed. "I'm . . . I'm going to go call Melinda back."

"You do that." She eyed the TV. "And I'm going to stop watching this stupid movie. I'm not in the mood for tales of true love tonight. Maybe I'll put on an action flick instead. Something with lots of blood and guts."

"Sounds much less romantic."

"And you and I are going to do a bunch of things together before I start the next book, okay?"

I managed to grin a little. "Is that a promise or a threat?"

"Both." She smiled back at me. "No excuses. I'm ready for some major Susan-and-Nikki time. But no more cutting school, or else. Got it?"

"I promise."

I went to my room, grabbed the phone on my bedside table, and quickly dialed Melinda's number.

"Where have you been?" she asked. "I was really worried about you."

"Thanks, Melinda. But really, you didn't have to be. I left after lunch. I wasn't feeling so hot. Then I ended up at the mall just wandering around. I . . . I guess I must have turned my phone off."

I had turned my phone off after I'd called my mother. So it wasn't a total lie.

"You're feeling better?"

Not even slightly. "Yeah. Much better."

"Larissa said you two had a fight today. What was that all about?" she asked.

I thought back to my convo with Melinda's brunette BFF-in-waiting. "A disagreement. She doesn't like me very much."

"Don't worry about Larissa."

"She thinks I'm not a very good friend to you and that I'll never fit in with the Royal Party."

"Well, she's wrong."

"She also thinks I'm trying to date Rhys."

There was a long pause. "Are you?"

My grip on the phone tightened. "Of course not."

"I guess I just don't get why you didn't tell me you already knew him."

"It's no big deal, okay? I forgot, that's all. It's been a while." A few days could count as a while, right?

"What do you think of him?"

"I think he's . . . different." *Very* different.

"I know! So totally different. He seems so, like, unaffected by everything to do with popularity. I think he'd be just as happy hanging with anyone, whether they're with the in crowd or not. He's really curious about everything and everyone at school." She cleared her throat. "Especially *you*."

"Me?"

"After you left, he kept asking me questions about you. What you're like, what you do, who your friends are. Stuff like that. I think he might be interested in you." There was a raw edge to her voice now.

My stomach wrapped itself into a tight ball. Rhys *was* interested in me. Interested in finding out how much of a threat I was to him and his faery friends. *Way* different from wanting to ask me out, which is what Melinda was making it sound like.

"You think so, huh? Well, I'm not interested in him, so end of story." I sighed. "How about we change the subject? How was your ballet class?"

"Strenuous." She sighed. "Ballet is way harder than I thought it would be."

"Are you going to have a recital or anything?" It was nice thinking about somebody else's life for a moment. "With a big pink tutu?"

She snorted at that. "Nothing's scheduled yet, but I'll let you know." There was a short pause, and then, "I really wish I didn't have to take these lessons."

"You could just say no, couldn't you?"

"I really can't. I have to do them. My parents insist."

"So now they want you to be a professional dancer or something? I thought they wanted you to be a doctor."

"They've changed their minds. Now it's all dancing, all the time."

That was kind of strange, actually. But it was nice to know I wasn't the only one forced to deal with things I didn't particularly want to. Not that I could compare my demonic problems with Melinda cramming her feet into satin ballet slippers.

"Listen, Nikki, can I ask you for a favor?"

"Sure."

"I know it's soon and Rhys only just started today, but I think I really like him."

Here we go again. What happened to changing the subject to something less potentially dangerous, like ballet? "Oh, Melinda, I don't know if that's such a good idea."

"Why? Because he's an exchange student?"

"Yeah. I mean, you don't want to start dating this guy one day and have him leave the next, do you?"

"I'm willing to take that chance. Look, I know he's in biology with you. See if he's even remotely interested in me, okay? Just be really subtle about it."

I bit my lip. I wanted to stop Melinda from being interested in the teenage faery king, but what was I supposed to say? I couldn't tell her the truth, and if I tried to argue with her, it would just look like I wanted to date him myself.

Talk about a rock and a hard place. At least I felt like I had a little control over this situation.

"Of course," I finally said. "I'll ask him some really good questions and find out what he thinks of you."

"Thanks." Her voice brightened. "And you know what? Forget about what Larissa said to you. She doesn't know you half as well as I do. I know you're a great friend and you'd never do anything to hurt me."

"I *never* want to hurt you." *Or anyone else*, I added internally.

"Ditto. Hey, I think I'm going to invite Rhys to my party. It's going to be great."

"Yeah, can't wait," I said, feigning excitement as best I could.

Melinda's party was this Saturday night. I just had to get through the gauntlet of four more school days first.

While I tried to get Rhys to stay away from my smitten best friend.

While waiting for word about what the demon council was planning on doing next about me and my highly unpleasant prophecy.

Without Michael as my boyfriend.

I'd considered having some Chinese food for dinner, but now I'd totally lost my appetite.

8

I got the strange feeling someone was watching me as I made my way to my locker on Tuesday morning. It was like a burning sensation on the back of my neck. When I turned I saw Chris Sanders standing halfway down the hall from me.

We stared at each other for a long, uncomfortable moment. He opened his mouth as if to say something, but then started walking in the opposite direction.

"I want to talk to you," he'd said to me yesterday. "It's important."

I didn't want to let him have any power over me, so I figured I should deal with him as soon as I could. I started to follow him, ready to demand he tell me what he wanted to talk to me about, when someone tapped on my shoulder.

Since I was already a ball of nerves, I let out a shriek and spun around to see who it was.

Rhys raised an eyebrow. "Did I scare you?"

Seeing it was him did nothing to calm my nerves. "No, but you surprised me. A little. That happens when people creep up behind me."

"I wasn't trying to creep."

"I guess you just come by it naturally." I eyed him. Today he wore blue jeans and a long-sleeved light blue T-shirt that fit tightly against his chest and arms. On his feet were new black leather shoes that looked designer. "So I have to ask—who helped pick out your wardrobe so you can fit in perfectly around here? Do you have a personal faery image consultant?"

"You think I fit in perfectly?" he asked, with a pleased expression.

"You blend. High-end blend. Your clothes look expensive."

"Money's not really a problem for me. And yes, my advisers helped me. A few are highly knowledgeable about the human world." When I didn't say anything to that, he asked, "So, did you learn more about the prophecy?"

I glanced at the other students in the hallway and moved toward a nearby corner where the lockers came to an end.

Rhys followed me cautiously. "Our conversation is shielded. You can tell me."

"My father thinks it might be false," I said.

"But there is one? For sure?"

"Yeah." I cleared my throat. "I guess you weren't lying, after all."

A smile twitched at his lips. "It's nearly impossible for a faery to lie about anything—it's in our nature to be truthful. Although, telling the truth or saying exactly what we're feeling or thinking sometimes gets us in trouble, even among ourselves."

"I'll keep that in mind."

"But it's what makes us superior to demons, really. Demons lie about everything." His lips curved some more. Was he baiting me? Trying to play games? I was *so* not in the mood this morning. Besides, I'd told enough lies recently that I couldn't exactly challenge his theory.

"Thanks a lot for your oh-so-valuable opinion." I scanned the hallway to see if I could spot Chris, but he was gone. I looked at Rhys again. "Did you know that prophecies are related by dragon oracles?"

He nodded. "Of course."

"And some of them live here in the human world?"

"Yes, they do. The prophecies given by dragon oracles are a valuable resource for demons and faeries alike."

I stared at him, suddenly realizing that out of everyone here at school, Rhys was the only one I could talk to about this who wouldn't think I was completely insane.

I exhaled a bit shakily, wanting to dislike him—this faery king alone in the human world investigating yours truly—but finding it just a bit more difficult.

As a king, my father lived a life of solitude with only servants around him, not friends and family. I sensed now that it was the same for Rhys. All alone after his parents died, with only his advisers to keep him company.

Maybe I just had a really good imagination.

In any case, I wasn't going to mistake empathy for a potential friendship with someone who might want to kill me someday.

"I have to go," I said, and turned away from him. Rhys grabbed my wrist to stop me.

"What did the prophecy say?" he asked. "I have to know."

"So you can figure out how much of a threat I am?"

His chocolate brown eyes turned serious. "Will you tell me or not?"

"Fine." I pulled my hand away from his. "It's pretty vague, but it says I'm supposed to destroy everyone. But if it makes you feel better, when I ultimately go supernova with my death ray, I promise to make a concentrated attempt to avoid the faery realm as much as possible."

He didn't say anything for a long moment. "And you think that the prophecy is false."

"It has to be. I don't have a death ray, at least not the last time I checked." Even as I said it, that edge of uncertainty crept in at the sides of my mind. I wanted to believe it was a lie, but how could I know for sure?

"It's not a good prophecy," he said.

"Thanks for the second opinion."

"You should get one of those."

"One of what?"

"A second opinion. If you're so sure it's false, you should have another oracle confirm that. It could help matters for you."

This hadn't even occurred to me. "I can do that?"

"Dragon oracles don't normally like to dispute each other's prophecies, but it would be worth a try." He crossed his arms and studied me for a moment, as if trying to come to some clear opinion about me. "I'm seeing a dragon oracle later this week."

I blinked at him. "You're *what?*"

"The dragon lives nearby, and it's another reason I'm here right now. One of my rites of passage is to meet with an oracle to receive a prophecy regarding my future as king. There are no dragons in the faery realm, and I preferred to visit the human world than travel to the dark ones. Besides, I can't stay in the dark worlds that long. It's just easier this way."

I was stunned. He had basically said that a dragon lived in the neighborhood as casually as if he was mentioning a local McDonald's. "Why can't you stay in the dark worlds?"

"I can visit but I wouldn't last long. For much the same reason your Shadow servant can't stay here permanently to be at your beck and call. Dark beings must stay in the dark worlds, and light beings in the light."

I didn't like Michael being referred to as a dark being, so I tried to ignore that. "What would happen to you?"

"I'd get weaker and weaker, steadily losing any magic or power I have until I might not be able to find a gateway home." He didn't look entirely comfortable discussing this with me. But he had said faeries were really honest, hadn't he? Maybe he felt compelled to answer my questions. It was surprisingly helpful, actually. "I can compare it to a human who scuba dives," he continued. "After an oxygen tank runs out, there isn't much time to get back to the surface before the human drowns. Faeries must stay in light worlds and Shadows must stay in dark."

"And demons?" I asked. "I know my father spent a couple months here before I was born."

"Demons are different," he said with a sour look. "The rules don't seem to apply to them. Which is why your father must maintain the barrier that holds them back. Otherwise, there's nothing stopping them from staying in other worlds for as long as it suits them."

A steady stream of students passed by us on their way to the first class of the day, the buzz of their conversations muted by the shield Rhys had put up around us. A familiar face caught my eye, though. I could have sworn I saw Michael in the middle of the crowd. I took my attention off Rhys for a moment to search everyone's faces, trying, and failing, to find him.

Knowing it had only been my imagination disappointed me.

I wished he was here. I missed him so much already and I had no idea when I'd get to see him again.

"What's wrong?" Rhys asked.

"Nothing." I shook my head, then chewed my bottom lip as I attempted to concentrate on the problem at hand. "So when are you seeing the . . . the dragon oracle?"

Even though no one was close enough to hear us, it felt so strange to talk about dragons out loud, like we were in a role-playing game.

"Soon," he said.

"How soon?"

He gave me a guarded look. "I'm not sure yet."

"Why? Not in a hurry to find out your future?" When he didn't reply to that, instead shifting his stance to look past me at the students breezing by, I continued. "So . . . what's the dragon supposed to tell you?"

His attention returned to me and a slow smile crept over his face. "Suddenly you're interested in me, are you?"

I crossed my arms. "Just call it morbid curiosity."

The idea of meeting with a real live dragon and having it confirm or deny the prophecy was surreal at best, but I could recognize an opportunity when it presented itself.

"The oracle will tell me many important things," he said simply.

That was vague.

"Can I . . . can I tag along? Get the oracle to give me that second opinion?"

He stared at me for a long moment as if considering this possibility. "Perhaps. I do need to know if this prophecy is true or not."

I glimpsed Melinda down the hall at our lockers. She'd definitely spotted me talking to Rhys in a semiprivate corner. I waved in her direction and she waved back, mouthing the words "What's going on?" to me. I shrugged back at her.

I returned my attention to the faery king. "This is way off topic, but you should know my friend likes you."

So much for being subtle. It was good that Melinda wasn't within hearing distance.

"Your friend?"

"You met her yesterday. Melinda?"

"Oh, right. I remember." He smiled at that. "She likes me?"

"I'm supposed to casually find out if you like her in return, but that doesn't work for me, since I know who you are and why you're really here. So I'm going to tell her that you have a girlfriend and so, even if you did like Melinda in return, you can't date anyone else. It'll be easier for her if you come off all honest and devoted. She won't take it personally that way."

He looked vaguely amused by my master plan. "It's not that far from the truth."

My eyebrows raised. "You have a girlfriend?"

"Is it that hard to believe?"

Hardly. If I looked at him as just a guy and not as a faery king with a fondness for sharp swords, Rhys really was megacute.

Melinda wasn't insane for developing a quick crush on him—not that I'd ever tell him that in a million years. "No, but . . . I don't know. I guess I'm surprised. You haven't mentioned her before."

"Well, it's more of a girlfriend in theory," he clarified. "A *fiancée* in theory, actually."

I scrunched my nose. "A fiancée? But you're only sixteen."

He absently dragged a hand through his short chestnut-colored hair, looking a bit uncomfortable with the direction of our conversation. "It's faery law that a king must have a queen. If he is unmarried when he takes the throne, the identity of his queen must be prophesied by an oracle."

"So that's why you're going to see the dragon."

"That's part of it."

"Matchmaking by a fire-breathing dragon. Sounds so romantic," I said sarcastically.

"It's not even remotely romantic." Rhys cleared his throat. "But it's something I have to do."

He wasn't looking forward to this unknown faery-girl matchup. I could hear it in his voice. He was being forced to accept and do things he didn't want to do out of responsibility and duty. I felt an odd sense of kinship with him there.

"It must be hard for you," I said with not an ounce of sarcasm this time.

He looked at me. "What do you mean?"

"Being . . . alone. Dealing with everything now that your parents are gone."

A shadow of pain went through his eyes. "How do you know about that?"

"I just know. I'm . . ." I swallowed hard. "I'm really sorry."

"I'm not looking for your pity."

"I'm not pitying you."

The hurt disappeared from his eyes, replaced by something harder and less vulnerable. He turned away from me. "I'll let you know when I'm seeing the oracle. That is, *if* I decide to let a half demon join me for such an important appointment. But if I were you, I wouldn't count on it."

Without another word, he walked away, leaving me standing there alone.

9

For the rest of the week I tried to act as normal as possible and put the prophecy as far out of my mind as I could. Every day I'd wait for something horrible to happen and was both relieved and slightly surprised when nothing did.

I told Melinda that Rhys was already taken and, while disappointed, she took it in stride with an optimistic "They'll probably break up."

The faery king attended school every day, although I wondered why he bothered. He didn't have to go to school at all, did he? But there he was in biology with me and also sitting with the Royal Party at lunch in the cafeteria. After how we'd left things on Tuesday, though, he stayed very quiet. He didn't ask me any more questions about the prophecy, which was fine with me, since I didn't know anything more than what I'd already told him.

Rhys continued to study me when he thought I wouldn't notice. I wondered what he was thinking, what he planned to do next. But nothing happened.

Thankfully, there were no more dissections to deal with after the frog incident. Mr. Crane was nice enough to let the students who bailed that day—there were four in total, including me and Rhys—do a virtual dissection on the computer.

I missed Michael more every day.

I swore I saw him a couple more times that week, a face in the crowd, but the moment I turned to look at him and ask why he was there, he'd disappeared.

My imagination was seriously distracting and not even slightly helpful.

I considered using my dragon's tear to find a gateway back to the Shadowlands so I could see Michael, but I stopped myself. He'd said if my father had anything to tell me, he'd come here. Until that happened, I wouldn't be a pest to either of them.

Just after school finished on Friday, I stood by my locker with Melinda. She was going through her list of things to do before the party tomorrow night. After the week I'd had, I was actually looking forward to it.

"I just realized you haven't picked a name for the gift exchange yet," she said.

"I haven't?"

She grabbed a cloth pencil case from the interior of her locker and shook it. "Remember, it's a ten-dollar limit to keep it fair for everyone."

I reached into the case and grabbed a tightly folded piece of paper. Pulling it out, I looked down at the name written on it.

Chris Sanders.

Well, that figured, didn't it?

"Somebody good?" Melinda asked with a grin. "No, don't tell me. It's supposed to be a secret."

I had to buy Chris a present. There weren't many things I could think of that were less awesome than that.

"Hey, Nikki!" I heard from across the hall. It was Rhys.

"Yeah?" I replied guardedly.

"Can I talk to you?"

"Uh, sure. Just a sec."

Melinda leaned toward me and whispered, "Rhys is coming to the party tomorrow night, too. Isn't that great?"

"Yeah. That's . . . that's great."

"He accepted the invite just this morning." She grinned. "I'm even being all tacky and putting up some mistletoe. It's going to be great."

"Nikki," Rhys said again, less patiently.

"Sounds important," Melinda said, not without humor. "Maybe he's broken up with his boring girlfriend and wants you to set things up between him and me."

The girl had a one-track mind. Did she ever think of anything more important than guys? "You never know."

"I have to get to my dance lesson in twenty minutes," she said, glancing at her watch. "I have another one tomorrow afternoon, but do you think you can come by my house at about five o'clock so you can help me with the decorations? I should be finished with ballet by then."

I forced a smile. "I'll be there."

"See you later," she said. And then her attention shifted. "See you at the party tomorrow, Rhys."

"Bye, Melinda," Rhys replied.

She walked away down the hall, and I could have sworn she was swinging her hips a bit more than usual. Melinda could have any guy she wanted, and she'd absolutely decided it was going to be Rhys. Fabulous.

"What do you want?" I asked Rhys, walking over to him. I didn't even attempt to make it sound superfriendly.

"I'm going now."

"Oh." I tried to ignore the sudden pang I felt in my chest. The only one in the human world I could talk to about non-human subjects was leaving. "Going back to Faeryville already? Just like that? One week and you've got all the information you need?"

"No, not leaving completely. I'm going to see the oracle. Right now."

Right now?

I'd pretty much given up all hope that Rhys would tell me when he was going. I'd asked him daily in class when he was seeing the dragon. He'd either changed the subject or ignored me entirely.

"Well?" he prompted after a moment. "Do you want to go with me or not?"

I stared at him. "I thought you didn't want me to come along."

"I don't."

"Then why would you do this?"

"Because if I ignore a chance to get to the bottom of your prophecy, I will have failed my people."

Despite myself, I couldn't help but smile. "Are all non-human guys so serious all the time?"

He frowned. "What do you mean?"

"Michael . . ." Just saying his name made me miss him even

more. It had been four long days since I'd last been with him, even though I'd imagined seeing him around the school a few times this week. "Well, he's always serious. Not much with the joking around."

"Michael is your Shadow servant?"

I flinched. "I guess you could call him that."

He raised an eyebrow. "If you want a jester to amuse you and tell funny stories, I suggest you look to someone other than a Shadow for that. And other than me, for that matter."

"That's not what I'm saying. I mean, I've seen you smile and joke around a bit."

"I used to be that way. But being king doesn't leave me a lot of time for having fun. Not anymore."

"So going to Melinda's party tomorrow night is just . . . more stern and serious research?"

He smiled at that, and it struck me then how rarely he smiled. Like Michael, he was much better looking when he did. "Humans are interesting creatures to observe in social situations."

I shook my head. "You *so* don't sound sixteen."

"And how does someone who's sixteen sound?"

"Like me." I grinned.

His smile widened. "I'll have to remember that."

Stop smiling, Nikki, I told myself. *Rhys is not your friend.* "So, uh, the oracle thing—"

"I have an appointment scheduled in an hour. Are you coming with me?"

I nodded. "I'm coming."

"Then let's go."

No more questions, no more chitchat. It was time to get a second opinion about my prophecy. Maybe I could get it in writing, like a doctor's note, to prove I wasn't going to destroy anything or anyone anytime soon.

"How are we going to get there?" I asked.

"I have a car and chauffeur waiting out front."

He was very organized.

"Thanks, Rhys. For . . . for taking me with you," I said awkwardly.

He gave a slight shrug. "You're welcome. Just don't tell my advisers about this. I don't think they'd understand my motivation."

Was he breaking the rules by doing this? Rhys the rebel. Who knew? I felt a strange sense of gratitude toward the faery king for letting me tag along. Otherwise, I would have had to find another dragon, and they weren't just listed in the Yellow Pages. Believe me, I'd already checked.

I followed him through the hallways to the front entrance of the school but I abruptly stopped walking when I saw somebody familiar.

"Mom?" I said with surprise. "What are you doing here?"

My mother, dressed in a knee-length white winter coat cinched at the waist, turned to look at me. There was a big smile on her face. She stroked her dark hair—a stark contrast to my blonde—away from her forehead and secured it behind her ears.

"Hi, honey," she greeted me. "I wanted to surprise you and pick you up today. I was just about to call your cell phone to let you know I'm here."

My attention moved from her to the person she'd been

talking to. The one who'd put the superchipper grin on her face.

"Hi, Nikki." Mr. Crane, my biology teacher, nodded in my direction.

My mom put her hand on Mr. Crane's arm. "I'm so glad I came inside the school. I got a chance to meet Nathan."

"Nathan?" I repeated.

She smiled and looked at the first-name-basis teacher in question. "He tells me you're improving in his class. Maybe bring that C you got last year in biology up to at least a B?"

"Or better," Mr. "Nathan" Crane said. "I think your daughter can do anything she sets her mind to. She's very bright."

I didn't like the way he was looking at my mother. He was looking at her like she was a . . . a *woman*.

Admittedly, a lot of men looked at her that way. She was only thirty-four years old, which, she constantly reminded me, wasn't that old at all. She dressed fashionably and she worked out regularly at the gym. At least he didn't mistake us for sisters. It had happened more often than I'd like to admit.

"I thought we could head to the mall," she said to me, "and maybe grab some dinner there?"

"I . . ." I looked at Rhys, who was keeping a low profile to my left. "I kind of already made plans."

"Plans?" she said curiously. Her gaze shifted to the faery king for a moment and then moved closer to me as she lowered her voice. "Is that the boy you mentioned to me the other day? Michael? Are you dating him again?"

I forgot to breathe for a moment. Inhale, exhale—it was a lost concept for me. My temples started to itch. I concentrated on not letting my emotions get away from me in case there was a random horn appearance. Why had I told her about that? Had Rhys heard what she just said?

"Uh . . . no. This is . . . um, Rhys." It sounded as strained as it felt.

"Oh, someone new. Very good. I firmly believe the best way to mend a broken heart is to focus on someone new and wonderful." She raised her voice above our conspiratorial whisper. "Nice to meet you, Rhys."

"Likewise," Rhys said.

No one else could know about me and Michael. I'd broken up with him to protect him, but if any rumors started, then his life would be in danger whether we were really together or not.

And I didn't particularly appreciate Mom making it sound as if I were doing the same thing she always did: lose one guy and replace him immediately before she had a chance to feel unwanted. That was *her* problem—she couldn't bear to be alone for long—not mine. Rhys most certainly wasn't Michael's replacement in my life. However, I couldn't exactly explain that to her without telling her everything else as well.

"So, anyway, we're out of here," I tried to say calmly. "I'll be home in a few hours, okay? Maybe we can do the mall thing another day."

"Susan," Mr. Crane said, "since it sounds like you're free, perhaps you'd be interested in grabbing an early dinner with me?"

She turned to him. "That sounds wonderful."

No, it did *not* sound wonderful. I felt the color draining from my face. My biology teacher was totally making a move on my mom. She'd been single—well, seeking a quick divorce from the last jerk, anyway—for only a week, and now somebody else was already asking her out? And true to her serial-dating record, she didn't seem to mind at all.

"Nikki, we need to go now," Rhys said.

"See you later, honey," Mom said. "Have fun."

Mr. Crane just gave me an awkward wave.

Without another word, I followed Rhys outside. There was a Lincoln Town Car waiting. The driver got out and opened the back door so we could get inside.

I couldn't believe this. Mr. Crane was totally going to be Husband Number Five, wasn't he? This was horrible.

Not that I didn't like him okay for a teacher. But as a step-father? I didn't want a stepfather. I wanted my *real* father.

The whole situation made my head hurt, and a simmering headache wasn't a good sign for proper Darkling management.

"So," Rhys began as the car pulled onto the road toward our unknown destination. "Michael isn't only your servant, he's your boyfriend, too? You know that's not allowed, right?"

That did it.

Stress coursed through me and I felt a popping sensation on the sides of my head.

"Oops." I reached up to touch my short spiral horns.

Rhys scooted back from me on the seat. "Uh, I'd appreciate it if you don't completely shift form in this car. It's rented."

I looked down at my hands. My talons glinted back at me. My eyes widened as I looked toward the chauffeur. Rhys followed my gaze.

"Don't worry about him."

"You put a glamour on us?"

"Something like that. He's driving us where we need to go, but he won't notice or remember anything out of the ordinary."

"Well, that's good," I said uncertainly. "Weird, but good."

"That sounds about right." Rhys just stared at me.

"Is it only the horns?" I asked, pointing at my face.

"And your eyes are red and glowing. And your hair . . ."

I nervously twisted a talon through my currently flame-red locks. Well, at least my wings hadn't unfurled. They might have broken through a window. Small blessing. I glanced at him. "You don't have to be afraid of me, you know."

"I'm not afraid."

"You look petrified."

"Do I?" He cleared his throat nervously.

"I'm not going to hurt you. I swear."

He didn't look convinced. "Let's just say I didn't expect this. Maybe I should have. I guess I got used to you looking completely human."

I grimaced. "I'm totally demonic, right?"

"Well, I wouldn't say that exactly. I . . . I saw a demon up close once. He was allowed into the faery realm to deliver a message to my parents. You look different from him. The eyes are the same but your hair is different." He tentatively reached forward to touch a lock of my red hair. "It's so soft."

"What did you expect?"

"Well, the demon I saw was completely bald. Shows off the horns better, maybe." Still looking uncertain and a bit freaked out, he ran his index finger up over my left horn. I grabbed his hand and pushed him away from me.

"Sorry. I was curious." Then he let out a short, nervous laugh, looking down at my taloned hand.

"I'll change back in a sec. I just need to calm down a bit."

"Think about, like, a bubbling brook," he suggested. "Or a unicorn—the one you saw the day we first met. Those are pleasant, calming images."

"I'm on it." I closed my eyes and willed myself to de-stress. After a couple of minutes it started to work. I felt a pinch and then a moment of painful wooziness as the horns disappeared. I touched my head to make sure and was relieved to feel they were gone.

"You need to keep an eye on your emotions, huh?" Rhys asked.

"I'm told it gets easier."

"It wasn't as bad as I'd expected, actually. The demon I saw before was really scary and ugly. You're . . . well, you're *not*."

"Not scary or ugly?"

"You're not ugly. Still scary, though."

True to what Rhys had said, even with such a strange conversation in the backseat, the chauffeur didn't glance at us in the rearview mirror once. He was focused only on the road ahead.

I eyed Rhys warily. "I freaked you out?"

"A little," he admitted after a moment. "But I also found it strangely interesting."

"Glad I amuse you."

He shook his head. "After observing you now for a whole week, I'm more confused than ever."

"About what?"

"My advisers are positive you're evil incarnate, based on

centuries of rumors about Darklings and our current knowledge of demons in general. Demons are our enemies, after all. I was convinced of it myself from the moment we first met. But . . ." His brows drew together. "But, now I'm not so sure."

The thought that Rhys wasn't entirely convinced I was evil was a strange relief. I felt myself relax for the first time that day. Just a little.

"And that's why we're going to see this oracle of yours," I said. "To prove it to you once and for all."

"And to prove it to you as well. If you were certain there wasn't any darkness inside you, I don't think you would have needed this trip. You'd know in your heart that you could never destroy anything."

I gritted my teeth, not liking that he seemed to know me so well, so quickly. "It's complicated, I guess."

"Just as complicated as you and Michael?"

I looked out the window as the road sped past us. "There is no me and Michael. Not anymore."

"Because he's your servant or because of the many rules and regulations your demon friends have against interspecies dating?"

"Because of lots of things."

He was quiet for a moment. "Just remember, there are solid reasons behind all rules, especially the ones that govern beings like Shadows."

I looked at him. "What's that supposed to mean?"

"I don't know. I've heard things—that Shadows can be dangerous, even more so than demons."

Even though Michael had told me the other day that some

demons were afraid of Shadows, I still didn't believe it. "You have no idea what you're talking about."

"Then I'll stop talking."

"Good idea."

I remembered leaving school with Michael on Monday. What was the last thing Rhys had said to me?

Just be careful with him.

Ridiculous.

I didn't say anything else, and Rhys didn't try to engage me in conversation. Shadows were dangerous and demons feared them? Sure, they were. That's why they were kept around as servants. It made zero sense.

A half hour later we reached our destination. The currently enchanted and, thankfully, oblivious chauffeur got out of the car and opened the back door.

"Wait for us here," Rhys told him.

"Yes, Your Majesty," the chauffeur replied without any hesitation.

"Follow me," Rhys said. "She's expecting us."

I had been so distracted by turning Darkling and by Rhys's reaction that I'd completely forgotten about where we were headed. I hadn't had enough time to mentally prepare myself for what was going to happen next—I was about to meet an actual *dragon*.

I took a deep breath and let it out slowly.

I really hoped the sweater I was wearing wasn't flammable.

10

"Come with me."

I looked up with surprise. A woman stood before us holding a clipboard to her chest. She was probably around forty years old, with light brown hair in a short flippy-yet-professional style. She wore a green blouse, which looked designer and fit her slim frame perfectly, and gray dress pants. She turned and walked through a door at the end of a short hallway.

Rhys began to follow her, but I grabbed his arm.

"Where is she taking us?" I asked.

"Down the hall."

"I see that, but . . . but is that where the dragon is?" I said under my breath. I was confused and Rhys was not exactly helping. I didn't understand why the car had dropped us off at a doctor's office. "Is there a secret passageway?"

He looked at me. "I find it charming how completely clueless you are."

I glared at him. "Gee, thanks."

"You're very welcome. Now, just come on. And stop worrying so much."

Easy for him to say.

Sticking close to Rhys, I forced myself to trail behind the woman as we went through a door. It led into a richly deco-rated room with a black leather couch across from a large black lacquered desk. On the wall were framed medical certificates.

One thing led me to believe that, despite all appearances, we were in the right place. Among folders and paperwork and a laptop computer, several small gold dragon sculptures sat on the desk.

The woman we followed moved to stand beside the desk near the gold dragons. She smiled and dipped her head toward Rhys.

"Your Majesty," she said. "Welcome."

"Thank you," he replied.

So she knew who Rhys was? Was she going to lead us to see the dragon oracle after a brief . . . I glanced around . . . checkup?

"What kind of doctor's office is this?" I asked, trying to remain calm, or at least appear like I was. I was grateful that my surge of apprehension about being there didn't feel as if it would trigger any Darkling shifts. At least, not yet.

Her gaze moved to me. "It's an office of psychiatric medi-cine. My specialty."

"You're a psychiatrist?"

"Yes, I am. My name is Irena."

"This is Nikki Donovan," Rhys introduced me. "*Princess* Nikki."

He said it very respectfully and not in the least bit mock-ingly. I did appreciate that.

Irena nodded. "The Darkling."

More apprehension. "You know about me?"

"Yes, of course." She touched her necklace, which held a large amber pendant. "King Rhys called ahead to let me know you might be joining him today. It's a pleasure to meet you."

She stood and extended her hand and I shook it, about to ask where the dragon was and what I should expect to happen next. But then I suddenly noticed that her eyes were the same vibrant shade of amber as her pendant. Like, the *exact* same shade. When she blinked, I could have sworn her pupils elongated.

It reminded me of something. Of a . . . lizard.

My own eyes widened at the thought, and I pulled my hand away from her.

"Hold on," I said. "You're a psychiatrist?"

"Yes."

"But not only a psychiatrist."

She smiled. "That's correct."

I'd expected the dragon oracle to be large and green and scaly. Not well dressed and well coiffed.

I forced myself not to cower away from her and launch myself to the safer side of the leather couch. "You're the . . . the . . ."

"The one you're here to see," she finished for me. "Yes, I am."

"Sorry," I managed. "I'm just surprised. You look so . . . uh . . ."

"Human?" Irena glanced at Rhys, who regarded my flabbergasted reaction with more than a little amusement. "It helps to look as human as possible when one wishes to fit in with other humans. I've maintained this form for so long that I barely remember my other one." She ran her finger along the spine of one of the small gold dragons. "But I do keep reminders around so I don't forget completely."

Rhys sat down on the leather couch. "Irena's lived in the human world for nearly twenty years. She even has a family here."

"A family of dragons?" I asked, trying to wrap my head around the fact that an actual fire-breathing mythical creature had a doctor's office thirty minutes from where I lived.

She shook her head. "I have a human husband and together we have a son."

"And they know who you really are?" I couldn't seem to stop myself from asking questions.

"My husband does. My son will be told when I feel he's mature enough to deal with it. Dragons and humans rarely produce offspring that is anything other than one hundred percent human, so it's not an immediate issue."

I was talking to a fortune-telling, future-seeing dragon in human form with a human family, and she made her living as a shrink. Well, something had to pay the bills, didn't it?

When I continued to stare at her in shock, she smiled. "But enough about me. Unfortunately, I only have a few minutes to spare today for you both before I must get back to my regular patients. I hope that will be enough time."

"I'm sure it will," Rhys said quickly.

Irena looked so totally and completely human. Then again, so did my father when he chose to have a human form. I'd seen him in demon form—coal black skin, expansive black leathery wings, large curved horns, and glowing red eyes. Same father on the inside, *way* different on the outside.

"Let's start with you, Princess." She pulled out the top drawer on her desk and withdrew a crystal sphere about the size of a baseball. "News of the prophecy has already reached me. It's a very serious one." She sounded surprisingly calm about it.

"Yes, it is," I said tightly. "So I'm here for a second opinion. It can't be true. But I'm worried what might happen next if I can't prove it's false."

She closed her eyes. "Let me see what I can find. I should be able to tell if the prophecy is clear or covered in a web of darkness and lies."

"Uh, that would be good. Thank you."

She held the crystal ball in the palm of her hand, and after a moment I saw a pulse of white light right in the very center of it.

"I have located the prophecy about the first Darkling in a thousand years," she said with a nod, but she didn't open her eyes yet.

The white light flickered to other colors—pink, green, orange. It was beautiful, really. But then it began to darken.

Irena shook her head, her forehead creasing. Her chest hitched. "It's . . . it's harder to see than I expected. I need to go deeper to gain clarity."

Shade by shade it grew darker until it appeared as if the crystal contained a solid, dark purple core.

Suddenly the center flashed from the darkness to a light so bright I had to shield my eyes. Irena's face grew strained and pale and a small gasp escaped her lips.

"Irena, is everything okay?" Rhys asked, concern in his voice.

"What's going on?" I asked him.

He shook his head. "It shouldn't be this difficult. She should already know the truth one way or the other."

"Something's blocking my vision. There's a thick wall around the Darkling prophecy. I can't see past it." Irena's eyelids fluttered and she cried out in pain. The crystal ball slipped from her grasp and I jumped as it shattered on the floor.

I didn't need Rhys to tell me that this wasn't normal. He'd moved from the couch and placed a hand on Irena's shoulder to steady her as her eyes snapped open.

"What happened?" Rhys asked.

She shook her head. "I'm not sure. I could see something, but not clearly enough to confirm or deny the prophecy. I'm so sorry."

Concern mixed with disappointment. While I wanted to know the truth, I didn't want it to cause anyone pain, and it was obvious that searching out my prophecy in the metaphysical ether—or whatever she had just tried to do—had not been big fun for her. To say the very least.

"Are you okay?" I asked.

"Yes, I'll be fine." She reached out to grab my wrist and drew me closer. She looked weary, and there was a thin sheen of perspiration on her forehead. "However, I did see something else—another prophecy. Princess, you are in danger. A darkness surrounds you and it is growing stronger."

"A darkness?" I asked. My mouth felt dry.

"It watches you closely now and in the future. One day, unless you're very careful, it will consume you entirely."

"The darkness," Rhys repeated. "Is that what might take her over so she will fulfill the Darkling prophecy?"

I gave him a look, thinking he was being sarcastic, but by his expression I could tell he wasn't. It was a legitimate question. After all, he'd taken me along with him today so he could learn the truth as well.

"No," Irena replied. "This has nothing to do with the first prophecy—it's a separate thing altogether. And the darkness comes from a source apart from the princess. I'm sorry, but my vision was unclear, so I can't give more specifics. There is very little about you that is clear, Princess Nikki. Perhaps your human side is what blocks my magic. That may explain why the first prophecy was shielded from me."

So this darkness thing was a *second* prophecy. I'd come here today to have the first one debunked, not to cash in on a two-for-one deal.

I just nodded, trying to take it all in and make some kind of sense of it. Being consumed by an outer darkness struck me as something straight out of a horror movie. Something that had the potential to keep me up at night worried about what was lurking under my bed or behind my closet doors.

"Did you see anything else?" I asked shakily. "Anything good?"

Irena squeezed my wrist. "I did see that there is a possibility the princess's light may, with effort, be enough to quell this darkness."

"Her light?" Rhys asked, confused. "But she's half demon. How is that even possible?"

"It's possible because her soul is pure." Irena's voice had

gotten steadily stronger as she spoke. "I saw no evil here you should be concerned with, King Rhys."

"Really?" Rhys sounded skeptical.

"Yes, really." Irena glanced at him. "You're surprised?"

"I . . . don't know. Maybe a little." His eyes flicked to me before he looked away, his expression still clouded with confusion.

I almost smiled. Out of everything horrible that had just happened—not being able to prove or disprove the first prophecy, almost making Irena's head explode, finding out that darkness stalks me in a shiny new second prophecy—the fact that she'd just confirmed to Rhys that I wasn't completely demonically evil almost made it worthwhile.

"This is all I can do for you today, Princess," Irena said. "I apologize for not having been more helpful."

I nodded, twisting my bracelet nervously as I went over everything in my head. "Thank you. It's a start."

Her pleasant, caring expression faded, and I realized she was now staring down at my wrist. She suddenly grabbed hold of my arm so hard, I couldn't pull away.

"You have a dragon's tear." The way she said it, her shock at noticing my piece of jewelry for the first time, made my blood run cold.

"It . . . it was a gift," I said quietly.

Irena raised her eyes to mine and hers were now pure gold with those long black slits. Any friendliness that had been there previously had vanished as if it never existed. Right then I knew I'd been wrong when I'd mistaken her for completely human. She wasn't. The magic poured off her now, making my skin tingle. I could practically see the green scales, the sharp spikes running along her spine, the long heavy tail whipping back and forth angrily, the wisps of smoke from her nostrils.

"The magic of one of my brothers or sisters dangles from your wrist. You wear the evidence of murder as if it means nothing to you. I didn't even sense it when you walked in here, which means you rarely, if ever, have used it. You take such an ultimate sacrifice for granted?"

"No, I . . . of course I don't." I flinched as her nails dug into my skin.

"Irena," Rhys said sharply. "Let go of her. *Now.*"

Irena clenched her straight white teeth, and I felt I could almost see the long, sharp incisors there, waiting for her to shift to her true form and take a big bite out of me. She let go of me so abruptly that I staggered back a few feet.

"Leave now, Princess," she said evenly. "King Rhys's reading is to be given in private."

I looked at Rhys. He nodded. "Wait in the hall. It's okay. I won't be long."

He looked disturbed by what had just happened. About what Irena had said? Or because he now knew a dragon had died to give me my pretty wrist accessory? After all, I'd already seen him get upset about a dead frog. This was . . . well, a bit bigger than that. To say the least.

Ten minutes passed, but it felt more like ten weeks before Rhys finally emerged from Irena's office. While I waited, I tried my best to process what I'd heard, but I didn't know where to begin. None of it made any sense to me. And none of it was particularly helpful.

"Here," Rhys said as he thrust something small and rectangular at me. "Thought you might want one."

It was Irena's business card with her phone number on it. Not that it was likely she'd ever want to talk to me again.

"Thanks." I shoved it into my wallet inside my backpack and scurried to keep up with Rhys as he quickly walked toward the waiting car outside. "So how did it go?"

"Fine."

"You got the answers you were looking for?"

He didn't look directly at me. "I did."

If nothing else, I was grateful to be with Rhys right now. No one else in the human world knew what I was going through, but he did. He might be able to help me make sense of everything. Plus, Irena had all but confirmed I was no threat to faery life. Maybe Rhys and I could be friends, after all. The thought gave me a weird sense of hope in the middle of a bizarre situation.

"Do you think I should find another dragon oracle and try again?" I asked.

"I don't know."

The flippant, disinterested way he said it was anything but reassuring. Snow blew past me as we reached the car and I felt the cold bite into me. "Is there something wrong?"

He looked at me. "What?"

"Are you okay?"

"I'm fine."

"Are you upset about the dragon's tear?" I covered it with my hand. "I feel terrible. I never would have worn it if I had known it would upset her."

"I don't care about your bracelet."

"You don't? But a dragon died."

"Did you kill it?"

"No. Of course not."

"Then I don't care."

He looked away as he got into the backseat of the car before I did.

I sensed a major chilliness between us. What happened? Had I said something to upset him?

I got in the car and tried to catch his eye. He was looking anywhere but at me.

Tears pricked at the backs of my eyes. I felt utterly alone at that moment.

There was a long pause after the chauffeur shut the door behind me. I sat as far away from Rhys as I could and put my seat belt on.

The car began to move, starting on the half-hour drive back to Erin Heights. I pressed my lips together, my arms crossed tightly in front of me.

"Look, I'm sorry," Rhys finally said after several minutes passed. "I know that was rough for you. You wanted a clean answer—to hear that the prophecy's a complete and total lie. I thought that's what you'd get, but it doesn't always work that way. Dragon oracles are never completely cut-and-dried when it comes to seeing the future. Even with the best readings there's always a great deal of interpretation that needs to happen. My advisers usually spend ages trying to decipher a dragon's visions. But . . . she didn't tell you it was absolutely the truth, either. There's still a spark of hope, isn't there?"

"A spark," I agreed. "A teeny, tiny, pathetic little spark."

His jaw tightened. "And yeah, I got answers. Mostly vague, and mostly not what I wanted to hear, either."

Despite his breaking the uncomfortable silence between us, I couldn't help but feel a major amount of tension in the car. Rhys wasn't happy right now, to say the least. Even less happy than I was, if that was humanly—faerily?—possible.

I struggled to find something else to say.

"Did she help you figure out who you're supposed to marry?" I asked.

He snorted. "You could say that. But she's wrong."

"You think she was lying?"

"No . . . not lying. Just . . ." He shook his head and sighed. "I figure she's unclear. She couldn't see your prophecy clearly, so I bet the same applies to mine."

Wow. Majorly unhappy reaction. Was this what had put him into cranky-faery mode? He obviously didn't approve of his intended. Maybe it would make him realize that getting married at sixteen was stupid and unnecessary, even for other-worldly royalty.

"So, what?" I asked, latching onto this as a good subject for us to discuss. "Is your future faery bride too ugly for you?"

Rhys leaned back against the head rest and studied the seat back in front of him. "That's not it."

"Too old or too young?"

"No."

I rolled my eyes, but smiled. This was why he was upset. He hadn't landed the perfect bride-to-be. "Her pretty faery wings aren't the right shade of sparkly lavender and pink?"

His eyes flashed with anger. "Actually, she doesn't have faery wings."

"She doesn't?"

"No. As a matter of fact, the dragon oracle tells me the girl I'm supposed to marry, the one destined to someday become the queen of the faery realm, isn't a faery at all."

Okay, that was surprising. Not a faery?

"She isn't?" I said. "Then who is she?"

His expression was severe as he turned to look me right in the eye.

"You," he said.

11

I stared blankly at Rhys for what felt like about three days.

"Me?" I finally sputtered.

He nodded.

"You're kidding, right?"

"Not kidding."

I laughed then, and it sounded slightly hysterical. "I'm not going to marry you."

"I'm not asking you to."

"Good."

He eyed me. "And you can wipe that horrified look off your face because it's obviously not true."

"Do I look horrified?"

"Yes, you do."

I grimaced. "Nothing personal, Rhys, but—"

He held up a hand. "Say nothing else. I shouldn't have even mentioned it to you. I'll find another dragon to help me."

"Second opinions are really important," I said.

He just glowered at that.

We rode the rest of the way back to Erin Heights in silence. Now I had even more information crowding my already full brain. Maybe that Irena chick should go see a shrink, herself. She was one crazy dragon lady.

Marry Rhys? That was completely ridiculous. Sure, over the last couple of days I'd started warming up to him a little. He knew I was a demon princess when no one else in the human world did—not including Chris, of course—and that was both reassuring and a bit scary, depending on the hour of the day. But that didn't mean I wanted to date him, let alone marry him and magically become the queen of the faeries.

Some of the books I'd studied in history class talked about arranged marriages. A few years ago, before my mom wrote about vampires and other monsters in love, she wrote historical romances, and a major plot point usually involved the heroine having to marry somebody she didn't want to in order for her family to survive and prosper.

But this wasn't two hundred years ago. It was now. And nobody, at least not in Erin Heights, got married because it had been arranged—especially not by a dragon in human form who saw fuzzy and indistinct images of the future.

Once we got back to town, I leaned forward so I could tell the chauffeur my address. He approached my street and pulled up at the curb. The sight was a relief after such a stressful, emotional day.

"Do you go back to the faery realm every day after school?" I asked Rhys, feeling strange at breaking the heavy silence between us but wanting to say something before I left.

"No."

"You stay in Erin Heights?"

"Yes."

"With who?"

"At a hotel."

"All by yourself?"

He nodded.

"Isn't that lonely?" I asked.

He raised his brown eyes to mine, and I saw there was now zero humor there. "Time for you to go, Nikki. It's been a long day."

"Wow, somebody's touchy, isn't he?"

"We've arrived at your house. Please get out of this car now."

I wasn't quite ready to move yet, or to follow the king's every order. "Are you still going to Melinda's party tomorrow night?"

"I don't know. Probably not."

The chauffeur exited the car and came around to my side to open the door. "You don't have to feel weird about this, you know. I'm not going to tell anyone. The dragon must have given you a false reading."

"I know that. There's no way she could possibly be right about this."

He sounded pretty darn certain.

"Oh, well, good," I said.

"And do you know how I know?" he asked, his teeth clenched. I hadn't realized it until then, but he was actually angry about this. "Because you're a *demon*."

"Half demon," I corrected.

"Whatever." He looked at me, and there was more distaste in his perusal than I remembered ever seeing before. "Demons are evil creatures of darkness and I want no association with them, now or in the future. I *hate* them."

I glared at him as my own level of anger rose. He was

basically saying he hated *me*, wasn't he? "Any particular rea-son, or just because hating demons is in fashion right now?"

He held my gaze steadily, but after a moment I saw his bot-tom lip quiver just a little bit and pain flicker in his eyes. "A demon killed my parents."

That unexpected statement knocked the breath right out of me. "Rhys, I didn't know—"

"Please, Nikki . . ." He shook his head and turned his face away from me. "Seriously. Leave me alone."

I wanted to say something but I wasn't sure what. Words escaped me. So instead, feeling sick inside, I did what he asked. I got out of the backseat and the door closed behind me. The car drove away and soon disappeared into the distance.

* * *

The whole next day, I tried to keep a very low profile. I stayed home, mostly in my room. I even caught up on some homework. As it was the beginning of the weekend, this was not over-looked by my mother.

She practically had to drag me away from my safe bedroom and English homework for a mother-daughter lunch early Sat-urday afternoon.

"Everything okay, honey?" she asked. I could tell she was still concerned about what had happened earlier that week—my lie about going to the mall with Melinda. Her trust in me was on shaky ground and would be for a while.

I missed Michael desperately. When he said he wouldn't

come to the human world to see me again until my father sent him, he hadn't been lying. Despite thinking I'd spotted him out of the corner of my eye a couple of times this week, it had been five whole days since I'd last seen him for real.

And Rhys . . . well, he obviously hated me. I figured it was mostly because his parents had been killed by a demon, leaving him all alone and forced to take the throne whether he wanted to or not. While I didn't think this was cause to hate an entire species—even if that species was *demon*—I couldn't really hold it against him too much. It still kind of bothered me, though. I didn't want to be judged because of something I had absolutely no control over. I was half demon and I wasn't going to be changing any time soon.

And the prophecy—make that *prophecies*—well, I had no idea what to do about them. The next time I saw my father, I'd ask if he could find another dragon to help me get to the bottom of things. Yes, that was the sum total of my fabulous plan of action. I was working on something better, but nothing was immediately coming to mind, unfortunately.

Add to that the fact that I knew Mom was still hurt, so I was trying my best to be a good daughter.

"No, nothing's wrong," I told my mother. I could tell she knew I was lying, but luckily she didn't press for more information. Maybe she figured it was simply the same boyfriend problems. "How was your date with Mr. Crane?"

"It wasn't really an official date."

"Dinner, then."

"It was nice. You're lucky to have him as a teacher."

She wasn't gushing about how wonderful he was, so I hoped that meant there were no wedding bells in her immediate future.

Finally some good news.

"Are you seeing him again?" I asked.

"We have dinner plans tonight." She looked at me innocently. "I know you're going to Melinda's party, so I figured you wouldn't mind."

Good news status removed.

"Why would I mind?" I said tightly.

She brightened. "I'm glad to hear it."

Admittedly, with all my distractions and problems, I hadn't been a stellar friend to Melinda lately, and I wanted to show her that I was helpful and reliable—at least *sometimes*. Besides, my only other choice at the moment was to hang out at home and feel sorry for myself.

I could still feel sorry for myself. But I decided to do it at Melinda's party, where I could make myself useful and where there would be loud music—the louder the better—to drown out most of my thoughts.

I got to her house just before five o'clock, but when I knocked no one answered. After a minute, I noticed the front door was unlocked, so I let myself in like I'd done a couple times before.

I was wearing a thin red sweater and black jeans under my winter coat. I forgot about adding any festive green to the outfit when I realized I didn't own anything other than a supremely tacky pair of green earrings.

Besides, green just made me think about Michael's amulet. And his eyes.

Before I could yell out Melinda's name to track her down in her huge house, I heard raised voices coming from nearby. It was two people arguing loudly.

"I hate this," Melinda said, sounding angry. "I keep practicing and practicing and I'm not getting any better."

"You are," an unfamiliar male voice soothed. "You need to trust your instincts."

Was this one of her dance lessons? I hadn't known she took them in her own house. That was convenient, wasn't it?

"Why can't you get someone else to do this instead of me?" Melinda asked.

"The power to do this is in your blood, Melinda. You need to work with me instead of fighting me all the time."

She laughed, but it didn't sound happy. "I thought you wanted me to fight you."

"I do, but . . ." He sighed. "You're only making this more difficult on yourself. You won't be ready."

"Ready? For what?" There was a mocking tone to her voice. "I haven't seen anything that makes me believe all the crazy things you've told me are even remotely true."

I didn't want to eavesdrop on a private conversation, but they were being so loud I couldn't help myself. It sure didn't sound like a discussion about dance lessons to me.

"You haven't been reading the books downstairs, have you?" the man said.

"I've read all the stupid books—the ones in English, anyway—and I don't believe any of it." She took in a shaky breath. "You're trying to ruin my life. Everything was great until I met you."

"Okay, that's enough." He sounded weary of arguing. "Today's lesson is over."

"Good. I have a party tonight—"

"A party?" His words twisted with sudden annoyance. "You need to forget about parties and friends and focus on what's important."

"It's not fair."

"Life isn't fair, Melinda. And you'd best get that through your head now so we won't have problems in the future. Your duty is to learn and to get stronger so you won't fail when the time comes to prove yourself. I'm counting on you not to let everyone down."

"Just leave me alone!"

The next moment Melinda came storming into the foyer and froze in her tracks when she saw me standing there. Her face was red and shiny with perspiration. She looked the least fashionable I'd ever seen her. She wore a black T-shirt, gray sweatpants that were a bit ripped, and Nike running shoes. Her long light blonde hair was pulled back in a tight braid, her bangs slicked to her forehead.

"Nikki, hey," she said. "I . . . I didn't know you were here already."

I felt confused and more than a little awkward. I knew I wasn't meant to overhear whatever they'd been arguing about.

"You told me to come early to help set up, so here I am. The front door was unlocked."

The bearer of the male voice entered the foyer behind her. He was tall and muscular and dressed in sweats. He had broad shoulders and dark red hair. He didn't look that much older than us—maybe a few years. His blue eyes moved from Melinda to me. They narrowed.

"Who are you?" he demanded. "What are you doing here?"

"I . . . I'm Nikki."

His expression shifted to a sour one, as if he smelled something funny coming from my general direction.

"She's my best friend," Melinda snapped. "Don't bother her."

"I thought for a moment that she was . . ." He trailed off, continuing to study me closely, then shook his head as if to clear it. "Never mind. I must have been mistaken."

"We're finished, aren't we?" she asked.

His jaw clenched. He might be sort of cute if he didn't look so miserable. "Fine, we're finished. But I'll be back tomorrow."

"But I need to—" she began.

"No arguments, Melinda. You still have a long way to go before you're ready. I'll be back tomorrow. Enjoy your *party*." He nearly spat the last word.

In silence, he turned and left through the doors behind me.

Okay, that was intense.

"Who was that?" I asked.

She cleared her throat. "Patrick? He's, um . . . he's my dance instructor."

I blinked. "He doesn't look like a dance instructor."

She laughed and it sounded shaky. "I know, right? Weird. But that's who he is."

I scanned her sweats. "I thought you were supposed to wear a leotard and ballet slippers for your dance lessons."

She looked down at her Nikes. "You've clearly never taken ballet, have you?"

"No, never."

"There you go. Uh, we only wear the fancy stuff for the recitals."

She was lying to me; it was so totally obvious. But I didn't understand why.

"Where are your parents?" I asked.

"Gone for the rest of the night, visiting friends from my dad's old fraternity." She looked relieved I'd changed the subject. "They told me that if there's any damage from the party, I'm grounded until I'm thirty."

"Do they know you and your dance instructor argue so much?"

She crossed her arms. "They're the ones who hired him in the first place. And Patrick and I don't argue, we *debate*."

"Sounded like a loud debate to me. And I don't think he liked me very much."

"Patrick doesn't like anybody." She walked over to the base of the staircase and leaned against it, trying and failing to look casual. "I'm sorry you had to hear that. He . . . he has his own way of coaching me, and whenever I want to change something he has a fit."

"He's kind of cute."

She scrunched her nose. "You think?"

I nodded. "I'm surprised you don't think so. You're normally the expert on these things."

She shrugged. "I guess I don't look at him that way. He's more like an annoying older brother."

"How old is he?"

"He goes to the University of Toronto. I think he's twenty or so."

"Ancient." I frowned. "Wait a minute, he's a student but he's a ballet instructor, too? Wouldn't that be a full-time job?"

Her eyes widened a little. "Like I said, he's weird. Anyway, I seriously need a shower. And time is flying. So . . ."

"Yeah, you go ahead. I'll hang out down here."

"Check out the kitchen. I have a ton of food in there and more to come. Feel free to sample. I'll be ten minutes, max."

I nodded as she ran up the stairs to the bathroom. I heard the door close behind her and the shower turn on.

Dance lessons, huh? Color me mega-unconvinced.

Concern swelled inside me at the thought that my friend was hiding something horrible. I'd been so busy with my own life that I hadn't even noticed she was acting strangely, but now that I thought about it, yeah, she had been. Distracted and worried. And I vaguely recalled her having some fading bruises on her arms and jaw that she'd explained away like they were nothing. And what had I heard her say to Patrick?

I thought you wanted me to fight you.

That didn't sound like the kind of conversation you'd have with your dance instructor.

I glanced up at the railing on the second floor. The shower was still going. I knew I should go into the kitchen and mind my own business, but I just couldn't.

Instead, I wandered through the house looking for clues, through the kitchen and down the hall where a framed family photo of Melinda and her parents hung on the wall. The door leading to the basement stairs was ajar. When I'd been here a few weeks ago, before Melinda had her dance lessons every day after school, it had been locked. I pushed it open and slowly descended the stairs.

It looked like a gym down there. Mats on the floor. A treadmill. Weight-lifting equipment. Not completely unexpected.

But there was other stuff, too, that I noticed at a glance. Things that began to totally freak me out.

For instance, there was a sword lying on the ground as if it had been dropped. Swords weren't a typical floor accessory, so to say it stood out to me would be putting it mildly.

A battered and ripped punching bag hung from the ceiling. The hilt of a knife protruded from it. Also a majorly unusual sight, in my humble opinion, for a home gym.

To my right there was a table on which a selection of sharp knives were displayed. One had a curved blade with what looked like rubies set into the hilt.

Next to the knives was a short stack of books. They looked old, with plain leather covers and yellowed pages. I reached out to open one and noticed my hand was shaking. The book fell open to a page with an illustration of a very familiar-looking horned monster with large batlike wings. My stomach lurched.

I closed the book and quickly went back up the stairs, trying to rationalize what I'd just seen. I think it was safe to say Melinda hadn't really been taking dance lessons, after all.

"This is in your blood, Melinda," Patrick had told her. "You're only making this more difficult on yourself. You won't be ready."

"Ready?" she'd replied. "For what? I haven't seen anything

that makes me believe all the crazy things you've told me are even remotely true."

I understood now what she was trying to say. She didn't believe in demons. All she'd seen was a bunch of illustrations in some old books. It was true what they say—seeing was believing. I knew if I hadn't seen everything I had with my own two eyes, then I'd never have believed it in a million years.

But it was true. Demons existed, and some of them were really evil.

The realization that was slowly dawning on me was good for one thing. Suddenly, my prophecies and my troubles with Michael and Rhys were the last things on my mind.

Melinda could never know I knew about this. And she could absolutely, positively never find out I was half demon.

My best friend was in training to become a demon slayer.

12

"I just want to have fun tonight and forget everything else," Melinda proclaimed as she came downstairs after freshening up from her secret (she thought) demon-slayer training session. She looked gorgeous, wearing a form-fitting short red dress I'd never seen before.

"Yeah, me too," I said, now feeling strange about being in her presence. But she didn't act any differently than she had before. She was the same Melinda as ever. She scurried around the house, putting last-minute touches on her decorations and ordering her party-planning assistant (aka, me) here and there as we prepared for everyone to arrive.

I watched her suspiciously. She seemed so normal. Was it possible I was overreacting to everything I'd seen downstairs? Was I worried over nothing?

"Hey, Melinda," I imagined myself saying to her. *"Is it true you're a demon slayer? And that Patrick guy is training you, even though you don't seem too happy about it?"*

"Yes, it's true," she'd reply. *"For a demon princess, and therefore my mortal enemy, you're very perceptive."*

"I'm actually only half demon," I'd try to explain.

"Doesn't matter," she'd say.

And then she'd kill me dead.

Was that why Patrick had given me the stink eye? Had he sensed I was a little bit demonic? And were Melinda's parents demon slayers, too? Was it the family business? They'd never looked at me strangely before, though, so maybe not.

Come to think of it, I didn't even know what Melinda's parents did for a living. I knew money wasn't an issue for them. Melinda had ordered a ton of food for the party, and a couple knocks on the front door announced caterers delivering platters of sandwiches and hors d'oeuvres.

Invited guests began to arrive at seven o'clock. By eight, there were forty or fifty kids in the house. Music blared from a variety of speakers, and the place was so loud I could barely hear myself think.

It was probably a good thing.

Melinda acted as if nothing had changed between us in the last couple of hours—and for her, nothing really had. After a while I could almost pretend that I hadn't overheard what I had; that I hadn't gone down to the basement and learned her big secret. But, unfortunately, pretending wasn't going to make this go away.

Maybe just for tonight.

I avoided Larissa, who, wearing a short, tight green dress, had glared at me so evilly upon her arrival that I thought I might get a scar on my forehead, or at the very least a welt. Her issues were her problem, not mine. I had my own issues to deal with, thank you very much.

I turned to go back to the kitchen and found Chris

Sanders standing directly in front of me, his arms crossed over his chest.

"I really need to have that talk with you, Nikki," he said. "I've put it off long enough."

Oh, great. I grimaced. "Now?"

"Yeah."

The gingerbread cookie I'd downed a few minutes before began dancing unpleasantly in my gut. I don't even want to say what the follow-up jellybeans were now doing at the prospect of chatting with Chris.

"Hey, Chris." Larissa approached us and snaked an arm around his waist. She held a glass in her right hand and took a sip. "Great to see you. You're looking mighty *fine* tonight. I'll have to find some mistletoe later, if ya know what I mean." She hiccupped.

What was in that glass? Melinda had threatened everyone upon entering the house that this was to be an alcohol-free party, otherwise her parents wouldn't let her have another one ever again. To me, though, Larissa seemed a bit tipsy.

In Larissa's defense, however, Chris *was* looking mighty fine. He had this effortless attractiveness about him that I couldn't help but notice from the first day I'd started at Erin Heights. This calm confidence only helped to ramp up his natural good looks a few levels.

I'd wondered back then if he had any flaws. I now knew they included a major sense of entitlement. If Chris wanted something—no matter what it was—he felt like he should have it. And if he didn't, he felt he should be able to *take* it, as evidenced by our situation in the back of the limo at Winter Formal.

Admittedly, I hadn't heard any rumors he'd tried anything like that before. If people hated Chris, it was because they were jealous of him, not because he was a bad guy who did bad things. Maybe the incident with me had been a onetime thing— at least, I hoped so. Or maybe nobody had ever said no to Chris before, like I had. Based on the drooling gaze Larissa had trained on him at the moment, it was possible.

"Hi, Larissa," Chris responded, although he didn't look directly at her. He wasn't looking at me, either. The floor currently held his complete and total attention.

"Am I interrupting anything?" she asked.

"No," I said at the same time Chris said, "Yes."

"I didn't know you were still seeing each other," she said.

"We're not," I said firmly.

"I . . . ," Chris began. "Look, I need to talk to Nikki in private. Do you mind leaving us alone?"

Ouch.

Larissa flinched before giving me the evil eye. "Yeah, sure. No problem."

Exit stage left.

If I hadn't been feeling a whole heap of uneasiness, I would have found it very difficult not to laugh.

Chris's eyes flicked to mine for a moment before he looked away again. It was as if he couldn't bear to maintain eye contact with me.

"Follow me," he said, and started walking over to the dining room, where all the coats were piled on the table. He grabbed his coat and put it on.

"Where are we going?" I asked suspiciously, not inclined to go anywhere with him just because he told me to.

"Out to the backyard. I don't want anyone to hear us talking."

He didn't want anyone to hear us discuss what he'd seen when I'd shifted to my Darkling form, thrown a big glowing ball of energy at him, and launched him out the side of the limo we'd been in when he'd forgotten what "no" meant.

Right. This was a discussion I had known was unavoidable, but now I'd finally decided how to handle it.

Denial. One hundred percent. I'd even worked out the convo in my head.

"Hey, Nikki," Chris would say. *"What was up with you turning all demonic during Winter Formal?"*

"Demonic?" I'd respond casually. *"Gee, sounds more like a nightmare than anything that could possibly have taken place in real life. I'm sure you were just dreaming."*

"But I saw—"

"YOU WERE DREAMING."

"Well, okay." He'd nod. *"You're absolutely right. Whatever was I thinking? Demons don't really exist. Oh, and by the way, sorry for being such an unbelievable jerk to you in the limo. You deserve much better."*

And that would be that.

Feeling a new surge of confidence, I grabbed my jacket and went outside with Chris. The yard was large and snow covered, with tall wooden fences and lots of trees around the edges. In the center was a pool—covered, since it was December—with a big slide. We didn't venture too far, instead staying on the patio near the doors.

Maybe it would be good to start this on a positive note.

"Here," I said, thrusting the small wrapped box at him that I'd pulled from my jacket pocket. "I picked your name for the gift exchange."

He hesitated before taking the present from me. "You didn't have to get me anything."

"It's not a big deal. Ten bucks or less. Rules are rules."

Ain't that the truth, I thought. And I had to follow them all now, didn't I? I hated thinking about rules, even little, meaningless ones. They only served to remind me why I was here at this party with Chris instead of anywhere else with Michael.

Chris cleared his throat and made quick work of the wrapping, revealing the stylish (not really) keychain with a Christmas tree on it I'd grabbed earlier that day at the mall. Could not have been more innocent or generic if I'd tried: $8.95 before tax.

"Thank you. I need one of these," he said politely, and tucked it into his pocket. "I have something for you, too."

"You picked my name?"

"Not exactly." He reached inside his jacket and drew out a rolled piece of paper, which he held out to me.

"What's this?"

"It's a drawing I did. I . . . I do art sometimes."

I looked at it skeptically. "You drew me a picture?"

"Uh, no, not exactly."

"Then what is it?" I dug my hands into my pockets and

tried to stay warm. Snowflakes were steadily coming down around us, and the backyard was dark except for one overhead light where we stood on the patio.

"Last week, at the dance," he began. "When you . . . you *changed* . . ."

"Changed?" I repeated. *Here we go.* "Changed my mind about dating you? Yeah, well, these things happen. It's not a big deal. It was our first date and it didn't work out. Let's just forget it ever happened, okay?"

He laughed a little shakily at that. "I remember exactly what happened."

"Not so sure you do."

"I do," he said firmly. "It's crystal clear in my mind."

"You were drunk."

"I'd been drinking, sure, but I wasn't drunk. You changed into something else."

"So did you," I said pointedly.

He cringed at the reminder. "I'm so sorry about that."

"You should be." I felt a flare of anger then, but I willed it away. I had enough problems to juggle without turning Darkling in the middle of Melinda's party. The mental image of the sword downstairs was enough to help me push any demon-shifting thoughts away.

"I didn't change the same way you did, though." He sounded so certain that it made me more nervous. "It was the most vivid moment in my entire life. When I saw you—your hair, your eyes . . . you had wings and horns, and . . . and a tail."

Yikes. I had a tail, too? How had I never noticed that little detail before? I guessed because it hadn't ripped through my clothes like my wings tended to do.

I forced myself to smile, but dread crept over me like an army of spiders. "Maybe you *were* dreaming. You might have hit your head on the pavement and knocked yourself out when you, uh, fell out of the limo. Wouldn't that make more sense?"

"Of course it would."

I let out a sigh of relief.

"But I wasn't dreaming *that* night." He held out the rolled paper to me again. "I *was* dreaming just before I drew this."

I studied him, trying to make sense of what he was saying. "I think I'm confused."

"I had a dream two weeks ago. It was so clear in my head that I had to get up in the middle of the night and draw what I'd seen in case I forgot it. Everything about it felt so real."

Okay. I'd play along for now. I finally took the sketch from him and slowly unrolled it, moving it more toward the light so I could see. I stifled the gasp that rose in my throat.

The sketch was pencil, detailed, and it was immediately clear to me that Chris was a talented artist. It showed a girl in the fore-front who looked a whole lot like me in full Darkling form, black wings stretched out behind her, with the unmistakable Shadow-lands castle in the background, dark spires reaching into the gray swirling skies like scary black arms.

An ice-cold shiver not caused by the winter night zipped down my spine.

How had Chris seen this? How had he even dreamed about this? Though he'd seen me in Darkling form in the school parking lot outside Winter Formal, he couldn't have ever seen the Shadowlands. It was impossible.

"What does it mean, Nikki? Why did I dream about you?" He sounded hoarse and upset and more than a little scared. "And what is that horrible place?"

"You drew this *two weeks* ago?" I said, my voice no more than a whisper. It was well before he'd seen me as a Darkling. Well before *I'd* even known I was a Darkling.

He just nodded. "I didn't realize it was you at the time. See?" He pointed at the drawing. "The darkness is blocking half your face. It was the darkness that made me wake up from the dream. It . . . it freaked me out . . . the way it started to block the light all around you."

Darkness.

I remembered what Irena had seen in my future. The darkness that surrounded me, that watched me. Was Chris confirming what she'd said? That the second prophecy was definitely true? Fear coursed through my stomach.

I rolled the sketch back up and handed it to Chris, but he didn't take it. "It's not me. I don't know what that is, but you have a vivid imagination. I guess you have a future as an artist ahead of you. Maybe comic books or something."

His brows drew together. "I don't know what the darkness is, but it wants you. It's dangerous."

"You're crazy, I think," I said evenly, trying to ignore the panicky feeling welling in my throat and threatening to choke off my words. "You might want to look into that."

When I took a step closer to Chris, he staggered back as though I frightened him. Was this fear the reason he'd been avoiding me since the dance? The thought didn't make me feel any better. In fact, it made me feel much worse.

He was quiet for a moment, and then he laughed so suddenly it made me jump. "You might be right about me being crazy."

I raised an eyebrow. "You think?"

"Maybe that would explain all of this," he said, shaking his head. "Maybe I should get my mom to prescribe me some meds."

"Your mom?"

"She deals with insane people on a regular basis. It's her job." He shied away from the piece of paper I held out to him. "No, keep it. Please. I don't want it anywhere near me."

"But what about—"

He put more distance between us. "Let's just forget we had this conversation, okay? I'm starting to realize how completely nuts I'm sounding. And I . . . I'm really sorry about what happened at the dance. I know you won't believe me, but I've never done anything like that before. So whatever happened, I deserved it."

I thought I'd be the one to walk away first, but it was Chris who left me standing there alone, breathing hard, my heart impersonating a jackhammer. I looked again at the sketch of the Darkling standing in a shadow with the castle behind her. I recalled what he'd said about his mother.

She deals with crazy people.

What did that mean? I knew Chris's father was a lawyer and his mom was a doctor. They had lots of money, just like Melinda's parents did.

Wait . . . Chris's mother was a doctor? A doctor who dealt with insane people and could prescribe medication?

My eyes widened. *Oh my God!*

I quickly went back inside and found where I'd hidden my purse in one of Melinda's kitchen cabinets. I dug into it to grab my wallet and pulled out the business card Rhys had given me when we'd left the dragon oracle's office yesterday. I hadn't looked closely at it then, but I did now.

DR. IRENA SANDERS, MD
Psychiatrist
905-555-6452

My hands shook, making the card hard to read.

Irena had mentioned her son—the one who didn't know the truth about his mother yet. She was waiting for him to be mature enough to deal with the knowledge that she was an immortal dragon living in human form. I'd assumed she meant he was just a kid, maybe seven years old, and she hadn't wanted to scare him at such a young age.

Actually, he was seventeen.

Irena was Chris's mother.

And, by the looks of the sketch he'd just given me, Chris had more than a little bit of dragon oracle in him as well.

13

I shoved the drawing and business card into my purse and went back to the party, feeling the least festive I'd felt in my entire life. It would take a lot more than fruit punch or finger sandwiches to help me recover from the revelation that Chris Sanders was half dragon and able to glimpse pieces of my life in his dreams.

"Oh, wow!" I heard Melinda exclaim from the dining room to my left, distracting me from my racing thoughts. "I love it. Thank you so much!"

I entered in time to see her throw her arms around the newly arrived Rhys—who I'd convinced myself wouldn't be at the party at all tonight, given how we'd left things.

"Nikki," Melinda said when she spotted me lurking nearby. "Look what Rhys got me for the gift exchange."

She held a small wooden jewelry box in the palm of her hand. It was delicately carved, with flowers on the lid.

So Rhys had just happened to pick her name, had he? What a coincidence. Although, I had a funny feeling Melinda had been in full control of who he ended up with. My best friend was definitely determined when she set her mind to a new goal.

After seeing her basement arsenal, knowing this did not ease my mind.

"Beautiful," I confirmed. "Looks like it cost a lot more than the ten-dollar limit, though."

"I'll never tell," Rhys said. He had a drink clenched in his right hand. Our eyes met for a moment before he quickly looked away, then downed whatever was in the glass in one big gulp.

He was forcing himself to stay in my presence rather than fleeing the room to get away from me. It was nice to know that was the effect I had on guys now. Really fabulous.

"Want some more?" Larissa asked him.

"No, thank you."

"Don't lie. You *totally* want some more," she slurred. "It's sooo yummy."

It was now painfully and pathetically obvious that Larissa was drunk. Was she feeling a bit uncomfortable and unwanted here at Melinda's party and had to find some liquid courage?

"Oooh, check it out," she said, pointing upward at Melinda's decorations. "Mistletoe!"

She grabbed Rhys and kissed him full on the lips. His eyes widened and he attempted to disengage from her. It took a couple of tries. The girl was strong. He then gave her a look that could only be described as unhappy as he wiped his mouth with the back of his hand and glanced at me.

I was not going to laugh. It was a struggle.

"Larissa." Melinda glared at her. "Can I talk to you, please? *Now?*"

Larissa's cheeks went red. "Uh, okay."

They left so Melinda could give her BFF-in-waiting the "keep your hands off Rhys" speech. Which meant Rhys and I now were in the dining room alone. Well, if you didn't count the fifty winter coats piled high behind us. I threw mine on the top of the heap. Everyone else had congregated in Melinda's massive high-ceilinged living room toward the front end of the mansionlike house. The music was so loud, I could feel it reverberating through the hardwood floors.

"So, I decided to come to the party, after all," Rhys said.

"I see that."

He eyed the plastic cup. "I have no idea what I just drank. Wine?"

"Probably."

"I've never tried human wine before."

"I guess this is your lucky day."

"It was kind of disgusting."

"Yeah, well, nobody's saying Larissa has great taste in anything."

He touched his lips. "She kissed me."

"Congrats. From what I've heard, you're one of many. You might want to floss."

He took a step away from me. "So . . . what's new?"

Yeah, this was a great time for awkward small talk with the faery king who hated me. "Irena's son is here at the party. And I already know him. Small world, or what?"

"I knew her son attended your high school. Chris, right?"

My heart skipped a beat. "You *knew*?"

"Of course."

My head throbbed, letting me know I wasn't doing a good job of controlling my stress levels. My Darkling form wanted to burst free and party. "Great. Thanks so much for the heads-up."

He looked confused. "Is that a problem?"

"Yeah, it kind of is."

I told him what had happened with Chris in the backyard. Despite my history with Rhys, I still felt desperate to confide in somebody who'd understand.

I showed Rhys the sketch. He studied it carefully before giving it back to me.

"It seems to confirm the second prophecy Irena told you about."

"I know. So what do you think I should do?" I asked, feeling hopeful in spite of myself that he'd be able to help me out or give me some sage advice.

"Why are you asking me?"

"Because you're the dragon expert around here."

"Dragons have scales, you know," Rhys said pointedly.

I looked at him. "What?"

"Green scales and spiky tails." He paused and then started to laugh. "Hey, I made a rhyme!"

"What are you talking about?"

"Dragons see the future." He nodded. "Unless it's all blurry. Then they just make stuff up, I think."

"That's not exactly what I asked you." I started to feel annoyed with him again. Why was I surprised Rhys was letting me down when I needed his help?

"Sorry." He grinned. "It's the wine. I wasn't sure how it would affect me, but now I see so, so clearly." He grabbed my shoulders. "Do you see, Princess Nikki? Do you? It's a strange world here with strange human people and none of it makes any sense to me."

I pushed his hands off me. "One glass of wine and you're already drunk? That's even more pathetic than Larissa."

"Faery anatomy." He shrugged. "S'different than humans. We have wine back home. It's made from strawberries and sunshine and a little bit of magic."

"Oh, brother." I rolled my eyes. "This is just perfect."

"Demons." He poked me in the shoulder hard enough to hurt.

I was grateful for the loud music. It helped drown out Rhys's scattered outbursts. "What about them?" I asked cautiously.

He made a face. "Hate 'em."

"Yeah, so you told me yesterday. Don't worry. I promise not to infect you with any demon cooties." I tried to move past him, but he grabbed my wrist to stop me.

"Not you. Don't hate you. Wanted to. And I sorta do sometimes, but you're not the one to blame."

"Blame for what?"

He inhaled deeply and it sounded shaky. "My . . . my parents."

I shivered. "I'm sorry they're gone."

"They were there one day, and then they weren't. And I had to become king whether I wanted to or not. My advisers . . . I don't think they like me. They respected my father and my mother, but they don't respect me. Maybe they never will. It makes me feel really alone." He frowned. "Why am I telling you this?"

"Because you're drunk and you don't know any better."

"Sometimes I don't want to go back. I wish I could stay here, where it's easy. Where people are nice. Where it's safe . . . unless you're a frog."

"You can't stay?"

He shook his head. "Not for long. I have duties. And my hotel suite—it's so empty and there are noises at night, but at least nobody bothers me there, asking me to make decisions that affect the entire faery realm. They think I'm the one to blame for everything bad that happens there."

He looked so dejected by this that I couldn't help but feel for how lonely he must be. "I can't imagine it's easy being a king."

"Would you want to rule the Shadowlands?"

"No," I replied honestly.

"If your father was murdered, you'd have to. You'd have no choice. You're his heir."

Murdered. I hated the sound of the word.

"You're right," I said. "I guess I would. How . . . how did it happen? With your parents?"

His eyes became glossy and he sniffed hard, swiping his hand under his nose. "They went to the Underworld. They were scheduled to have an important meeting with Queen Sephina. The demon who did it was caught and put in the dungeon there so he can be punished, but it doesn't change anything. My parents are gone forever." His voice broke.

"I'm so, so sorry."

Rhys looked on the verge of tears for a moment, and I touched his arm in a weak attempt to comfort him. The contact made him take a big step back from me. I was getting used to guys doing that, attempting to escape me in any way they could. I was trying very hard not to take it personally.

I snatched my hand back. "Sorry."

He laughed, still sounding tipsy from the wine, but there wasn't a lot of humor in the sound. "You're so weird."

"Me?"

"Yeah."

"Gee, thanks."

His smile turned into a scowl. "I really don't like you."

I tried not to let his harsh words bother me. "I guess you don't have to like me."

"But Irena said that you're my—"

I cut him off. "I don't care what she said. You know it's not true."

"I know. It's stupid. All my life—even before what happened to my parents—I've been taught to hate demons. They're evil and ugly and unpleasant."

I nodded. "Right. So I'm pretty much done with this conversation. I think I'm going to go join the rest of the party. Or maybe I'll just go home."

"Why are you going?"

I glared at him. "You just called me evil and ugly and unpleasant. That doesn't exactly make me want to hang out with you any longer."

"That's demons. Not you."

"I'm half demon." I sighed. "Why am I even having this conversation with you? You're drunk."

He frowned. "Am not."

"I don't do well with drunk guys. They tend to do or say things they end up regretting." I went to walk past him, but he stepped in front of me. I put my hands on my hips. "Move, please."

The corner of his mouth twitched into a half grin. "Or what?"

"Or I'm going to punch you in the stomach."

"Violent."

"Well, I *am* a demon."

"Half demon." Now he was the one reminding me.

"Whatever. Now please move."

"Well . . . unfortunately there's a little problem," he said.

"What?"

He pointed up. "That."

I looked up to see the mistletoe dangling from the ceiling where I'd hung it three hours before.

"Okay, but what does that—?"

Rhys kissed me. It took me so much by surprise that I didn't realize what had happened until it was almost over. When he pulled away, he held my shoulders and leaned back from me, his brows knitting together, his expression filled with dismay.

"I really, really didn't want to like that," he said.

"Rhys—" But before I could say anything else, he kissed me again and pulled me closer. The fact that I wasn't pushing him away was a little disturbing. In fact, after another moment I realized I was kissing him back.

If I'd known mistletoe was this dangerous, I never would have helped Melinda put any up.

"The last time I saw her, she was over here," someone said. Then I heard a gasp.

That was when I finally shoved Rhys back from me and peered over his shoulder. Melinda stood in the kitchen staring at us with wide eyes.

Next to her was Michael.

14

"Nikki," Melinda said after a long moment of silence passed among the four of us, despite the loud music reverberating through the house. "Your friend Michael stopped by. He said he needed to talk to you."

"Uh, thanks," I managed.

She cleared her throat. "You're welcome."

She sounded pleasant and polite, at least on the surface. However, the glare on her face said another thing altogether. It was a mixture of disappointment and major betrayal. If eyeballs were capable of slaying demon princesses, I would already be dead.

Larissa would be happy to know the position of Melinda's best friend might be up for grabs, after all. My stomach sank. I'd promised her a thousand times I wasn't interested in Rhys, and here I was kissing him at her party.

That probably didn't look good, did it? I could only blame the mistletoe for so much.

I couldn't bear to look at Michael yet. What was he doing here?

"Melinda—," I began.

She gave me a frozen smile. "I have to get back to my guests. We'll talk later, okay?"

Without another word, she turned and left.

That was not a conversation I was looking forward to. She was going to kill me.

I really hoped it wouldn't be literal.

"Princess." Michael's voice was strained. "I'm very sorry to come here unannounced, but it's urgent. Your father sent me."

"What's wrong?" I finally forced myself to look at him. His attention was focused on something down by my feet.

"Queen Sephina and the rest of the council have requested a meeting with you."

"Why?"

"She wishes to learn more about you and wants this to happen face-to-face. Prince Kieran's report didn't satisfy her curiosity about you or the prophecy."

I'd felt as if this was coming. Kieran did mention the potential of my meet and greet with the demon council. However, I'd tried to put it out of my mind, hoping it wouldn't happen any time soon.

"When?" I asked.

"Immediately."

My eyebrows went up. "Now?"

"That is generally what *immediately* means." Michael's eyes flicked to Rhys. "Why? Am I interrupting something you feel is more important?"

"I don't think I appreciate your tone, Shadow," Rhys said.

"His name is Michael," I corrected.

"Right. *Michael*." Rhys still managed to make it sound like a bland label rather than a name.

Michael glanced up at the evil mistletoe hanging above us before his gaze returned to Rhys. "I apologize if my tone is anything less than respectful, King Rhys."

Rhys smiled thinly. "Apology accepted."

Again, there was more unsaid than said in the room at the moment. I could feel it as sharply as if it were raining needles.

"Is the demon council waiting for me in the Shadowlands like Prince Kieran was?" I asked.

"No. They request that you travel to the Underworld castle, where they've convened to discuss the prophecy in detail."

I looked at Rhys, who'd flinched at the mention of the place his mother and father had been murdered.

"You don't have to go if you don't want to," Rhys said. "As princess of the Shadowlands, you're entitled to veto any request that doesn't come from your own kingdom."

I thought that over. It sounded a bit too simple an answer, actually.

"What happens if I say no?" I asked Michael.

"Is that what you're saying?"

I shook my head. "I . . . I just want to keep my options open."

"Your father agrees with King Rhys," Michael said. "That you shouldn't go."

"Really?" I didn't know why that surprised me.

"Then there's no problem," Rhys said. "Nikki will stay here."

Michael's expression darkened. He nodded. "Then I should leave."

"Wait," I said as he turned away from us. "No, Michael, don't go."

He stopped and looked at me.

"You told me my father doesn't want me to go, but you didn't answer my question. What will the council do if I don't meet with them? Will they be upset?"

Seemed to me that denying a council of demons a request, even though it might be within my right to do so, could come with a price tag. I just wanted to know how expensive it would be.

Michael pressed his lips together as if unsure whether or not to answer me. "Your father despises the council. He doesn't say this out loud, of course, but it's obvious to me he does. They're the ones who create all the laws that govern the dark worlds, after all."

Yes, the laws that said if he ever tried to contact my mother again, she'd be in danger just because of their romantic history. And I was fairly certain that was only the tip of the demonic iceberg when it came to my father's issues with the council.

"I'm not too fond of them, either," I said.

"No, but . . . I think this hatred has clouded King Desmond's better judgment. He wishes to deny them this request, but it's at his own peril . . . and yours, too. The queen is simply curious about you right now, that's all. But if she's refused this meeting . . ."

"What?" I prompted.

"I'm afraid of how she might react. Queen Sephina, and the

Underworld as a whole, has a great deal of power . . . much more than the Shadowlands ruler. Your father maintains his hold on the barrier and the castle all by himself. He has no support. But the queen, well, she has the support of the entire Underworld *and* Hell."

"You think she could nullify Desmond's reign over the Shadowlands if she wanted to?" Rhys asked, sounding troubled about this possibility.

Michael nodded. "If she was provoked."

A chill spread through me. "Does my father know this?"

"I'm sure he does. But he refuses to acknowledge it. His hatred blinds him to the real threat here."

"So we have to do what the queen wants or else?" I said lightly, trying to ignore the dread that had suddenly enveloped me.

"Yes, I think so."

The rebel in me resisted this idea. But she'd grown very tired and beaten down over the last week, so I now doubted myself. "Do you think I should go?"

"The queen has given her royal word that no harm will come to you."

Rhys snorted. "And you believe her?"

Michael's eyes narrowed. "I will go with the princess and ensure her safety."

"How can you ensure something like that? You're only her servant, aren't you?" At Michael's highly unfriendly glare, Rhys's eyebrow raised. "Oh, wait a minute. I think I get it."

"You get what?"

"Why you look so disturbed right now. It's not just because of the queen's request of the princess." Rhys's gaze flicked up to the mistletoe. "Don't be jealous, Shadow. A kiss under the mistletoe means nothing."

"You think I'm jealous about that?"

"I think it's very possible." Rhys shrugged, amusement sliding behind his brown eyes. "However, I suppose if it *did* mean something, it wouldn't be any of your business, would it?"

I really wanted him to shut up.

"I am the princess's servant," Michael said flatly. "Nothing more. Besides, there are more important issues to deal with right now than petty jealousies."

Rhys cocked his head to the side. "It's very interesting to me, this demon council of yours and the laws they create."

"Oh?"

"They make sure demons are forbidden to date humans. Demons can't date Shadows, either. But, well, there just isn't any rule that says they can't date faeries. Why do you think that is? An oversight?"

Michael's lips thinned. "It's probably because no demon would ever be interested in a faery. After all, they're so easily broken."

"You might be surprised about that." Rhys's eyes swirled, evidence that he was more agitated by this conversation than he wanted to let on.

Okay, that was more than enough. "Michael, let's go."

Michael looked surprised. "You're sure?"

"Yes, I'm sure."

"We must see your father first. He'll be able to open a gateway for us to the Underworld. However, he won't be happy about your decision."

"You're probably right. But that's not going to change my mind. I won't let him make a mistake that'll cost him the entire kingdom. Or worse."

"Fine, then let's go." Michael turned and, without waiting for me, began walking through Melinda's house toward the front door.

Rhys grabbed my hand before I followed Michael out of the room. "I don't trust him."

I frowned at him. "Who, Michael?"

"Shadows are dangerous."

"So you were trying to tell me before. Are there any Shadows in the faery world?"

"No. Their souls are too dark to survive in a light world. Your servant is the first Shadow I've ever met. But my mother used to warn me to stay away from Shadows, that they couldn't be trusted."

I yanked my hand away from him. "I trust Michael more than anyone else I know. He'd never hurt me. And his soul isn't dark."

Rhys nodded then, a quick motion of his head. "If you say so."

"I do."

His eyes were guarded. "Nikki . . . what I said about the kiss . . ."

"It was because of the mistletoe and it meant nothing," I said quickly. Maybe a bit *too* quickly. "I totally and completely agree."

"That's . . . what I figured."

"Wish me luck."

"Good luck. And please try to be careful around that Shadow of yours."

"Are you going to tell me to be careful around Michael every time I say good-bye to you?"

His lips twitched. "It's entirely possible."

I never would have guessed it from the last time we'd seen each other—when he'd basically thrown me out of his car because he hated demons—but actual concern for me was now in Rhys's eyes.

I hadn't wanted him to hate me, but I didn't want him to like me, either. That made things much more complicated than I wanted them to be.

✳   ✳   ✳

While looking for a gateway to the Shadowlands, Michael walked so quickly I had to jog to keep up with him. I drew my winter coat closer around me to block out the chilly night.

"It was the mistletoe, you know," I said.

He stopped so abruptly, I bashed into him. "Pardon me?"

"That . . . what you saw back there. It was because of the mistletoe. It's a human tradition, that's all."

Yeah. It sounded pretty weak to me, too.

"I know about mistletoe," he said.

"Oh, well, good. Then there's no problem."

"Why would there be a problem?"

I chewed my bottom lip. "It was just a kiss. It didn't mean anything."

He started walking again. "I was confused, of course. I thought he was attacking your mouth with his lips and I should protect you. A *kiss*, you say? That's what it's called?"

I grimaced. "I never knew you were so good at sarcasm."

"I guess you don't know me half as well as you think you do." He stopped again and turned to look at me. Snowflakes drifted softly down between us in the moonlight, and I could clearly see the hurt in his eyes he'd been trying to hide. "Fine, I'll admit it. I wasn't exactly thrilled to walk in on that. But it's not like I have any right to say anything. All I am is your servant. I understand that."

My cheeks felt warm, despite the cold. "That's not all you are to me."

His jaw tightened. "You know, I think it's good you've moved on already. And so quickly, too. What is it? Five whole days? It's amazing, really."

More sarcasm. It confirmed that he was incredibly mad at me.

"I haven't moved on," I tried to explain. "Rhys is just . . . just . . ."

He waited, dark eyebrows aloft. "Just what?"

"I don't know."

"You like him." It wasn't a question.

I rubbed my forehead, which had started to throb, warning me to remain calm. "He's the only one here who knows about me. He knows what I'm going through. He makes me feel less . . . I don't know. Less alone."

"I can understand that." Michael nodded. "Plus, without

him you wouldn't have had a chance to see the dragon oracle yesterday."

"Right. Not that it did me any good." I paused. "Hey, how did you know about that?"

"I saw you leave the school yesterday with the faery king and overheard your plans. Magical cloaking and glamour tricks don't work on Shadows like they do on humans."

A bolt of shock went through me. "You were there?"

"Of course. With the prophecy looming over your head, I couldn't just leave you without any protection at all. Especially with King Rhys nearby. I was deeply concerned he might try something." He snorted. "Little did I know what he'd end up trying."

"You've been *here*?" I said again.

"Yes. Some of the time, anyway."

It suddenly made sense. "I knew it. I saw you . . . or, I *thought* I saw you a few times this week out of the corner of my eye, but I just assumed it was my imagination."

"You saw me?" He seemed surprised.

"I thought I did. But then when I looked closer, you weren't there."

He touched his amulet. "I can stay hidden when I concentrate. It's an ability I recently discovered. I can blend into the background of almost any room and become unnoticeable."

"Because you're a Shadow?"

He nodded. "I know I'm not very good at it yet, if you saw me when I didn't want to be seen. I haven't had much chance to practice."

So even when he wore his amulet, Michael still could take on the consistency of a shadow if he wanted to. I wasn't sure how I felt about that.

"Why didn't you say anything to me?" I asked.

"It was better for me to stay at a distance, ready to step in if necessary." He shrugged. "It wasn't ever necessary. But that's how I knew you'd be at your friend Melinda's tonight. When your father told me about the demon council's request, I immediately knew where to find you."

My throat felt thick. I wanted to be angry at him for not letting me know he was nearby, but I couldn't summon the emotion. Michael had been here all week, when I'd been missing him. After I'd had to end things between us, he still stuck by me to make sure I was safe, trying to blend into the background like any good servant would.

The thought made me want to cry.

"Here we are," Michael said after another minute passed in silence. He'd found the swirling gateway near some garbage cans behind a variety store. We hadn't needed to use the magic from my dragon's tear to find it this time. Michael's amulet pulsed with soft green light in the darkness.

I touched his arm. "Thank you for watching out for me, Michael. Really."

He nodded but didn't meet my eyes. "It's my duty, Princess."

15

"I'm going," I said firmly.

"No, Nikki, you're not."

"Yes, I am." I could do this for hours. It had already been about ten minutes since Michael and I had arrived at the castle, only to be met by my father's very stubborn opinion that I shouldn't do what Queen Sephina wanted me to do.

"They can't force this meeting," he argued.

"But if I don't go, the queen will be mad."

"Then let her be mad."

"I won't let her hurt you."

"Hurt me?" My father looked sharply at Michael. "What have you told my daughter about this?"

Michael had his hands clasped behind his back. "Only the truth, Your Majesty."

His eyes flashed demon red. "I assign you one thing, to keep my daughter safe, and this is what you do? You convince her to go to the Underworld and put herself at risk?"

"Queen Sephina has assured her safety," Michael said, with no weakness in his voice at the reprimand. "The greater risk is if she doesn't go."

"Greater risk to whom?"

"To you, Your Majesty, and you know it."

My father looked shocked at that. "So this is what I get for allowing you so many freedoms here, more than the other servants? You've begun to think for yourself?"

"I've always thought for myself," Michael said. "I just rarely expressed it out loud before. I know you hate the council, but denying them this request will make them angry. All the queen wants to do is meet Princess Nikki in person. I think if she does, it will be obvious to her and everyone there that the prophecy is false."

"You *think* that, do you?" He looked at me. "And what do you think?"

"I think Michael's right," I said as firmly as I could. "So you can argue with me all night or you can open up a gateway for us so I can go and get this over with."

My father's expression shadowed as he paced over toward the huge fireplace, which blazed so brightly it was almost blinding in the otherwise dark room. It was the only thing about the cold, dark castle I'd found that had any warmth or personality to it. I didn't like to think that my father had been stuck here, never being able to leave, since before I was even born. It was like being in prison.

"I wish I could go with you," he said finally.

"Me, too." It was so warm in the room that I peeled off my winter coat and draped it over the back of the nearest chair.

His eyes rested on Michael for a second. "Please give my daughter and me a moment alone."

"Of course, Your Majesty," Michael replied after a brief

hesitation. With a last glance at me, he turned and left the room.

"As you can see," my father said after a moment, "despite what Michael is, I give him many freedoms here. He's earned that much from me."

As usual, that made me bristle, ready to defend Michael. "Because he's a servant?"

"Yes, but also because he's a . . . a Shadow." He looked worried. "Other than visiting the human world recently, Michael has never left the Shadowlands. After his parents died, I promised to take care of him."

"You knew his parents?"

He nodded. "I did. His mother and father died when he was less than a year old. It was shortly before I traveled to the human world and met your mother. My father didn't approve of my taking a Shadow child under my protection, but he couldn't change my mind."

"You were stubborn," I said.

His eyes caught mine, and there was an understanding there. He was just as stubborn as his daughter. "I suppose I was. But I knew what would happen if Michael stayed in the Underworld."

"What?"

"He either would have been exterminated—"

"Exterminated?" I yelped.

"Shadows, especially males, are . . . regarded cautiously. There has been scattered evidence that they can pose a threat to demonkind if they choose to. Alternately, they are forced to become servants somewhere in the Underworld. If you think servants have a difficult life here, it is nothing compared to what I've witnessed elsewhere. Please believe me when I tell you it's safer this way for him."

So he was saying Michael was lucky to be here. And maybe he was right.

"Why would demons have Shadow servants if they're dangerous?" I was still trying to make sense of what he'd said, coupled with what Rhys and Michael had said, about Shadows.

"Because Shadows can be specifically assigned through magic to a certain demon—much as I've done with you and Michael." He sighed at the reminder of his unfortunate decision to pair me with a really hot eighteen-year-old guy with beautiful green eyes. "Most are highly obedient, very hard workers, and protective of their master. But other Shadows . . . well, others are different."

"Different how?"

"Shadows are forbidden by law to use their abilities in front of demons. Most Shadows are completely unaware their own powers even exist, and it's best it stays that way." My father leaned against the edge of the large black table that still had the big crack through the middle of it from the last time I was here. Another thing we shared was our temper. "You told me Michael used his power to protect you just after you first met, correct?"

I remembered being attacked by a demon with a big knife and Michael stopping him by throwing a burst of energy, green like the color of his amulet, at the murderous thug. The use of power had drained Michael, and it had taken him a while to recover.

I just agreed, choosing not to mention Michael's new-found ability to fade into the background if he wanted to.

My father's expression became more serious. "I wasn't even aware he knew of his powers. I'd never mentioned them to him in case they might cause problems. Though he did it to protect you, it's still against the rules."

"This place has a lot of stupid rules."

"I know." He gave me a serious look. "Just . . . please keep an eye on him, Nikki. As much as I'm worried about you making this journey to appease the queen, I worry for Michael as well. He's never met another of his kind before."

I nodded. "I'll do my best to keep him away from any bad influences."

A slight smile moved across his expression. "You'll protect both of us, will you?"

"I'll try."

He placed his hands on either side of my face before leaning over to kiss my forehead. A lump of emotion formed in my throat. I'd never had a real father before—one who made me feel like he cared what happened to me.

"I don't agree with your decision to meet with the queen at her whim, but I'll respect your wishes this time, only because she's promised you will come to no harm. Queen Sephina may be many things I don't care for, but I know her to be truthful."

"Thank you," I said.

"You can call Michael back in here now," he said.

"Michael!" I yelled.

My father actually laughed out loud at that. "No, not like that. With your telepathic bond."

"Oh, that."

Michael . . . are you there? I projected the thought, hoping he was close enough to hear me.

::Yes, Princess?:: It was always jarring to hear him in my head, but strangely reassuring at the same time.

I have full approval to head to the Underworld.

::Good. And you and your father are finished discussing me again?:: There was a wry tone to the words.

I would have smiled at that if I wasn't still thinking about everything I'd just learned about Michael, and about Shadows in general.

For now.

::Then I'll be right there.::

Shadow 101 class was over for the day. I didn't like most of what my father had told me. He said a lot of things so casually, like there was nothing bizarre about the dark worlds and his own strange and archaic way of looking at certain things—like servants and freedom and adhering to rules. I'd never agree that anyone should be forced to be a servant, no matter who or what they were—it was just wrong. And forced to repress their powers? Kept from meeting more of their kind in case they would be influenced in any way?

I preferred the idea that Michael should be in charge of his own life without anyone telling him what he could and couldn't do.

This was not the first time I'd been told Shadows were potentially dangerous. But as I turned it over in my mind, I realized that demons were *also* dangerous. So were faeries. And so were . . . *humans.* We were all in the same potentially perilous boat, weren't we? I figured, as long as nobody decided to bash the other over the head with the oars, we'd be okay.

Still, I couldn't help but feel uneasy about it all. I'd seen Michael use his abilities, and, yes, he'd been very powerful. But I never would believe he could be dangerous to anyone who didn't completely deserve it.

Another minute went by before Michael entered the room. When he saw me, he smiled, and that guarded expression he'd had since seeing Rhys kiss me under the mistletoe lifted from his eyes. He had a really amazing smile.

My heart skipped a beat.

I'd admit it, I liked Rhys. Despite the evidence that I probably shouldn't, I couldn't help myself. But how I felt about the faery king paled in comparison to how I felt about Michael.

On our official visit to the Underworld, Michael would be going as the Shadowlands' princess's personal servant. I knew better than to wear my "Freedom for Shadows" or my "Michael's Sort-of Girlfriend" T-shirts. I didn't know the demon council, but I did know they were not beings I wanted to mess with.

I didn't want to go. This wasn't something I was looking forward to in any way, shape, or form. I was going because I was afraid of the consequences of not going. They would not only affect me but also my father and the entire Shadowlands kingdom—and in turn that affected the human and faery worlds. Talk about pressure.

Duty called. I could handle it. I'd make a charming, wonderful impression on the council, and everyone would become good friends.

It was possible. Not probable, but *possible*.

And here I thought Melinda's Christmas party was the toughest thing I'd have to get through today. Wrong. So very wrong.

My father squeezed my hand in his, then released me. He waved his arm at the wall, I felt a wave of power waft over me, and a moment later a gateway appeared five feet from us, much like the one he'd opened to send Kieran back home.

"You can still change your mind," he said to me. "You don't have to go."

Before I took another step, I considered that. I could leave now. Head back to Melinda's party, to my seminormal life, and try to mend things with my best friend. I still had to figure out what to do about the fact she was probably, if not definitely, in training to become a demon slayer. *That* was important.

But I'd have to deal with it another day.

"We'll be back as soon as possible," I said.

Then I summoned up enough courage—pushing past the dread that crept up inside me and wrapped itself around my throat like an ill-fitting turtleneck—to walk through the gateway. It did help to know Michael was right behind me as the vortex swept us away from my father's castle and into the very heart of the Underworld.

16

Based on my limited experience with the Shadowlands—gray stormy skies; scary black castle; sharp, rocky ground beneath my feet; and cold, dry winds—I'd expected an even more desolate wasteland for the Underworld. But I'd been wrong.

The Underworld looked like a city. A big one, with paved streets and tall chrome-and-glass skyscrapers looming all around me. I could barely see the skies above where the gateway let me and Michael off on a long, pale sidewalk, but what little I could see appeared to be reassuringly blue.

"You're getting stronger, Princess," Michael commented.

"Oh?" I looked at him before realizing I had his arm in a death grip. I released him. "Sorry."

He smiled. "It's okay. It's my first time here, too, at least that I can remember. So it is a bit strange, isn't it?"

"That's an understatement," I said.

Again, that smile of his was totally distracting. I found myself very quickly lost in it, forgetting for a moment that we'd just entered a completely different world. But I was jolted out of my daze when he suddenly pushed me back a few feet behind him.

"What are you—?" I began, when I turned to see what had prompted him to block me.

A blonde woman now stood in front of us. An unfortunately *familiar* blonde woman.

"I was asked to wait here for your arrival," my aunt Elizabeth said. "Welcome to the Underworld, Nikki."

The fear and surprise caused pain to sweep through me, and I knew my horns had formed because of the burning, tingling sensation on either side of my head. I clenched my fists and felt the sharp talons dig into my skin. A small, unconscious hiss slipped through my rapidly sharpening teeth at the sight of the woman who'd nearly succeeded in murdering me and my father only last week.

"What are you doing here?" Michael growled.

Elizabeth's eyebrows went up as if surprised by our visceral reaction to her. "Prince Kieran sent me to fetch you both and lead you to the castle. Otherwise, would you be able to find your way without a guide? I don't think you have a map."

"Why would he send *you*?"

"Because no one else was available."

Michael shook his head. "I don't like this, Princess. We're leaving. Sending Elizabeth after what happened is a show of major disrespect to you and King Desmond."

Elizabeth's lips curled. "So protective, Shadow. It's good that you're doing your job, but you have nothing to fear from me. Despite our rather . . . *unpleasant* . . . history."

"You tried to kill me," I said tightly, when I finally found my voice.

"And I was soundly punished for it," she replied. "My brother will never allow me to return to the Shadowlands. I accept my banishment and I'm doing what I can to make amends. I want you to know how deeply I regret what transpired last week." She reached out a hand toward me.

Michael placed himself in front of me. "Don't come any closer."

"But I wanted to demonstrate that you have nothing to fear from me. The banishment makes it impossible for me even to touch my niece now."

Michael's lean muscles were tense as he held me back, but we didn't move as Elizabeth reached her well-manicured hand out toward me. When she was about six inches away, I heard a zapping sound, similar to what happened if I inadvertently touched Michael's amulet. She yanked her hand back and shook it out, pain crossing her beautiful face.

"See?" she said. "You're completely safe. Any closer and I might have lost a finger."

"That *is* oddly reassuring," I said.

"Please, come with me." She turned and began walking away. Michael didn't make any immediate move to follow her.

"We can leave right now and go back to the Shadowlands," he said, his worried gaze sweeping over my partial Darkling shift. He reached down to squeeze my hand. "Your father will be furious to know the council sent Elizabeth to meet us."

I concentrated for a moment and felt my horns and talons disappear. I was getting better at controlling my shifts. Practice makes perfect, after all.

"No . . . let's keep going. We're here now. She can't touch me."

"I really don't like her."

"That makes two of us."

Despite my brave(ish) words, seeing Elizabeth with no warning had freaked me out. So I tried to focus on something, anything, else. As we tentatively followed Elizabeth at a safe distance, I craned my neck, looking at the tall buildings around us.

If I didn't know we were in the Underworld, I would swear it was New York City. Mom had taken me on a trip to visit her publisher there a couple years ago. This was similar, only I didn't see any tour buses or big neon billboards, like in Times Square.

There was one major difference, though. In New York, there were crowds of people and the streets were filled with traffic. There were sounds and smells—both good and bad—and an energy that infused the city from corner to corner.

Here was none of that. No sirens, no traffic—no cars or taxis, either, parked or driving—no crowds. No one, seemingly, but the three of us. That such a large city was so silent and empty gave it an eerie ghost-town feel that sent a shiver through me.

Where is everybody? I asked Michael telepathically.

::I don't know. The Underworld is a very large place—bigger than anything you can imagine. I guess everyone's really spread out. Doesn't explain why it's completely deserted, though. We can leave—::

No, we're staying. For now, anyway.

Michael stayed close to me, keeping watch for potential threats. But there was nothing and no one other than Elizabeth, walking quickly on high heels that *click-clacked* along the sidewalk, the cloaklike blue dress she wore swishing around her slim legs.

I remembered when I'd first met her—she'd seemed so nice, so helpful, so caring. My mom was an only child, like me, so the thought of finding not only my father but my aunt as well had been amazing to me.

Unfortunately, she'd been one big lie wrapped in a beautiful blonde package. I think she'd single-handedly taught me the lesson not to trust anyone I met, or anything they said, before I got to know them better.

We finally came to a building that seemed to be made entirely of gold, and it reached so far into the sky that I couldn't even see the top of it.

"Here we are," Elizabeth announced. "The castle."

"This is a castle?" I said.

She nodded. "Queen Sephina changes the appearance of the Underworld's core frequently. All you see around you can change at her whim. Right now it's a city. Six months ago this was forestland. A year ago it was a tropical island."

She changed her surroundings like she might change her outfit? "So she gets easily bored?"

"Her daughter, Princess Kassandra, is the one who requests the changes when she visits. And"—Elizabeth sighed heavily—"what Kassandra wants, Kassandra gets."

That sounded interesting. Someone who made Elizabeth sigh with frustration and annoyance? I liked this Princess Kassandra person already.

Despite my feet really wanting to rebel and head back through the gateway to where I knew it was safe, I followed Elizabeth and Michael through the huge glass doors at the front of the building. They led into an expansive lobby with white marble floors. The walls looked like mottled silver and reflected our shapes, without detail, as we walked through. To the left of the doors was a fountain, and a hundred feet in front of us were elevators.

"Where is everybody?" I asked. My voice echoed off the metallic walls.

"The council is upstairs right now."

"No, I mean . . . everyone else. Like, the people, or demons, who live in the Underworld. Outside was empty as well. Where are they?"

"The Underworld is made up of many divisions, Nikki," she explained patiently, as if this was something I should already know. "This particular one represents the kingdom—the core. For security reasons, only royals and our servants and guards are allowed here, unless we choose to invite others. So yes, it can seem a little underpopulated at times."

"You could say that." I glanced at Michael.

"Although, it's much more populated than the Shadow-lands." Elizabeth shook her head and laughed. "Honestly, I don't know what my brother does to fill his years there other than read from that massive library of his, chat with his servants, and walk the halls of that boring castle. At least I was able to come and go at my leisure. And since his magic is all used up by maintaining the barrier, he can't even use it to change his surroundings to something more interesting.

"Oh, I'm sorry," I said as the anger rose inside me. "Are we politely chatting about my father? The one you tried to poison so you could take over his throne?"

Her laughter died away and she cleared her throat. "Yes, well, I guess there's no need to drum up the past, is there?"

The look she gave me was filled with extreme hatred for me—since I'd basically ruined her master plan of taking over the Shadowlands and letting her boyfriend Kieran have an all-access pass to the human and faery worlds.

There was an edge of fear there, too, and I didn't think it just had to do with the prophecy that may or may not be true about me. I'd proven the last time I saw my aunt that my power as a Darkling was bigger than hers as a demon. She hadn't liked being defeated, especially by a sixteen-year-old.

Even now, standing ten feet away from her, power began to move along my arm and into my right hand. I instinctively wanted to protect myself against somebody who'd tried to hurt me and my father. She'd taken Michael's amulet away and nearly killed him as well. To say Elizabeth and I would never be good buddies was putting it mildly.

"You said the council is upstairs?" Michael asked, as if trying to divert my thoughts from ones of zapping my aunt into the next dimension. Literally.

"They are." She walked over toward the fountain, sat on the edge of it, and dipped her hand into the shallow water.

"Princess Nikki has arrived," she said. After a moment, she nodded. "Very well."

It was a gazer. A big one. I guess it worked similar to an intercom.

Cell phones were easier in my honest opinion. Way more portable than a magical pool of water.

"They'll see you now." Elizabeth got up and walked toward the elevator.

My breath caught in my chest. Just like that. No preparation time. No nothing. I had to meet with the demon council. I looked at Michael for support.

He shrugged at me.

Yeah. Real helpful.

Elizabeth glanced over her shoulder, and a smile snaked across her face. "Oh, it looks like Fernando is coming to say hello."

"Who's Fernando?" I asked.

"Princess—" Michael's voice sounded strained. "Do not move."

"What?"

I suddenly heard the sound of scratching on the marble floor, a sound that got closer and closer, along with something like wet, slobbery breaths. Then a low, throaty, threatening growl. I turned to my right slowly, very slowly, to see the scariest thing I'd ever seen in my entire life.

It was big, the size of a full-grown lion. Its lips curled back from long, razor-sharp yellow teeth. Its fur was coarse and black and its eyes were glowing demon red. Its long swishing tail had a sharp point to it, like an arrowhead.

"Don't worry, he's very friendly," Elizabeth said evenly.

Michael's hand clamped down on my wrist, tight enough to hurt, but he didn't move, either.

I seriously was going to pass out.

My Darkling power—the energy and magic I'd had at the ready a moment ago to defend myself against Elizabeth—

suddenly vanished. Where did it go? I felt completely helpless to defend myself.

Whatever this monster was, had it drained me of my power? Just like that?

The monster continued to growl at me as it got close enough to sniff my shaking hand. Tendrils of smoke wafted from its nose and a steady stream of drool dripped from its jowls.

Elizabeth said this thing was friendly? Didn't seem that friendly to me. Actually, it looked *hungry*.

"Hey . . . *Fernando*," I said, trying to keep my voice steady. "Nice puppy."

"Puppy?" Michael managed. "That thing's a *hellhound*. I thought they were extinct."

I gulped. "Nice, uh, hellhound. Who's a cute hellhound? You are! Yes, you are!"

But instead of being charmed by my awkward puppy love, the monster growled again and moved to block our path to the elevator. Elizabeth waited nearby with an amused expression on her face at my fear of the Underworld castle's family pet.

"He won't hurt you," she said. "Just walk toward me."

Was she serious? Or was she trying to get her revenge by letting this thing rip out my throat?

What do you know about hellhounds? I asked Michael telepathically.

::They're just as dangerous as they look.::

That's what I was afraid of.

"Fernando!" another voice called out. "There you are!"

Out of the corner of my eye I saw someone approach us, making a beeline to the beast. It was a pretty girl who looked around my age, with wavy waist-length dark hair, vivid blue eyes, and pale porcelain skin. She wore a short black skirt and a flowy white blouse. When she got to the hellhound, she fearlessly grabbed one of its pointed batlike ears and tugged.

"Leave them alone. Bad boy." She pointed in the direction she'd come from. "Shoo!"

I half-expected the monster to attack her, but it didn't. Instead, its growl turned into a whine and it padded out of the lobby without another red-eyed glare in my direction.

She'd saved me. I'd been a few seconds away from becoming half-demon kibble, I just knew it.

"Thank you," I managed, my voice sounding strained.

"Not a problem," she said. "You're Princess Nikki, right?"

"Yeah. But just Nikki is fine."

She grinned. "Then you can call me just Kassandra."

"Kassandra," Elizabeth said. "You'll have a chance to talk to Nikki after she meets with the council. I need to take her upstairs now."

Kassandra rolled her eyes, her smile remaining exactly where it was. "I'll handle it, Elizabeth."

Elizabeth looked confused. "You'll handle what, dear?"

"I'll take Nikki upstairs. You can leave us now."

"But—"

"I honestly can't believe Kieran sent you to meet Nikki when I could have come instead. He's so unbelievably thoughtless." She looked at me and seemed a bit embarrassed. "My brother's always been a serious pain."

"Kieran's your brother?" I asked with surprise.

She nodded. "Unfortunately."

"So you're the princess here," I said, stating the obvious. Another demon princess, just like me. Although I didn't think Kassandra was anything like me if she had to live here, if Kieran was her sibling, and if she was able to boss around hellhounds as easily as if they were troublesome Chihuahuas.

"I am. That's why I'm so excited you're here. I've been dying to meet you."

Elizabeth cleared her throat. "Kieran wanted me to help out today."

"No, Elizabeth," Kassandra said patiently. "Kieran is simply trying to keep you busy so you stay out of his hair. Leave. Now. Or I'll tell my mother you didn't follow a direct order from me, and you know what'll happen then."

"Fine, have it your way," Elizabeth snapped, and with a glare Kassandra didn't see, my aunt walked out of the lobby and disappeared through a set of doors to my far left.

Interesting. Elizabeth had to take orders from someone my age. I liked the sound of that. Then again, Elizabeth had said Kassandra gets what she wants when she wants it, right? In this case, she was a very helpful asset.

Kassandra shook her head. "Of all the places she could have been banished to it had to be here. I really cannot stand your aunt. Neither can my brother, for that matter. These days, he tries to be anywhere she's not."

"Sorry to hear that."

"No, you're not."

"No, maybe I'm not."

Kassandra looked about ready to burst with excitement.

"I can't tell you how great it is to have you here. How long are you staying?"

"As soon as the meeting's done, I'm leaving." I wrung my hands, feeling some serious stage fright at the prospect of being presented to the council.

Her smile deflated. "Really? I'd hoped to show you around a bit. Can't you stay longer than that?"

I glanced at Michael, who silently stood close to me, but not too close, carefully observing my conversation with the Underworld's demon princess. "Well . . . maybe a bit. Like, a *tiny* bit."

I had to admit, the thought of hanging out with her, getting to know her, appealed to me. She might be able to give me some tips.

"You're all stressed about the prophecy?" she asked.

"Big-time stressed."

"I think it's really cool, actually. I wish I had a prophecy about me. This place is boredom central and finally something is happening that's got everyone excited." She glanced at Michael, her gaze resting for a moment on his amulet, and her eyebrow went up. "You're a Shadow?"

He looked at me but didn't say anything in reply.

"His name is Michael," I said.

"Your servant."

I pressed my lips together. "Well, I guess you could—"

"I wish I had a Shadow servant. My mother won't let me have one, but they're way cooler than the demon ones. Demons can be so cranky and demanding. I've heard Shadows are extremely obedient, not that they have any choice. Once they're assigned to you, they're compelled to follow your orders no matter what. Is it like that for you?"

I cringed. "Well . . . I don't know. I . . . I guess so."

More evidence that Shadows had no control over their own lives. I'd compelled Michael to follow my wishes once before, and it was only because I had no other choice. I would never order him around on a regular basis.

She started to walk a slow circle around him. Michael didn't look the least bit comfortable under her close scrutiny. "Is it true you can speak to your assigned Shadow telepathically? That would be so handy."

::You don't have to tell her anything.:: Michael projected to me.

She seems nice enough, I sent back. *Although, I don't like how she's looking at you.*

::Like I'm a trained rat in a cage?::

She doesn't know any better. It's kind of sad, actually. For her.

"Telepathy, huh?" I said aloud, playing innocent. "Really? Never heard of that. But it would be kind of handy."

"That's too bad." She looked disappointed. "Oh, well. Some rumors are true, some aren't. I'd still like a Shadow of my own one day."

Michael's expression soured. ::She's a spoiled brat. Actually, this attitude is what I expected from you before we met and you showed me differently. Like she owns the world and everyone in it.::

I'll tell her you think so.

His brows immediately knitted together with concern. ::I don't think that would be a good idea, Princess.::

Then it's good that I'm totally kidding.

"So, Kassandra . . . you live here?" I thought it might be a good idea to change the subject.

"I go to school north of here, but I'm on break right now."

"You go to school?" I don't know why I was surprised by that. Demon teenagers needed an education, too.

She nodded. "It's a boarding school, which means I don't have to live here very much. Classes are a pain but there are loads of other students to hang around with." She sighed. "Being here feels like a punishment. Nobody to talk to, nobody to hang out with. But I go back in a week. Can't wait. You go to school, too?"

"High school."

"That's in the human world, right? So you go to school with a bunch of humans?"

"Mostly."

"Mostly?"

"Well." I cleared my throat. "Right now the king of the faery realm is going there, too, which cuts down on the human-only class list."

"King Rhys?" she said immediately.

I nodded. "That's the one."

Her expression grew grave. "His parents were murdered two months ago."

My heart ached again for Rhys's loss. "I didn't know it was that recent."

"It happened right here in the castle."

I looked around and felt a sense of foreboding. "How did it happen?"

"The king and queen came here for a meeting with my mother," Kassandra continued. "There's a lot of bad blood between faeries and demons—it goes way back. I studied it in my history class, but I never really paid much attention to it. Anyway, my mom wanted to mend things and maybe move toward a new and bright future of peace between the worlds. So they arrived and they were attacked and killed right in the lobby before the guards could do anything but drag the murderer away and throw him in the dungeon. That's where he is right now." She pointed at the ground and, despite the grim story, she grinned. "It's kind of exciting, isn't it?"

I looked at the spotless white marble floor and felt a bit sick. "There's a dungeon down there?"

"Yup. The castle sits directly on top of it. It's a small one compared to those in Hell, but don't worry, the prisoners are kept tightly locked up at all times."

Yeah, that's a comforting thought. I met Michael's gaze and held it for a moment.

He gave me a concerned look. ::I guess that's where they send anyone who breaks the rules.::

Let's be on our best behavior and get out of here the minute we can.

::Good idea.::

"Anyway." Kassandra's voice cut through the suddenly quiet lobby. "We should get going or my mom will wonder what Elizabeth has done with you."

"Does your mom know Elizabeth tried to kill me?" I asked. "*And* my father?"

She nodded. "She knows a bit. What Elizabeth has said about it, anyway."

"And what's that?"

"That Elizabeth wanted to be queen of the Shadowlands," Kassandra said. "My mother respects demons with drive."

"So it's okay with her? Attempted murder?"

That earned a noncommittal shrug. "We don't chat about stuff like this since she knows I'm not interested in politics. But she's letting Elizabeth stay here, so obviously she doesn't feel threatened or anything, if that's what you're asking. I mean, it's *Elizabeth*. She's fairly useless, all things considered. Frankly, I'm surprised she even tried anything vaguely ambitious."

It was on the tip of my tongue to tell Kassandra that her brother was the one who pushed Elizabeth into her poison-administering evil ways, but I decided against it when I saw the look Michael was giving me. I didn't need telepathy to get that he thought I'd said enough on the subject. After all, I'd just said I wanted to get out of here ASAP. But it was a demon princess's prerogative to change her mind. Frequently.

Best behavior. That was me.

The door to the elevator opened as Kassandra approached it. After a look at Michael, who had his arms crossed in front of him and seemed as if he was ready for anything, I followed Kassandra into the carriage. Michael stayed beside me.

"Does your Shadow ever speak?" Kassandra asked with amusement.

"When I choose to," Michael said curtly.

"Good to know." She shifted her gaze from him to me and

studied me curiously for a moment. "You're freaked about this, aren't you?"

"Define freaked."

"Scared to death about meeting the council."

"That about covers it."

She smiled. "The last demon they called before them is sitting in the dungeon right now while they decide what his sentence will be. They found him to be impolite in the presence of the queen."

I sucked in a breath. "I'm going to throw up."

"My advice?" she said. "Just let them talk at you. Smile and nod. As long as you don't attack anyone—"

"Which I won't," I interjected.

"—then it'll probably be fine."

"Probably?"

She shrugged. "Depends what mood they're in. The counsel members' bites are sometimes worse than their bark, so be careful."

This coming from someone who had a hellhound as a house pet.

After a minute, the elevator door opened. Kassandra got out and we followed her.

It was a room as large as the lobby, and at the end of it was a long black table with five beings seated at it. They had been discussing something loudly until the door opened; after that there was complete silence. I could clearly hear my footsteps as I trailed after Kassandra. I desperately wanted to grab hold of Michael's hand for courage, but I restrained myself.

"Wait there," a woman sitting in a large plush chair said to us abruptly, and Kassandra stopped walking. The conversation continued in hushed tones.

I was close enough now to see who was at the table, and honestly, it was like something out of a nightmare or a horror movie. Fear shot through my body as fast as a shiver. They weren't all human—or at least, they weren't all in *human form*. I knew none of them were human to begin with. After all . . . it was a *demon* council, right?

I felt Michael move close enough to me that his fingers brushed reassuringly against mine.

::Don't worry. It's going to be okay.::

You sure about that?

::I know this must be strange for you, Princess, but it'll be fine. I promise.::

He sounded so certain that I relaxed a little. Only a little. I wanted to lean against him for support, but I didn't. I stood, straight as a column, as I waited for the demon council to call me over.

Kassandra turned. "So typical. They're making you wait just so you sweat it out a bit more."

"Who are these . . . these demons?" I asked.

"The one on the far right, that's my mother—Queen Sephina," she said, indicating the woman in the tallest chair, who basically looked like a grown-up version of Kassandra. She was, thankfully, in human form at the moment. Dark hair was piled on top of her head and threaded with gold and jewels that sparkled under the lights.

To our left, halfway between us and the table, was a three-foot-tall gold and white stone statue of the queen herself perched upon a marble pedestal. It was a perfect likeness.

"She's the leader of the council," Kassandra continued, "and whatever she says goes. She's superpowerful; her magic is the strongest of any demon I know—except my father, of course. She's got a soft spot for my brothers, especially Kieran, and gives him almost anything he wants."

"*Almost* anything?"

"He isn't allowed to go to the human world, and it's something he's always wanted. That's where she draws the line. She's afraid he'd get into major trouble there."

I wondered what would happen if the queen decided to let him have free rein. Would she be able to force my father to open the barrier so the prince could pass through the Shadowlands to the worlds beyond? And, if so, what would happen then?

"How many brothers do you have?" I asked.

"Three. Two are traveling right now elsewhere in the Underworld—one's on his honeymoon, actually. And you've already met Kieran." She nodded toward the table.

Prince Kieran was seated to the queen's left. His attention was fixed on me even though his mother was saying something to him. His light blue eyes glittered.

"I have." I didn't expand on that thought because if I did, it would sound like this: *I have and I hate his guts.*

"Next to Kieran is Groden." He was in demon form. Ashy red skin, glowing eyes, thick curved horns. Along his pointed right ear he wore a multitude of golden earrings and there was another one through his nose. "He's usually drunk and mostly disorderly. He's been on the council pretty much forever—since my grandmother was in charge. Rules and laws are his thing—he loves coming up with new ones. My mother thinks he's annoying, but she can't kick him out."

"So he's responsible for making the rules?" I thought about all the rules that had made life difficult for both me and my father. Stupid rules that, when broken, could lead to horrible and deadly punishments.

"He's the one. The woman next to him is Florencia." She was in human form and appeared middle-aged, with a skunk-like streak of white hair in the middle of her shoulder-length dark locks. "She's the one you have to watch out for. Groden makes up the rules, but she enforces them. A real by-the-books kind of demoness. Another interesting factoid about her is that she was supposed to marry your father years ago."

That got my full attention. "Really?"

Kassandra nodded. "It was an arranged marriage. It was right before you were born, not that this was known until just this past week, of course. Anyway, rumor has it when King Desmond came back from his trip to the human world to take over the throne of the Shadowlands, he refused to marry Florencia, even though refusal of an arranged marriage is rare. I don't think she's ever forgiven him for that." She paused. "Your father must have really been in love with your mother. I've heard he's never even dated anyone since then."

I swallowed hard. It only helped to cement what I already knew. "Really?"

"Really."

This might be the reason for the icy-cold daggers Florencia was sending in my direction with her glare.

"She seems nice," I said.

Kassandra snorted. "Yeah, as nice as my brother's hellhound."

"That was *Kieran's* hellhound?"

"Yeah. But I think Fernando likes me better. Hard to tell with hellhounds. They do make great guardians, though."

"I felt my power drain when it was near me earlier. I thought it was my imagination."

"No, it's a trait of hellhounds. They absorb the energy of any demon outside of the family they protect."

"Only demons?"

"Yes. Or, I suppose, Darklings, too."

Michael looked at me, his forehead furrowed.

::You lost your power?::

Only for a minute. It's fine. I'll just make sure I avoid Fernando for the rest of my visit here. I'm more of a cat person, anyway.

"Okay . . . uh, who's the . . . the last one there?" I asked nervously. It was the council member I'd tried not to look directly at, since he, or she, was totally freaking me out. It didn't look like a demon *or* a human. Even though it did look slightly humanoid, with arms and shoulders and a face, it also looked like a cockroach. Seriously.

A wave of repulsion washed through me.

"Oh, him?" Kassandra said casually. "That's Beasley. He's my father's representative."

"Your father?"

She nodded. "The king of Hell."

My eyes widened. "Your father is the *king of Hell?*"

"He is. He's got so many names that nobody knows what to call him, so most people just call him the king. I call him Daddy. Not that I ever get to see him, since he and Mom got divorced. She hates his guts. She's not too fond of Beasley, either, but he's actually really nice."

Information overload was making me queasy. "If you say so."

"Princess Nikki can approach the council now," Kassandra's mother called out sharply.

My hands started to shake, and I clasped them together. I could do this. I was brave. I wasn't afraid. The queen had promised I would be safe. All they wanted was to meet me.

Just a meet and greet. Friendly. Happy. All was well with the worlds.

I put one foot in front of the other as I moved through the room. Michael kept pace with me.

"Nikki," Kassandra called after us. "Servants aren't permitted to approach the council. You need to have your Shadow wait back here with me."

"No," Michael said. "I won't leave the princess's side."

He said it so definitively that she looked surprised. "You're saying *no* to me? Nobody says no to me."

His green eyes met mine. "I will do as Princess Nikki wishes, of course."

"You're staying with me," I said without missing a beat. "That is what Princess Nikki wishes."

A half smile appeared on his lips. "Good."

"Fine, have it your way," Kassandra said stiffly. "Well, good luck."

I hoped I wouldn't need it. Luck hadn't exactly been much of a friend to me lately. I mean, look where I was.

17

"Your servant must wait at the back of the room," were Queen Sephina's first words to me, echoing what her daughter had said. She had a cool, commanding, and intimidating voice.

"I want him to stay here with me," I said weakly, then forced myself to sound more confident. "In fact, I insist."

Her lips thinned. "I see."

Would that be enough to get me thrown in the dungeon for being rude? I really hoped not.

There was silence for a long, uncomfortable moment. All of the council members' attention was fully on me. It was like back in grade six, when I had a part in the school musical and it was time for my solo. Only then did I realize I had horrible stage fright, making my singing voice sound a whole lot like I'd inhaled a balloon full of helium.

The cockroach's antennae twitched as he stared at me through big, creepy black eyes. I made a mental note to bring along a large can of Raid if I ever had the misfortune of coming here again.

I waited for my inevitable punishment.

Nothing happened.

"Princess Nikki." Kieran spoke up, glancing at the other council members. "We are pleased you agreed to meet with us today."

"It's . . . it's my pleasure," I lied. May as well be as nice as I could after putting my foot down about Michael staying next to me. This was about first impressions—or maybe second impressions—after all.

"We've been discussing you a great deal since news of your existence first reached us," he said. "It was a shock to learn King Desmond had a half-human daughter all these years. From what I gather from Elizabeth, it was a shock to him as well."

"It was. He had no idea I existed."

"Has he been in contact with your human mother?" Florencia asked unpleasantly.

Such a simple question for such a touchy topic. One that could tilt this meeting to a very dark place if I handled it wrong. But there was no reason to lie about this.

"No," I replied. "In fact, he insists I don't tell her anything about him . . . or about the fact I'm half demon."

"A wise decision." Queen Sephina nodded. "So your mother was unaware that Desmond was a demon prince when they met?"

"She had no idea at all. And she never will."

It hurt to say it out loud. Was I giving up hope that I could find a way for my mother and father to get back together? No. But right now I had to appear that I believed that to be a hundred percent true.

Florencia shook her head. "Such shameful behavior for all involved in this disgusting situation. It sickens me that

Desmond would display such poor judgment. A human female? It's no wonder the barrier exists. Otherwise, perhaps all demon males would run off to have romantic flings in the human world. I don't care if Desmond was young at the time, it's simply not acceptable."

Why? I thought. *Because he didn't want to marry a sourpuss like you when he came back?*

I felt Michael eyeing me. Had I projected that thought telepathically, or were my thoughts written all over my face? The latter, I figured. Sending telepathic messages to him actually took more effort than just thinking. I tried to keep my face as pleasantly expressionless as I could.

"Florencia," Queen Sephina said with a warning edge. "Please, mind yourself. Princess Nikki is our guest here and will be treated with respect. That respect extends to her father as well. King Desmond will be dealt with another day."

"Of course." Florencia lowered her head in a small bow. "My apologies to the queen and to the princess."

"What do you mean, he'll be dealt with?" I asked cautiously.

The queen gave me a slight smile. "It is we who are asking the questions today, not you."

"But . . ." It would be better if I said nothing, but one of the main reasons I was here today was to make sure my father was safe. "It happened a long time ago, and there's no reason it should be held against him anymore. It was no big deal."

"No big deal?" Florencia sputtered. "He broke the rules forbidding a demon to be with a human—and the result was a Darkling child prophesied to destroy us all. He's lucky we haven't thrown him in the dungeon retroactively for his crimes."

"Rules," Groden piped up, scratching his cheek with the sharp black talon on his index finger. "I believe there should be a rule for anyone who dares to wear blue on a Wednesday. It's simply not right." Without waiting for a reply, he scribbled something down on a piece of parchment in front of him with a feathered quill. "Or purple on a Thursday. *Blecch*. Punishable by one year in the dungeon."

The gigantic cockroach appeared to have no opinion so far but continued to study me through large glassy black eyes. I wondered if he could actually talk, or if staring creepily was his chosen mode of communication.

"King Desmond made a very poor decision," Kieran said coolly. "While in the human world, he was lucky he wasn't discovered to be a demon. He could have come face-to-face with a slayer. Then what would have happened when the former king died? Elizabeth would have been forced to take the throne at the same age you are now, Princess."

I glared at him. Wouldn't he have loved that? Then he would have gotten what he wanted seventeen years ago instead of having to wait to find a break in the barrier. It was almost funny.

However, the talk of "slayers" did keep me from laughing out loud.

"Slayer?" I said, trying to play dumb. "What's that?"

Kieran rolled his eyes. "Exactly what it sounds like, of course. There is a secret society of humans who lull themselves into a false sense of security by training to kill any demon who might dare to enter their precious light world. In certain families, the firstborn children are believed to have special abilities from birth to help them become slayers of our kind. The tradition and supposed power is a mystery, but we believe it originated in the Middle Ages, when humans went on their quests and crusades. But with the Shadowlands barrier intact, I would imagine they've been very bored for a very long time. All that training and no opportunity to slay anything." His lips twisted. "It is a dream of mine to come face-to-face with one of these slayers. I think it would be a great deal of fun."

It was a lot of information to take in all at once. So Melinda was the firstborn child of a family that had a long demon-slaying history?

"Kieran, please. That's quite enough." Queen Sephina folded her hands on the tabletop.

He jutted his bottom lip out in a pout at being reprimanded. "But Mother—"

"Kieran," she snapped. "Enough talk of the human world. Your whining grows more tiresome with every year that passes."

He slouched and looked away.

I wanted to save it as a Kodak moment. If only I'd brought my camera.

Queen Sephina sighed. "Princess Nikki, we are a very understanding council. We see the shades of gray when others might only see black and white. What your father did was wrong, especially since he was aware of the rules. At the time he was a stubborn and impulsive young man. I know he's changed greatly over the years and has taken his duty as king of the Shadowlands very seriously. However, I do believe, had he been given the choice, he would have chosen to remain in the human world with your mother—"

Florencia let out an annoyed *harrumph*.

"—and this decision would have not only put humans at risk but also exposed the existence of certain gateways of the demon worlds to this slaying society Kieran speaks of."

"So these slayers," I said, trying to get it clear in my head. "They know demons definitely exist?"

"Yes. Those who are aware keep the existence of the dark worlds, as well as the faery realm, a secret from others of their kind. It's the best way. Should they happen to discover or create a gateway here, it would be extremely unpleasant for all involved. It is my duty to protect the Underworld from any unpleasantness like this. Desmond understands this now—that one's royal duty must precede all else."

Anger ignited inside me at her dismissive attitude toward my father's pain.

"I think Desmond should be executed for breaking such an important rule," Florencia stated bluntly. "A *human* woman. I still cannot believe it."

"No, he shouldn't," I snapped at her, then clamped my mouth shut at her surprised look.

My anger turned quickly to fear. Did Florencia have the power to punish me? Kassandra had warned that she was the enforcer of rules. Hell hath no fury like a demoness scorned.

Queen Sephina sighed. "And after his execution, then what? The power of the Shadowlands would shift to his half-human daughter, confining her within the castle walls until her own death. As one raised in the human world since birth, she would not make an adequate queen."

While I didn't want to take the throne—in fact, it was the

last thing I wanted—I did bristle a little at the accusation that I'd suck at it. Just because I was half human didn't mean I wouldn't try my very best.

Groden cleared his throat. "There is also the ever-looming threat of the prophecy. Would it, perhaps, be vengeance for her father's execution that triggers the Darkling to destroy us all?" He eyed me and Michael uneasily, breathing hard enough that the gold ring through his nose bounced. "I propose a rule that no Darkling shall ever become queen. Punishable by beheading!"

He scribbled this down on his parchment.

Queen Sephina rolled her eyes. "Unfortunately, such a thing cannot be governed by law, Groden. She is Desmond's heir by blood."

"So what?"

She looked slightly exasperated with this debate. "Royal blood cannot be challenged. Princess Nikki is heir to the Shadowlands throne for as long as she lives and breathes. The prophecy changes nothing when it comes to this matter."

"I think the prophecy is a lie," I said.

Five sets of eyes widened and tracked to me. Florencia gasped out loud.

"You wish to challenge the prophecy?" Queen Sephina asked.

"I . . ." I licked my dry lips. I hadn't exactly expected such a dramatic reaction. I hadn't even known I was going to say that until I did. "Well, yes. I challenge it. I'm . . . I'm here to prove that it can't be true. I have no intention of destroying anything or anyone."

"Intentions are different from future actions," Kieran said.

"You can't predict what will happen based on how you feel at this particular moment. Besides, the prophecy was related directly to me. It is true. I would swear on my own life and the life of my mother."

The queen patted his arm. "Of course, my son. The palace oracle has never been wrong before."

I bit my lip, finding the direction of this "meeting" to be stomach-churningly bad. I opened my mouth to say something else.

::Princess,:: Michael projected to me before I spoke. ::Let them discuss among themselves. Don't give them a reason to extend this any longer than it has to be.::

He was telling me to stop attempting to put my foot in my mouth. The less said, the better. This was only a meet and greet.

Got it.

Sephina leaned back in her chair. "I wish to see your Darkling form."

I gulped. "Now?"

"Yes."

Again, performance anxiety crawled through me. "I can normally change form when I'm feeling emotional"—I had that covered, but I still felt weakened from being in that hellhound's drooling, power-draining presence—"but right now . . . uh, I'm not sure if I can."

"Then let me help you." Queen Sephina's eyes glowed red, and I felt a wave of magic flow over me. I gasped as all my muscles tensed, my limbs tingling with the force of her pulling my Darkling form out from inside me.

The change was fast and shockingly painful. The sides of

my head burned as my horns appeared. My talons grew. My muscles became leaner and firmer. My black wings tore right through the back of my red sweater as if it wasn't any stronger than tissue paper. My hair grew longer, thicker, and changed to a bright, fiery red I could see from the corner of my eye. When I traced my tongue over my teeth, I confirmed that I sported sharp canines, like a vampire might have. And now that I was aware of its existence—yes, I also definitely felt a tail. Yikes.

"This is your Darkling form?" Kieran raised an eyebrow, his gaze sweeping the length of me. "You look much the same as before, only now you are more beautiful."

Gee, lucky me. A compliment from Kieran. However, it was one that only succeeded in creeping me out.

More *beautiful?* I projected the thought toward Michael: *He's crazy.*

Michael hadn't moved an inch from my side since we'd approached the council table. His hands were clasped behind his back. ::Yes, Kieran is clearly crazy. I think you're equally beautiful in either human or Darkling form.::

My heart swelled at that. The council probably wouldn't approve if I threw my arms around him and kissed him right then, would they?

Nope. They'd likely throw us both in the dungeon.

I couldn't see myself, but I'd turned fully Darkling a couple of times before—wings and all—and I felt much the same as I had then. Stronger, more powerful . . . and way angrier. My fear mostly faded away, replaced by an annoyance that the council would make me do this—parade myself before them and let them judge me as though this was a demon beauty contest. It was now obvious this meeting was only to show me who really had the power in the room—them, not me, and I wasn't supposed to forget it.

"This is it," I said, holding my taloned hands up to either side as I turned around in a slow circle. "What you see is what you get."

"You have your father's wings," Florencia said wistfully.

I shifted my weight to my other foot. "I'll take that as a compliment."

The queen's eyes narrowed as her gaze swept over me. "How do you intend to destroy us when you still look so very human?"

I rolled my eyes. "I'm not going to destroy you."

There was some visible tension around her mouth. "The prophecy was very clear. The first Darkling in a thousand years—"

"Wait a minute," I said, interrupting her, which was probably a big no-no. Taking Darkling form meant losing some, if not all, of my human fear of the council. It also brought a sense of clarity and objectivity that I didn't normally have. "Are you *sure* I'm the first Darkling in a thousand years?"

"Of course we're sure," Kieran said bluntly. "There is no other."

I thought it over. "Correct me if I'm wrong, but I don't think the prophecy says, 'Nikki Donovan, the first Darkling in a thousand years.' Or even, the 'Darkling daughter of the Shadowlands' king.' It just said the *first* Darkling. How can you be positive it's me?"

There was total silence in the cavernous room for a long moment.

"There has been no other Darkling child *but* you," Queen Sephina said evenly. "If there had been, I would know."

"Maybe or maybe not," I challenged. "Any Darkling who feared for its life would probably try to keep its existence under wraps, given what little history I've heard. I don't think a Darkling would stroll through the Underworld wearing an 'I'm a Darkling, Ask Me How!' T-shirt."

Michael studied me. ::You're right, Princess. This is a strong argument against the prophecy. But still . . . please be careful what you say. Don't provoke them.::

I'll try my best.

"It's impossible," Florencia interjected. "No demon, aside from your father, has visited the human world in a thousand years. The Shadowlands prevent casual travel or communication between the dark and light worlds. You're speaking nonsense, child. You must take after your mother."

I shot her a withering look that she reflected right back at me.

"Nobody except my father in a *thousand years*?" I asked, doing my best to sound as respectful as possible, despite the anger bristling under my skin. "With all due respect, I find that hard to believe."

"Desmond had permission from his own father to visit the human world," Florencia countered. "A foolish decision on the former king's part, knowing how impulsive his son then was."

I shook my head. "There *has* to have been some kind of

communication, some contact. This city looks just like a human city. The way some demons dress is very similar to how humans dress"—I pointed over my shoulder toward the back of the room—"like Princess Kassandra's outfit, for example. I could have bought the exact same thing last time I was at the mall. Even the way you talk—it's all very human. To me, that means you must have had *some* contact more recently than a thousand years ago to influence things, even if it was just a little."

"We haven't," Kieran said bluntly.

"Sure we have," said the cockroach.

18

All eyes turned to Beasley.

He shrugged his buglike black shoulders. "I mean, there's all that paperwork that needs to be filled out and submitted to King Desmond, and he takes forever to approve anyone for a trip beyond the dark worlds. He's fastidious, I'll give him that. But don't deny it, Your Majesty. Scouts and servants are *often* sent to fetch samples of the human world—books, movies, food, drink, clothing—for us to study and enjoy." He leaned back in his chair. "Besides, the Shadowlands is not the only place to find a gateway to the human world."

This got Kieran's full attention. "It's not?"

"Beasley," the queen hissed. "This is not the time to discuss this."

"But doesn't Prince Kieran know this already?" Beasley asked. "There are other gateways scattered throughout the Underworld and Hell. Hidden ones. It stands to reason, at one time or another, they may have been discovered by a wandering demon who could have been swept away, never to return again."

"Tell me, Beasley, where are these hidden gateways?"

Kieran asked curiously, leaning toward the bug at the end of the table.

"Let us change the subject, please," the queen said.

"They're *hidden*, Prince Kieran. Which means they're not easily found. Frankly, I don't know where they are. Not that I'd ever be interested in traveling to the human world. I don't think they'd welcome me with open arms."

I thought of Rhys and his ability to hide his pointed ears and wings enough to fit in. "Can't you do a glamour to look human?"

The cockroach looked at me. "Afraid that's not one of my talents. Besides, when you're as gorgeous as I am, why would you ever want to look any different?"

I blinked.

Beasley laughed. "I'm kidding of course. I'm fully aware I'm hideous. I'd be there three minutes before finding myself on the wrong side of a demon-slayer's sword."

Good point.

I suddenly got a mental image of Melinda facing off against Beasley. She hated bugs. She was afraid of spiders. But could she kick demon butt?

It wouldn't be a pretty sight.

Would she kill a demon who looked scary but wasn't a threat? How did that work? I'd only just met Beasley, but so far he seemed fairly personable and helpful, despite his appearance.

I couldn't deal with the demon council right now *and* think about Melinda. The whole thing made me feel seriously seasick.

Groden slapped his hand against the table. "I propose a rule that all secret gateways be revealed to any demon wishing to do a little interworld sightseeing. A penalty of death to all who conceal their locations!"

"Beasley," the queen said sharply, apparently disturbed by the direction of this discussion. "You're saying you believe there may be demons living in the human world even as we speak?"

"I'm saying it's possible," Beasley replied, his antennae twitching. "We know there are dragons living there already, so why not demons as well? The possibility is enough for me to lean toward Princess Nikki's argument that the prophecy may not be about her at all."

"It was related to me the day the Darkling would have turned sixteen and come into her powers," Kieran said.

"Possibly a coincidence," Beasley replied. "Besides, just look at her. She's way too adorable to be as destructive as the prophecy says she is. Those horns could not be cuter."

Cockroaches were now my absolute favorite insect.

Okay, I lied. They weren't. But I'd make an exception for Beasley.

I returned my attention to the queen. I waited, holding my breath, for what she'd say next. She studied me for a full minute, her gaze moving over my Darkling form, taking in all my extra demonic accessories as if appraising me for auction value.

"Very well, you may leave us now." She flicked her hand and I felt magic sweep over me, changing me back to human form. I staggered backward as momentary but severe pain lanced through me. Luckily, Michael caught my arm and steadied me before I fell.

The queen stood up from behind the table and approached

me. I willed myself not to back away from her. She grasped my hands and kissed me on either cheek.

"Please give my regards to your father," she said.

"Sure," I said breathlessly.

So that's it? I glanced at Michael. *We're free to go?*

His expression was guarded. ::I think so.::

Queen Sephina continued to hold my hands in hers. She peered at me as if expecting me to show suddenly that my true face was even uglier than Beasley's. Her gaze slowly moved down to my wrist.

"You have a dragon's tear," she said with shock.

A chair scraped against the floor as Kieran rose to his feet. "A dragon's tear? A real one?"

I was surprised Elizabeth hadn't told him already. She'd been well aware of the gift I received from my father.

"It's very beautiful," Queen Sephina said, holding my wrist tighter.

I tried not to pull away from her. "Thank you."

"Did your father give you this?"

"He did."

She nodded. "I'd heard he slayed a dragon when he was no more than your age. It was an accomplishment that branded him as a future king, despite his stubbornness in many things. It makes sense that he would give it to you."

My father had been the one to kill the dragon who shed the tear I now wore on the chain around my wrist?

"Well, some fathers hunt deer," I said, repressing a shudder. "My father hunted dragons. Same difference."

"Hardly. Dragons are very dangerous and magical creatures. Only three dragons have been slain in recorded history, and your father is responsible for the most recent. This tear is very precious. I hope you realize and appreciate that."

"More and more every minute."

"You have given me much to consider here today." She finally released me. "My daughter will see you back to the Shadowlands gateway. Good-bye."

Without another word, she turned dismissively away from me and went back to her chair. Now that she wasn't sitting in it, I noticed it had a gold sheen and was speckled with the same jewels she wore in her hair. Was it her throne?

::Let's go, Princess. Wouldn't want to outstay our welcome.::

It was an excellent idea. I turned, and Michael and I walked away from the council and toward the elevator, where Kassandra waited for us. I still felt on edge.

Did that go well? I asked. Now that my Darkling form was gone, so was my confidence.

::I think so. They asked fewer questions than I thought they would.::

Did I do okay? I think I talked too much.

::You stood up for what you believe in. You didn't take everything they said with your head lowered like many would. I was impressed.::

Despite the compliment, a lump formed in my throat. I'd stood up for what I believed in, but I couldn't stand up and tell them how I felt about Shadows—how I felt about Michael in particular. I wasn't that brave. And I couldn't put him in danger.

So, what now?

::Now we do exactly as Queen Sephina suggested. We leave.::

Lead the way.

Kassandra grinned as we approached and got in the elevator with her. "See? That wasn't so bad, was it?"

I was still breathing. I wasn't currently redecorating a dungeon cell. I'd let the demon council check me out and I'd challenged the prophecy, enough to put doubt in their minds about it. It definitely could have gone worse.

I was surprised I hadn't thought of the possibility there might be another Darkling around somewhere, either now or some time in the past millennium. It was a reassuring thought, and I allowed a small measure of relief to flow through me. Is that why Irena couldn't see the first prophecy for herself? Because it was so vague and maybe not even about me at all?

Whatever the reason, now I could go back to my semi-normal life, where all I had to deal with were faery kings and jealous demon-slaying best friends.

Still major problems, but ones I could at least deal with in the human world, not here.

"It's so cool you have a dragon's tear," Kassandra said as the elevator slowly began to make its way down to the lobby. "Can I see?"

I pulled up the sleeve of my sweater—now ripped and a bit drafty in the back, thanks to my unscheduled wing appearance—and showed her the bracelet.

Her eyes widened with appreciation. "It's gorgeous."

"Thanks."

"Can I have it?"

I looked at her. "What?"

"I have lots of jewelry," she said. "I could trade you for something else. Anything you want."

"Uh . . . I don't really think so."

She frowned as if confused by my refusal. "But I want it."

I shrugged. "Sorry."

Rolling the crystal between my thumb and index finger, I felt the cold weight of it. I didn't like how the crystal had been obtained, and I didn't like that my father was the one who slayed the dragon in the first place, but I wasn't planning on trading it to anyone.

She twirled her hair. "In school, in dragon studies, we learned about their tears. Dragons can teleport from place to place and between worlds no problem, they always have. So it's rumored that their one and only tear—a solid piece of their life magic—gives the wearer the ability to do the same."

I hadn't known that. "You think having this means I can teleport wherever I want?"

"I think so. Cool, right? I'd love to be able to do that." Her gaze slid back down to my wrist.

::Princess, please say nothing else,:: Michael's voice warned in my head. ::I don't like the way she's looking at your bracelet.::

But she can't have it.

::Remember what Elizabeth said about Kassandra when we first arrived? What Kassandra wants, Kassandra gets.::

She's not that bad. She'll just have to take no for an answer for once.

Even though she was a bit of a spoiled brat, I kind of liked

Kassandra. She'd been helpful and friendly and was full of information. But I was better safe than sorry. A lot of girls seemed
superfriendly on the surface, but when it came to something
they wanted, they were different. Kind of like Larissa. And
she wasn't even a real demon underneath it all, like Kassandra was.

The doors opened on the lobby and we got out of the
elevator.

"You don't have to leave right away," Kassandra said,
finally tearing her eyes from my bracelet. "We can hang out for
a while first."

"We really should be leaving," Michael said.

Kassandra looked at him sharply. "I wasn't speaking to you,
Shadow."

I flinched as I did whenever anyone treated Michael like
he was a lesser being. I'd promised myself I'd be on my best
behavior, but it was on the tip of my tongue to defend him.

"Kassandra," I began. "Michael's—"

::No, Princess. Say nothing. Let's just leave.::

I bit my lip.

"Michael's right," I said instead. "I'm kind of tired, and it's
actually, like, late at night back home, so . . . can I take a rain
check?"

Her expression soured and her eyes again darted briefly to
my wrist. She couldn't get the bracelet and she couldn't get me
to stay. It must have been a shock for someone used to getting
anything they wanted. "Whatever."

Maybe I wouldn't be best friends with the only other
demon princess I'd met, but I wouldn't let her suddenly sullen

attitude bother me. I'd met with the council, and other than finding them mostly unpleasant—although Beasley was nice enough for a six-foot-tall talking cockroach—I thought it went okay.

Now I wanted very much to go home. I looked at Michael, and he met my gaze and held it. He'd been so amazing this whole time—despite our shaky start after the "mistletoe incident." I didn't think I could have done this without him. I felt it deeper now than ever before—there was more between us, something superstrong that couldn't just be pushed aside and forgotten about, no matter what the rules were or who made them.

If somebody on the demon council could push back against all the stupid rules Groden came up with, maybe he or she would change things. Make them better.

Maybe I could try to get on the demon council someday.

I'd never even wanted to run for student council before. I turned the channel when politics of any kind came on television. But here I was thinking about it for myself?

Sure. Why not?

Pondering this bizarre but somewhat hopeful thought, I approached the exit of the Underworld castle.

Suddenly, Michael stopped walking and spun around on his heels. I turned my head to see what had grabbed his attention and froze with fear.

It was the hellhound. It had entered the lobby again. However, the hellhound wasn't approaching me slowly and ominously like last time. It was racing fast across the lobby, drool flying from its snarling mouth and sharp fangs, its red eyes locked solely on me.

"No, Fernando! What are you doing?" Kassandra shouted, and I couldn't mistake the panicky sound to her voice.

As the hellhound got closer, my power fell away in one weakening *whoosh*. There was nothing at my fingertips to protect myself, not even a spark of energy. My bracelet felt dead and cold on my wrist. I couldn't have turned Darkling at the moment if my life depended on it.

And it did.

The hellhound wanted to kill me. I'd never been more sure about anything before in my life.

"Michael!" I turned so fast to run that my legs got tangled up and I fell hard to the ground, smacking the side of my head on the cold marble floor. I scrambled backward, trying to escape.

"Princess!" Michael yelled.

The monster launched itself at me, flying through the air.

A pulse of green light emanated from Michael's amulet and focused directly on the beast, surrounding and freezing it in mid-pounce, its talons only inches away from slicing deep into my throat. It was then knocked hard to the side, where it fell to the ground, sliding across the lobby floor before hitting the wall. It didn't move again.

The hellhound was unconscious. Or dead. I didn't know.

Michael dropped heavily to his knees and I crawled over to him.

"Princess, are you okay?" he asked. His amulet and his eyes had lost their color, just as they had the last time he used his power—they were gray now instead of green. It was like he used up an entire battery charge for one of those powerful pulses of energy.

"Oh my God, Michael . . ." I was breathing hard and trembling, my heart beating so fast I could feel it through my entire body. "You saved me."

"Are you surprised?" He managed a weak grin. I grabbed his hands and they felt very cold.

I looked over at the fallen hellhound. "I think you killed it."

"Good," he said grimly.

"I guess Shadows don't have their powers drained by hellhounds like demons do."

"Lucky for us."

"Yeah."

A glance at Kassandra showed her holding a hand over her mouth in shock, her eyes wide at what she'd just witnessed.

Then an alarm began to blare.

I stroked Michael's dark hair off his forehead. "Are *you* okay? Are you going to pass out?"

"I don't think so." His skin had turned pale and ashen. "I just need a couple minutes to recover."

"Take as long as you need."

There was the sound of footsteps then, and several men approached us—some in human form, some in demon. They wore uniforms, black with gold details. I figured they were some kind of guards. They looked at me and Michael, then at the still hellhound, and then at Kassandra.

"What happened here?" one guard asked.

"Fernando, my brother's hellhound, attacked Princess Nikki. But . . . but her . . . her Shadow servant stopped him." Kassandra hesitated. "I . . . I witnessed him use his power."

You're a hero, I told Michael telepathically. *My hero. Now let's get out of here.*

He looked worried as the guards got nearer. ::I have a feeling that's going to be a problem.::

What?

::Let Kassandra take you back to the gateway. Go back to your father.::

What are you talking about? You're coming with me, aren't you?

He didn't answer me. The next moment the guards grabbed Michael firmly by his arms, yanked him to his feet, and dragged him forcibly across the floor toward the elevator.

I ran after them. "Where are you taking him?"

"To the dungeon," a guard replied without looking at me.

"The *dungeon*? But why are you—?"

Before I could demand any other answers, the silver elevator doors closed between us. I was in shock. I placed a shaking hand on the cold silver door before turning around to look at Kassandra.

"I'm sorry, Nikki," she said. "I know he was your servant."

My eyes burned. "Why are they taking Michael to the dungeon? He didn't do anything wrong. He saved my life!"

"Yes, but . . ." She pulled on her hair nervously. "He's a Shadow. They aren't allowed to use their powers at all, and especially not in front of demon royalty like us."

"Are you crazy? If he hadn't, the hellhound would have killed me."

"I know. But what he did is against the rules. The reason he did it doesn't matter. My mother's enforcing all rules to the letter these days, especially after . . . after—"

"After what?"

"After what happened to the king and queen of the faery realm. My mother won't let something like that ever happen again. Especially not here in the castle."

"But that doesn't make sense. A demon killed them."

"No." Kassandra shook her head. "They were killed by a Shadow."

19

A *Shadow* killed Rhys's parents? That revelation knocked the breath out of me. I couldn't even speak for a moment.

"Why would a Shadow do something like that?" I finally asked.

Kassandra tore her attention away from the body of the hellhound. "I honestly don't know."

"Rhys . . . ," I began. "King Rhys . . . he told me it was a *demon* who killed his parents."

"Then he hasn't been told the truth—not yet, anyway. Maybe his advisers assumed it was a demon."

"And this Shadow—"

"Jonas," she said quietly, as if afraid someone might over-hear. "His name is Jonas. I've heard the guards talking."

"Why would he kill Rhys's mother and father?"

She shook her head. "I don't know. I've heard it was simply to show how powerful he was. How dangerous. And a warning that Shadows shouldn't be kept as servants. Crazy, right?"

The last part didn't sound crazy to me, but the rest of it did. "And he's in the dungeon right now?"

"Yes. The strangest thing was, he didn't even resist when

the guards tried to capture him. He went quietly. He killed the faery king and queen and just stood there waiting to be arrested. He's being watched very carefully. The castle's security has been in an uproar ever since it happened. I know they were already nervous about the possibility of your bringing your servant here, but they couldn't do anything about it."

"Michael's nothing like this . . . Jonas," I said, tears welling up in my eyes. "He'd never kill anyone."

"He killed Fernando." She flinched at my look, then shrugged. "I know. It sucks, but your Shadow broke the rules. The guards are just following protocol set up by my mother."

I looked at the elevator door again, concern for Michael sweeping through me. "So what am I supposed to do now?"

Kassandra approached the fallen hellhound and patted him gently on his side. "Poor boy. He was normally really well behaved. I mean, sure, hellhounds are completely vicious by nature, but they rarely attack unless ordered. I don't know why he would have done that. Kieran's going to be very upset. Fernando was his favorite pet."

"Kassandra." I tried to get her attention. "What should I do?"

She stood up and brushed off her hands. "I don't know. What do you want to do? Go home? Or we can still hang out for a while. I can take you on a tour of the castle."

"I . . . uh, no. I mean, about *Michael*. How do I get him released?"

She looked at me blankly. "He's been arrested for using his power in front of us. The guards have taken him down to the dungeon."

"I understand that. But there has to be a way around it. He saved my life."

She crossed her arms and studied me. "And that was really brave, but it doesn't change anything. He's gone now. There are plenty of servants to choose from, anyway, so don't worry about it." She was quiet for a moment. "Hey, are you thirsty? We could grab something to drink."

"I'm not thirsty. I want to get Michael out of the dungeon." I could barely control the anger that simmered just under the surface of my skin. How could she be so calm and matter-of-fact about this? I felt my Darkling power finally return, crackling down my arms. "I don't think you understand what I'm saying. I don't want to drink anything. I don't want a tour of the castle. I want to get Michael. He's being imprisoned for saving my life. Funny how I don't think he deserves being thrown in the dungeon."

"But that's just the way it is."

"I don't care!" I raised my voice, and she looked surprised at my outburst. "I need to see the queen right now."

Kassandra blinked. "She doesn't usually get involved with this sort of thing."

I was either going to burst into tears or go into a rage. I hadn't decided yet. But the fury I was feeling coursed through my body, and I felt myself start to change into my Darkling form again—this time under my own power, so it didn't hurt as much.

Her eyes grew large with alarm. "What are you doing?"

"Have you heard about the prophecy?" I asked her. "The one that says I just might be the one that will bring about the destruction of pretty much everything and everyone?"

She swallowed. "I thought you said there might be another Darkling it applies to."

I fisted my hands at my sides. "Maybe I was wrong. Let me just put it this way: if I don't see your mother very, very soon, I can't be held responsible for what I might do."

She stared at me for a long moment before a smile spread across her face. "Oh, this is so awesome. She's totally going to freak. Sure. Follow me."

As Kassandra approached the elevator, it opened up again and we got in. My wings brushed against the side of the door. Had my sweater not already been ripped, it would be now. I was glad I had left my winter coat back in the Shadowlands.

Kassandra scanned me from horns to toes. "So a Darkling looks half demon and half human, huh?"

"Probably because that's exactly what I am."

She cocked her head to the side. "When my mother found out you existed, I'd never seen her so worried about anything before. It's as if she's expected a major issue like this to happen for a while. And you're it."

I could use that. As much as I didn't like the idea that people were afraid of me before they'd gotten to know me, if I could use it to save Michael, then it would totally be worth it.

The doors opened after a minute, but it wasn't the council room where we'd just been. It was a large, luxurious loft apartment. Several demons in white uniforms, much different from the guards, wandered around dusting and vacuuming and carrying trays. Queen Sephina was sitting on a long white sofa reading a piece of parchment. She looked up at us with surprise as we entered the room.

"Kassandra . . . Princess Nikki . . ." Her gaze swept over my Darkling form. "I thought you'd already left."

"Mother," Kassandra began, "something bad happened downstairs."

"What?"

"Fernando. He . . . he attacked Nikki."

Queen Sephina placed the parchment on the seat next to her and stood up. "Oh my. Are you all right, child? Are you injured?"

"I'm fine," I said.

"That is a relief to hear." She shook her head. "I never should have allowed Kieran to bring that beast into the castle. Hellhounds make horrible pets—one never knows when they might turn on their keeper or anyone else. Please, Princess Nikki, accept my sincere apologies for any stress this may have caused you. There's no excuse for an ill-trained hellhound."

"Her . . . her Shadow servant saved her," Kassandra said.

Queen Sephina's eyebrows went up. "Is that so?"

"Yes." I blinked as I tried my very best to be patient. My eyes burned but I wouldn't let myself cry in front of this woman. I was certain she'd consider it a sign of weakness.

"He used his *power* to save her," Kassandra said. "It triggered the alarm, and the guards came and took him to the dungeon."

"Oh, I see." Sephina pursed her lips. "I'm very sorry to hear that. But he should have known better." She shook her head. "Thank you for telling me. And Nikki, again, my apologies for any distress you've been caused."

"I want Michael released," I said simply.

She tilted her head to the side. "Excuse me?"

"Release Michael. My . . . my *servant*." I cringed as I said the word aloud, but that was what they labeled him. "He doesn't deserve to be thrown in the dungeon for saving my life."

See? I could sound calm, cool, and collected. I was stating the facts. No threats or hissy fits would be necessary to get what I wanted. Queen Sephina would see reason. She had to.

"I'm sorry, but that's not possible," she said. "He broke a very specific and important rule about Shadows. The penalty for this is death."

Death?

Panic ripped through me. If I wasn't already in Darkling form, I would have shifted in no time flat. Adrenaline coursed through my body.

"No." My voice was strained. "There has to be another way."

She absently picked a piece of lint off the sleeve of her embroidered robe. "I understand that, to an outsider, rules like this one may seem harsh. But they're in place to protect the precious existences of all demonkind, especially the royals who call this castle home. We can't have our safety disrupted by any Shadow who would yield his power without permission. Especially after what happened the last time."

"Last time," I said. "With the king and queen of the faery realm."

The queen's lips pursed. "Yes. An accident that only confirmed my feelings about Shadows and how unpredictable they are. I no longer allow Shadow servants in my castle. I see now that I shouldn't have made an exception today, either."

My legs felt weak and my stomach churned. "If you

hadn't made the exception, I would be dead. He saved my life!"

"He should feel very proud of himself, then." She reached over and squeezed my hand reassuringly. "It shows him to be a very loyal servant. However, all Shadows, no matter where they reside, should be well aware of the rules. That he broke this rule to save you does not matter. All that matters is that it was broken."

Why was she saying these things? How could I make her understand? "But, Your Majesty—"

"No, Nikki," she said, cutting me off. "To quote a human expression you might be familiar with, servants are a dime a dozen. You will easily find another who suits your needs."

"Isn't there anything I can say to make you change your mind?" I asked, knowing I was beginning to sound like a broken record.

"No," she said firmly.

"But that's not fair." My voice cracked. "How can you live in a place with so many stupid rules?"

Her brow furrowed. "My patience is wearing thin with you. My decision is final. You are a guest in my kingdom, and you're now beginning to overstay your welcome. Perhaps in the human world the rules are more lax, but I assure you, the Underworld has run in perfect order since I became queen, and it's because of these rules you find so distasteful."

Anger flooded through me and power moved down into my hands, which began to glow red. "I'm not leaving here without Michael."

I'd never felt more certain about anything. It wasn't as if

Michael had killed the hellhound because he didn't like it or it had been standing in his way. He'd killed it to save my life. So what if he used his power for something like that?

And yeah, the human world had plenty of idiotic laws and rules, too, but at least if you were unjustly arrested for something, you could make a phone call and get a lawyer. You were presumed innocent until proven guilty no matter what the circumstances.

Here, there was none of that. Despite the squeaky clean white, silver, and gold veneer of the Underworld, a place that looked more like a high-rise luxury condo than a castle, I now saw the darkness just underneath the shiny surface.

During the council meeting, Queen Sephina had said she saw the world in shades of gray rather than stark black and white, but she'd been lying—either to me or to herself. There was no compromise here for anything, was there?

Kassandra said her mother had worried about me and my prophecy. Well, I'd make her worry. If she thought I was the Darkling who could destroy her kingdom and leave it in ashes, then I'd use that fear to get her to release Michael. I wasn't leaving him here to be executed for saving my life. Not a chance in . . . well, *hell*.

Queen Sephina's gaze moved to my glowing hand. "And what, precisely, do you intend to do right now?"

"Whatever I have to," I said flatly.

"Your father won't be pleased that you've made such a fuss here today. This was supposed to be a pleasant meeting."

"A pleasant meeting? Demanding that I show up and be grilled by you and your friends?"

"I'm sorry you feel that way." But she didn't look sorry. She looked annoyed.

"I never should have come. I wanted to let you see that I'm nice and not somebody you have to worry about. But maybe I was wrong about that. Maybe you *should* worry."

She studied me for a long moment. "Kassandra, dear, what shall I do about your new friend? She's very headstrong—a great deal like her father, in fact. However, I've never seen anyone get so distraught about the fate of a servant. She looks positively ready to explode."

"You're right. It is a bit strange." Kassandra watched our discussion with a look that was either troubled or excited. I wasn't sure which.

"I'd prefer not to explode," I said, and a swirling red and orange energy ball began to form in the palm of my right hand. Maybe I'd bust a lamp or two to show I was serious. "But whatever does the trick. I'm not afraid of you."

"You should be." Queen Sephina eyed my show of power and then smiled thinly at me. "Enough of this nonsense, child."

She waved a hand at me, and every ounce of my power and strength disappeared in the blink of an eye. I lost my Darkling form and stumbled forward, bracing myself on the edge of the white sofa so I wouldn't fall.

"What—?" I managed, gasping for breath. It was one thing to change back with my own power, but to have my power forcibly yanked away from me was much more painful.

Queen Sephina shook her head. "Are all humans this rude and disrespectful? You may be powerful, but this is my castle, my kingdom, and I hold dominion here. Please don't forget that again, or you'll be very sorry."

I looked down at my hands. They were normal human hands. No talons, no glowing power. I looked up at Queen Sephina. She must have seen something in my eyes because her expression softened and she patted my face.

"This Michael is just a servant, child, and a Shadow one at that. His life is meaningless. Now go home. I'm sure this will all seem much better tomorrow."

She picked up the parchment. A quick glimpse told me it contained the rules Groden had been jotting down during the meeting today. More proposed rules for her to approve or deny to help the Underworld run in perfect order. Unbelievable.

Without another word, the queen turned from us and went into an adjoining room.

I felt an arm come around my shoulders, and Kassandra led me toward the elevator. I felt numb and defeated.

Michael, I sent out telepathically. *Are you okay? Please answer me.*

But there was no reply. We must have been out of range.

"My mother can be a serious pain," Kassandra said. "People say I'm just like her, but I don't believe it for a minute."

"I need to go," I said. "I need to talk to my father."

He'd be able to do something about this. As king, he could demand Michael's release.

Or would he? He also stuck very closely to the rules. He may have been a stubborn, dragon-slaying rebel at one time, but he was different now. He'd let Michael slide the last time he'd broken this particular rule, but would he do it again?

Maybe he'd use this as an opportunity to get rid of him once and for all.

I shuddered at the thought.

"I don't get you," Kassandra said, frowning. "I've never seen anybody so concerned about the fate of a servant before. It's almost as if you . . ." She blinked and her brow furrowed. "It's as if you . . . you really *like* him." Her voice hushed. "You like him as more than just a servant, don't you?"

Uh-oh. More broken rules coming my way.

"No, of course not," I said quickly.

"You *do*. I can't believe I didn't realize it before. But he's a *Shadow*. It's against the rules."

My mouth felt dry. Kassandra studied me soundlessly, apparently stunned at her successful mental investigation into my social life.

The elevator door opened in front of me, and I stepped inside. Kassandra made a move to get on with me.

"No," I said as firmly as I could. "Stay here. Please. I'll see myself out."

I half-expected her to call for security and have me arrested as well. She didn't. A moment later the doors closed between us and I felt myself begin to move downward.

20

Unfortunately, the elevator didn't stop at the lobby level. It came—or rather, *lurched*—to a stop at the same floor the council meeting had been on. The room seemed empty now.

I hissed out a breath of frustration and looked around the elevator for buttons or something to make the doors close again. No buttons. No numbers. How were these things controlled? By royal command?

Finally, I got out. Maybe there was a gazer I could use to contact somebody to help me. Demonic technical assistance.

The moment I got off the elevator, I heard a deep voice.

"Sorry to divert you from your course, but I wanted the chance to speak to you. In private."

Prince Kieran casually leaned against a support beam to my left, by the small statue of his mother. A quick glance behind me confirmed the elevator doors had closed.

Dread engulfed me. "You stopped the elevator here?"

"I did."

I guessed I was right about the "royal command" thing. "What do you want?"

"Your servant killed my hellhound."

"Your hellhound almost killed me."

He flinched. "That was an unfortunate mistake. Elizabeth was supposed to be watching him, but she was distracted and Fernando got away from her."

"Elizabeth?" I said, my stomach sinking. "Oh, well, that explains everything. You both want me dead, don't you?"

"Let's not be overly dramatic, Princess. Anything that happened between you and your aunt in the past is just that. The past."

"The past?" I repeated. "It was a week ago."

"Ancient history." He smiled. "Besides, that regrettable incident had nothing to do with me."

"You're such a liar!" I blurted out before I could stop myself. "You were in on it. You wanted Elizabeth to kill my father, too. Don't even try to deny it."

"You have no proof of any such allegation. And saying these things in my castle is very disrespectful."

"Your *mother's* castle, you mean," I corrected.

His neutral expression slipped a little to show something much less pleasant. "I am the prince here."

"I swear, if you try to hurt me, my father will tear your head off."

The cool, handsome exterior was again back in place. "My mother promised King Desmond your complete safety during this visit."

"Then let me leave." Being stuck here with Kieran of all people made me more nervous than I already was.

"But I haven't gotten to my point yet."

My eyes narrowed. "Then get to your point."

"I have the strangest feeling that you don't like me very much, Nikki."

I just glared at him. "Still waiting for that point."

"Very well." His gaze moved down to my wrist. "I want your dragon's tear."

I automatically slapped a hand over the bracelet and took a step back from him. "Forget it."

"You have no idea what you have there. It's wasted on your simple half-human mind. If you give it to me, freely, then the power will be mine."

"Give it to you *freely?*"

"Yes." His smile held. "A dragon's tear must be handed on to its next owner freely for its power to properly transfer. It cannot be stolen, because then its magic will become dormant. Your father gave it freely to you, and now I want you to give it freely to me."

"So you can do what with it?"

"I want to be able to travel among worlds with ease."

I inhaled sharply. "And why would you want to do that?"

"Just because."

No, not just because. I'd seen Kieran's eyes light up when Beasley mentioned the possibility of secret gateways during the meeting. He'd wanted Elizabeth to take over the throne of the Shadowlands so he could be given permission to travel to the human and faery worlds whenever he wanted.

"I don't know you very well, Kieran, but I get the feeling that you're not happy being only a prince."

"Whatever do you mean?" he asked innocently.

"Maybe you think you're stuck here, while your mother is

the queen of the Underworld and your father is the king of Hell. What does that leave you? Endless days of plotting and planning, while they're the ones with all the power. Not to mention, now you're stuck putting up with Elizabeth all the time."

"Elizabeth *is* a growing nuisance," he said grimly. "Your father not only punished her with banishment to the Underworld, but he punished me as well."

"I think, and this is just a guess, that you want my bracelet so you can go to the human world and take over. So you can be, like, the king there." It sounded ludicrous as my jumbled thought turned into words, but Kieran's expression of surprise only confirmed it as the truth.

"Is that what you think?" he asked.

I nodded.

"And would that be so bad?" he countered. "The human world is in disrepair. They fight among themselves and have for millennia, with their separate countries and policies. They have been slowly and steadily destroying their precious resources— the water, the air, the wildlife. Their world is dying a little more every year. They need someone like me to help make things right again."

I laughed. Despite everything, I couldn't help myself. "Prince Kieran, the savior of humankind."

His eyes flashed red. "Don't mock me."

"So, okay, you go to the human world and you become the king. What if anyone opposes this idea?"

"I will exterminate them," he said simply.

I stifled a gasp of shock. "I want to leave now."

"And you'll give me your bracelet?"

I looked at him as if he was crazy. Pretty sure he was. "Uh, no. *So* not going to happen."

He was silent for a moment. "And what about your Shadow?"

"What about him?"

"He will be executed. It normally takes a few months before the punishment is administered to one imprisoned in the Underworld dungeon. This is much more time than it would take if he was placed in one of Hell's dungeons—they're more efficient in dealing with prisoners there. However, I will make sure your Shadow has only hours left here."

My skin felt cold and clammy. "You can't do that."

"No?" He raised a black eyebrow. "I listened in on your conversation with Kassandra and my mother just now through a one-way gazer. You're desperate to find a way to have your . . . *Michael* . . . released, and yet no one will help you. But I can help you, Nikki. I have something you want and you have something I want. We can make a trade."

Trade my bracelet for Michael's freedom?

The dragon's tear had helped me locate a gateway to the Shadowlands the other day. It helped me change and maintain my form as well as focus my power and strength when I concentrated on it. Kassandra thought it could do much more than that. Was it really possible for the bearer of the bracelet to easily teleport from world to world?

If so, it would give Kieran exactly what he was looking for—a chance to travel to the human world as simply as stepping into another room. All without being forced to ask my father for permission to travel beyond the Shadowlands.

Michael was in the dungeon right now, out of my tele-pathic range. Was he scared? Angry? Did he think I'd already left him behind? Did he know that he had only hours to live unless I could find a way to release him?

I twisted the bracelet, feeling the cool crystal tear beneath my fingertips. It never seemed to warm to my body temperature just by wearing it—it grew hot only when it was used.

Had my father slayed this dragon in self-defense? Or had he gone out in search of a dragon to kill for the sport of it? It made a big difference to me. I didn't like the idea that he'd hunt down a magical, immortal creature just to end up with a small crystallized piece of power that could ultimately fall into the wrong hands.

Kieran tapped his foot as he impatiently waited for my reply. The sound of his hard-soled black boots echoed off the smooth floor and metallic walls.

"Is there something else, anything else, I can trade for Michael's freedom?" I asked quietly.

"No," he said without hesitation.

I felt the sting of tears because I knew then I couldn't do it. I *couldn't* give Kieran the bracelet. It was a horrible realization, but I felt the heavy truth in it.

If I gave him the bracelet, I knew beyond a shadow of a doubt that many humans would die because of that decision. If I didn't give him the bracelet, only one person would have to die.

I wanted to be selfish and hand over the piece of jewelry, but I knew I couldn't. Kieran could never have it.

I'm so sorry, Michael.

Kieran must have seen the answer in my tear-filled eyes because he shook his head. "Wrong decision, Princess."

"But what if I—"

I couldn't even finish the sentence. Kieran grabbed my throat and slammed me into the support beam behind me. It knocked my breath away.

"You're making a grave mistake. Even if I can't have your bracelet, I'll still find a way to enter the human world. Now that I know there are concealed gateways, I need only to locate them. It may take a bit longer than I'd hoped, but I'll find them. So you see, not handing over that dragon's tear is ultimately a futile, meaningless act. You could get something that you want right now. I guess your Shadow doesn't mean as much to you as I thought he did."

"Let go . . . of . . . me," I managed, clawing at his hand, but it didn't make a difference. He held me up effortlessly, off the ground, to show me just how strong he was.

At least until I sliced my newly formed talons into his arm, drawing blood so dark it looked black—demon blood. He yelped out in pain and released me. I fell to the ground, choking and sputtering, but forced myself up as quickly as I could, my hands clenched, ready for a fight.

"You're the one who heard the prophecy about me first, right?" I said. "Aren't you afraid it's true?"

"Oh, please." Kieran grabbed the front of my sweater tightly. "You think you're that important, little girl? You're not."

I hadn't expected that reaction. "What?"

"The palace's dragon oracle won't let me get close enough to kill him and procure myself one of those precious tears you have, but his family is still vulnerable. He was willing to do whatever he had to in order to protect them, even manufacture a false prophecy and shield it from other nosy oracles."

"So the prophecy *was* a lie. I knew it."

He shrugged. "It could easily be true. The last Darkling was a dangerous creature that nearly fulfilled a prophecy much like this one. But you're not so tough, are you?" He shoved me hard and I went flying backward, hitting the beam again. I think I lost consciousness for a minute. I wasn't sure. The world alternately darkened and sparkled all around me as I gulped mouthfuls of oxygen.

"I do have another hellhound," he said as he looked down at me. "Perhaps a short time locked in a room together might change your stubborn mind. But if Dimitri gets hungry, that's fine, too—the dragon's tear will shift to neutral when its owner dies, so I will be able to claim it for myself."

"I thought you said you didn't want to kill me," I managed.

"No. I said my mother ensured your safety to your father." He scratched his chin. "I'll blame it on Elizabeth. Desmond will be furious. He might even break the Shadowlands barrier and wrench himself out of that castle to seek vengeance on her. See? It's a win-win situation for me."

Once I got my breath back, I forced away the fear that swirled inside me and concentrated on changing to my Darkling form. It came on quickly and surprisingly easily, and I rose to my feet as the strength began to flow. My hands clenched and glowed with power.

"Really?" Kieran said. "You think you can fight me?"

Anger pushed past my fear. "I think I can try. I stopped

Elizabeth when she wanted to kill me, but maybe she didn't fill you in on all the unflattering details."

I did feel weakened and bruised from being tossed around like Kieran's rag doll, but an energy ball quickly formed in my right palm, a baseball-sized globe of swirling red, orange, and yellow. Without hesitating, I threw it directly at the prince.

But Kieran easily deflected it with a flick of his wrist. It exploded off to the side, leaving a black scorch mark on the smooth white floor.

"I am much more powerful than Elizabeth," he said. "She used her power in an attempt to gain love and acceptance— foolish needs that handicapped her. My power is meant for much greater things."

He came at me. I expected him to shift to demon form, but he remained in his human one. He grabbed my arms, then swept his leg under mine, knocking me to the floor. Then he pressed the hard sole of his shoe onto my throat so I couldn't move. I struggled to breathe.

He shook his head as if disappointed in me. "Sixteen-year-olds should stay in school and not get in my way. It's very detrimental to their health."

I felt helpless and afraid, not just for myself but for Michael. If I couldn't even save myself, how was I supposed to save him?

Then I thought about my mother. She'd be so worried when I never made it home from Melinda's party. I should have told her about my father when I had the chance, even if he didn't want me to. I knew she'd accept the demon him, accept the demon half of *me* . . .

No, I couldn't let Kieran win. I gathered every remaining

ounce of my power, but I knew with a dark, sinking feeling it wouldn't be nearly enough.

Then I heard a thud and Kieran whipped his head around. Kassandra stood behind him, in front of the now-open elevator doors. She held the statue of Queen Sephina in her hands— the statue she'd just used to whack him in the head.

He frowned at her. "What do you think you're—"

"You've always had a really thick head, Kieran," she said.

She whacked him again. Harder. This time it worked. His eyes rolled back and he fell to the ground beside me. I scrambled away from him and looked up at Kassandra.

She flexed her hand. The head of her mother's statue had broken off and rolled over to rest next to her unconscious brother's nose. "Ow. I think that hurt me more than it hurt him."

"Wh-what are you doing?" I managed. My throat throbbed from having Kieran's boot clamped down on it.

"Helping you," she said.

"Helping me?" I was confused and dizzy. "Why?"

She rolled her eyes. "Just accept it, okay? Now do you want me to help you rescue your boyfriend, or what?"

21

Kassandra turned toward the elevator, then looked over her shoulder at me.

"Are you coming?" she asked.

With a last glance at Kieran, sprawled out on the floor of the council meeting room, I ran to the elevator and got in with her.

"Just for the record?" she said. "It's because I think this is romantic. You and the Shadow."

My mouth felt dry. "I never actually admitted to anything like that."

"You didn't have to. It's obvious to me what's going on."

"Did you know what Kieran was planning to do?"

"No." She grimaced. "I *was* mad at you for totally dismissing me upstairs in my mother's quarters, you know. But I thought I'd follow to make sure you didn't try anything crazy, that's all."

I rubbed my bruised throat. I'd nearly died. I think I was in a little bit of shock. "I'm glad you did."

"Kieran wanted your bracelet?"

"You knew that?"

"It's a guess." She shook her head. "My brother is such a jerk sometimes."

"He tried to kill me."

"This really isn't your day."

I swallowed. "Thanks for stopping him."

"I've felt like clobbering my brother over the head with something heavy for a while. This just gave me a good excuse." She smiled at me. "So here you are, single-minded in your determination to save your Shadow boyfriend from the dank, nasty dungeon." She paused. "Which actually is neither dank nor particularly nasty. It's all glass and silver like the rest of this place. I helped with the design ideas."

I leaned against the side of the elevator, hoping to recover my strength quickly. "He's not my boyfriend. It's against the rules for a demon and a Shadow to be together."

"So what? Like I said, I think it's kind of romantic . . . in a bizarrely inappropriate way." She bit her bottom lip. "I fell for somebody inappropriate myself last year. A guard. When my mother and Kieran found out, they nearly had a conniption. She said he wasn't good enough for a princess. I was stubborn and told her I didn't care what she thought. We were . . . we were going to run off together, but she sent him away, and I'm never allowed to see him again. He's now a guard for one of Hell's dungeons. I have no idea which one—there are so many of them."

"I'm sorry."

Her expression had shadowed with what were apparently painful memories. "Yeah, me, too. So let's just say I understand how you're feeling. Really. And anything I can do to mess up either my brother's or my mother's life is major fun for me."

So Kassandra felt a bond with me due to us both liking guys who didn't meet our families' approval.

"You're really going to help me?" I asked hopefully.

"We're headed to the dungeon now, so that is the plan. But first you have to make me a promise."

I eyed her warily. "What?"

She twisted a finger through her long dark hair. "If I ask a favor of you someday, I want you to say yes, no matter what it is."

"What favor?"

She shrugged. "I don't know yet."

"Okay, that's vague. How can I agree to something like that? You could ask me to kill somebody or steal something or—"

She sighed. "Fine. I promise that whatever I ask for, nobody will get hurt. Okay?"

I let out a long shaky breath as I thought about it. "Then okay. You do this for me, and I'll owe you one. Cross my heart."

"Good." She smiled as the elevator came to a halt. "Here we are. Just follow my lead."

"But what are we—?"

Before I could finish my question, the door opened to the dungeon level. As Kassandra had warned me, it wasn't at all what I would have expected. It was bright and modern looking, with sheets of glass and silver walls. Kassandra walked off the elevator and quickly headed toward a glass desk.

"Princess Kassandra," the guard on the other side said with surprise. "What are you doing down here?"

"I'm here about a prisoner," she said confidently, as if she strolled down to the dungeon level on a daily basis.

"Which one?"

"The Shadow."

His expression turned to shock. "Jonas? He isn't allowed visitors, not even you, Princess. He's much too dangerous."

"No, not him. The one who was brought here just now. Young, tall, dark hair. Killed my brother's hellhound?"

"Oh *that* Shadow." The guard nodded. "What about him?"

"I want him released and pardoned of all charges. He's going to be my servant now."

"Kassandra—," I began, but I stopped talking when she gave me a look that told me to shut my mouth.

"Even though he's officially your servant, Nikki, it doesn't matter in the dungeon," she explained to me. "Any connection like that vanishes between these walls. Therefore, it's easiest to transfer him to me here."

Was that why I wasn't able to talk to Michael telepathically after he was taken from the lobby? I was worried now. Kassandra could be playing me, trying to take Michael away for real.

"You're sure about this?" I asked her pointedly.

She grinned. "Everything's going to be fine."

I had no choice but to trust her. That was a scary thought.

The guard frowned at us. "Maybe I should contact the queen and see if this is okay. After what happened to the hellhound, that Shadow has proven he could be just as dangerous as Jonas."

Oh no. He couldn't contact Queen Sephina. She'd never approve this.

"Are you questioning my authority here?" Kassandra snapped.

The guard blanched. "No, I'm just saying—"

"What you should be saying is 'Yes, Princess, whatever you say, Princess.' You will follow my royal orders as clearly as you follow my mother's. Now I suggest you don't get me angry. Release the Shadow to me right now and don't waste another minute of my valuable time."

He stood up quickly. "Yes, Princess. Follow me."

"That's better."

Being a spoiled brat seemed to have some advantages. I could learn a few lessons from Kassandra on how to get what I wanted when I wanted it.

Kassandra tugged on my hand and I looked at her.

"Say as little as possible," she whispered. "And just keep playing along, okay?"

I nodded.

We trailed behind the guard through two locked sets of doors that led to the main dungeon area. We walked past room after room, each fronted by a thick glass wall that clearly showed the interior of the cells. Many were empty, but others contained a prisoner—some of whom were in human form, some in demon form, and some who looked more monstrously akin to Beasley's physical appearance. I didn't look too closely at the latter. I already had a full schedule of nightmares to look forward to in the weeks to come, thanks to this little field trip to the Underworld.

Finally we came to Michael's cell. He stood at the glass wall, his eyes widening as he watched our approach. My heart drummed wildly, and I felt relieved that he seemed unharmed. His eyes were still gray, his amulet still dull. He hadn't recovered yet from using his power.

"Princess," he said. His voice was clearly audible, even from behind the thick glass separating us.

I didn't say anything. I fought to keep my expression neutral.

Michael, can you hear me? I sent telepathically.

He just looked at me searchingly, his right hand held up to the glass between us, and didn't reply. Kassandra had been right. Our princess-servant connection was gone while we were in the dungeon.

This had to go as smoothly and as quickly as possible. The moment Kieran came to, he wasn't going to be a happy demon prince.

"You're sure about this, Princess Kassandra?" the guard asked, then flinched at the glare he received. "Just checking."

"Yes, I'm sure. The Shadow's very . . . interesting, don't you think? He'll make a nice addition to my personal staff." Kassandra fixed a cool smile on her lips. She moved toward the glass and looked closely at Michael. Now that she knew he wasn't only a servant to me, her curiosity had obviously been piqued.

"What's happening?" Michael asked with concern, his attention focused on me. His forehead furrowed as if he was concentrating on sending me a telepathic message, but of course I didn't hear it, and I couldn't explain to him verbally what was going on.

"What's happening is, this is your lucky day." Kassandra tapped the glass between them. "Nikki has decided you're too much trouble for her, so she's giving you to me. You'll be my servant now, Shadow." She grinned. "My mother is totally going to freak over this."

She was good. Very believable. I wondered if they had drama class in her demon boarding school. A part of me, though, still had trouble believing she was only faking this. If she was serious about using this opportunity to take Michael away from me, I didn't care if the prophecy was a lie or not. *Destructo* would be my new middle name.

"She's *giving* me to you?" Michael repeated with disbelief. "Princess, is this true?"

"Yes, it's true," I said simply, trying very hard to play along and not say anything that would get us in any more trouble.

"Why?" There was a catch in his voice that almost undid me.

He really believed this? Without a moment's doubt, he believed I would give him away to somebody else, as though he were a trading card I'd put up on eBay for the highest bidder?

Had I given Michael that much doubt about how I felt?

Between breaking up with him and kissing Rhys, I couldn't really blame him.

"Lots of reasons," I finally replied. "Your major tendency to get into trouble. Lurking around my school and not bothering to tell me. Breaking the rules. It's too dangerous to keep you as a servant. You should be thanking me. If I didn't do this, you'd be executed for killing that hellhound."

"I see."

He was angry, too. I could hear it in his voice and see it in his eyes as he glared through the glass barrier at me. It was a strange relief that he wasn't just taking this news without any glimmer of emotion. It meant he cared. About me. About himself. I was glad he was mad.

"Let's go," the guard said sharply. He had a handheld electronic device and he punched something into it that popped open the glass door to Michael's cell. "Princess Kassandra wants you pardoned so she can put you to work. I'll make sure you're pardoned, but if you get in any more trouble, I'll personally eliminate you, Shadow. I've had enough of your kind lately."

There was no time to waste. I began walking out of the dungeon, following the guard. Michael was behind me and Kassandra behind him. Had Kieran woken up yet? How much time did we have to get to the gateway?

I felt Michael's eyes on me, disappointed and confused about why I'd so easily given him away to someone I'd just met. I was desperate to tell him everything, but it would have to wait a couple more minutes.

"You there!" someone shouted from a cell as we passed. We were only a few steps from the locked door leading to the front of the dungeon where the elevators were. "Stop."

I turned to see a man with his hands pressed up against the glass wall of his cell. He was tall and had green eyes, dark hair, and a full beard.

"I've been waiting for you," he said. "I knew you'd come."

A chill went down my arms at the way he said it. "Who, me?"

He grinned to show off white teeth. "No. *Him*."

He was looking at Michael.

"You've been waiting for *me?*" Michael asked suspiciously.

"Yes."

"Who are you?"

"Someone who knew your father." The man stroked a hand over his chest, over his amulet, nearly identical to Michael's.

I inhaled sharply. It was the other Shadow—the one who'd killed Rhys's parents. I felt a sliver of fear.

"Keep quiet, Jonas," the guard said. "You've caused enough trouble."

Why weren't we walking? The guard was still fiddling with his handheld device. I tried the first door leading toward the elevators, but it was locked.

"Can we get this opened?" I asked.

The guard nodded. "Just a sec. I need to finish this pardon before we'll be able to pass through with the Shadow. Next time, please call ahead."

Michael shook his head. "I think you have me confused with someone else. My father died a long time ago."

"Yes, he did. He was murdered because he refused to be a slave to demonkind. And look at you." Jonas's eyes narrowed. "He'd be ashamed that his only son has accepted that fate without a fight."

"How do you even know who I am?"

"Because you look exactly like your father. You're from a strong line, a royal line, one that was exterminated because of that strength. You could lead us out of this slavery, out of this treatment at the hands of demons. They took away our land and they took away our freedom, and they slaughtered the ones who wouldn't comply, both then and now. How can you sit back and not want to do something about that?"

The guard rapped on the glass and looked at Kassandra. "See what we have to put up with down here, Princess? But this glass is strong enough to hold anyone, so don't worry."

"Do I look worried?" she replied. "Just hurry up."

"Yes, Princess."

Jonas's gaze moved to Michael's grayish amulet. "Looks like you've used your power recently. That's a good start. But do you know how to replenish your energy now and become even stronger than you were before? I bet you don't even know half of what you can really do."

"Why did you kill the king and queen of the faery realm?" I asked.

His green eyes moved to me. "Because the opportunity presented itself. And because I needed to come here to this dungeon and wait until this moment arrived. I've been waiting for you, Michael."

"You know my name?"

"Of course."

Michael shook his head. "And you knew I'd be here?"

"Yes," Jonas replied.

"How?" I asked.

His unfriendly green eyes moved to me. "It was a prophecy related to me several years ago, but it was very specific. It stated that Michael, the young Shadow prince whose kingdom was stolen from him, would be imprisoned here. Now. If I wanted to find him, to meet him, then I had to set in motion several events to get myself here. So I did what I had to do."

A prophecy? About Michael?

Jonas smiled at the shock on my face. "Did you think prophecies only concerned those who currently are royalty? Do you think a Shadow is so worthless a creature that he does not have any power or influence at all?"

"Of course that's not what I think." I glared at him, the initial shock burned away by a flicker of hot anger.

"So you chose to be brought to this dungeon because of this . . . this prophecy that said I'd be here, too." Michael's voice was filled with confusion.

"Yes. Do you think these demons could contain me if I didn't wish to be here?"

"I . . . I don't know."

"Don't let them fill your head with lies. That's what demons do—they lie."

"Enough," the guard barked, finally pocketing his handheld device. "Let's move on."

"Yes," Jonas said. "I'm ready to move on."

He held his hands to either side of the locked door and closed his eyes for a moment. A pulse of green light moved from him to the door itself. A moment later, it flew open, the glass shattering and falling to the ground like sugar. Kassandra shrieked loudly. Or maybe it was me.

Then Jonas took off his amulet, lifting the gold chain over his head, and threw it onto the cot along the side of the cell. My heart beat faster. A Shadow wasn't ever supposed to remove his amulet. When Michael's had been taken away from him, he'd lost his solid form and had begun fading away to nothing. It was a punishment, not a choice. But Jonas removed his willingly? What was he trying to do? Kill himself?

"Watch and learn," the Shadow said before swiftly moving through the doorway into the wide hallway where we stood.

The guard immediately tried to grab him, but his hands slipped right through Jonas's body—it now had no more substance than a ghost. Instead of looking distraught by this, Jonas looked amused.

He glanced at Michael, who'd automatically moved in front of me, blocking me from harm.

I struggled to swallow the lump in my throat. How could anyone accuse Michael of being dangerous? Everything he did was to protect me—even now, when he truly believed I'd just given him away to someone else. It only made me want to protect him in return.

"What do you think you're doing?" Michael demanded.

"Demons have kept many things from Shadows because they're afraid of us," Jonas said. "Our amulet gives us form and function and strength; we're led to believe that without it we're helpless and will fade to nothing." His jaw clenched. "But the truth is, in our Shadow form we can be more powerful than any demon."

The guard was calling for backup, panic gathering in his voice.

"Watch and learn, my prince," Jonas said again to Michael. He held his hands at his sides, palms up.

I could barely believe my eyes as I watched Jonas's form

turn dark and formless until there was nothing left of him but a moving shadow on the floor.

Another guard ran up to us. "What's going on?"

"Jonas. He . . . he's escaping. I think," the first guard said, looking confused. At that moment, an alarm began to blare, same as the one that sounded after Michael killed the hellhound.

"Michael." I touched his shoulder. "Be careful."

"Just stay behind me," he snapped.

"What about that one?" the second guard asked, looking at Michael. "He's a Shadow, too, isn't he?"

The first guard's attention was fully on Jonas's shadow. "Forget him. It's Jonas who's the problem. But I don't know how to capture him when he's in this form."

I gasped and pointed at the guard's leg. The dark shadow was now crawling up it. The guard tried to brush it off, but it was impossible.

"Do you see?" Jonas's voice was still clear. "In this form they can't hurt us. They can't stop us. However, without our amulets, we need to maintain our energy a different way. We do this by absorbing the energy of others—I did this with the faeries who were foolish enough to believe there could be peace between them and the demon worlds."

The guard took quick, short breaths as the shadow swirled around him like a tornado, darkening in color and gaining opacity until it obliterated his entire form. A few seconds later it became transparent again and I could see the guard's face, his eyes wide and terrified. Then the guard's eyes rolled back so I could only see the whites, and he fell backward to the floor.

My heart hammered against my rib cage. Kassandra clutched my arm—her face was pale with shock.

The second guard staggered back. "He's . . . he's dead!"

The sound of the alarm made it hard to hear anything else; hard to *think* about anything else. I felt frozen in place. It had all happened so fast—less than twenty seconds from beginning to end.

Jonas rematerialized in front of Michael. His eyes now burned bright green and a smile spread across his face. "Do you see?"

Michael nodded, his jaw tight. "Yes, I see."

"Join me. We can change the worlds."

Michael's gaze moved to the dead guard. "Did my father do that as well? Drain demons and faeries for their energy?"

"Your father . . . ," Jonas said, and sighed. "His friendship with a demon prince prevented him from taking the necessary steps that would have made a difference to us all. That friendship ultimately led to his death. I won't make the same mistake, and neither should you."

Was he talking about my father? He'd mentioned that he knew Michael's parents, but were they friends, too? Was that why he felt the responsibility of looking after Michael all these years?

Had my father been protecting Michael from other demons? Or from the chance he'd meet another Shadow like Jonas?

When Michael didn't answer right away, Jonas reached past him and grabbed me. I tried to pull away, but there was nothing to pull away from. He had no substance. He could grasp me, but I couldn't fight against him in return.

"You're only half demon," he said, cocking his head to the side. "I wonder what you'd taste like."

"Let go of her!" Michael demanded.

"I heard what she said before. She'd give you away as if you were no better than an inanimate object. Why would you care about someone like that?"

Michael's eyes flicked to me. I could see the pain and doubt there.

"Michael—," I began.

But I couldn't finish what I was trying to say. Jonas had turned to shadow form again, and as he swirled around me, I started to feel the strangest draining sensation. He was absorbing my energy, the same as he'd done to the guard.

It had killed the guard.

I fought hard against it. I focused on my dragon's tear bracelet to help give me extra strength, and it began to work. The draining stopped, but only for a moment. Then it started again, worse than before. Jonas was very strong. He'd done this many times before, hadn't he? And not just to Rhys's parents and the guard.

It didn't hurt. Despite my fear and panic, it felt only like I was growing more and more tired. All I wanted to do was close my eyes and go to sleep.

Kassandra held a hand to her mouth as she watched with horror.

Again I thought of my mom. And my dad. And Michael and Melinda . . . and an image of Rhys flitted through my mind as well. So much for promising him I'd be careful. I was going to die the same way his mom and dad had.

Out of my narrowed vision I watched Michael take off his amulet and throw it to the side, his attention focused on me and the dark tornado that now surrounded my body. He looked uncertain for a moment, but his brow creased as if he was concentrating very hard on something. The next moment he darkened to a formless black shadow that sank to the floor and moved rapidly toward me.

"Excellent," Jonas said. "You're a natural at this, my prince."

"Thank you for showing me what we can do," Michael replied. "All of these years I had no idea."

Had Michael decided to join Jonas? They could so easily drain demons of their energy, and I couldn't see any way to fight back other than using my bracelet to prolong the inevitable.

No, Michael wouldn't do that. He *wouldn't*.

Wouldn't do what? Choose to be a prince rather than a servant? Choose to have his freedom rather than be at the mercy of someone like me giving him away any time it pleased me?

But I didn't think of Michael as my servant—I never had and I never would. No matter what. I wished he knew that without any doubt.

This had to be the second prophecy that Irena told me about—the darkness consuming me. Jonas was going to kill me.

I was close to losing consciousness now, and I knew when it happened, that would be it. I'd be dead, drained of all my energy to help feed a Shadow.

Then I felt something. It was as if Jonas's shadow was being pulled away from me.

"What are you doing?" Jonas growled.

"Stopping you," Michael snarled back.

"You'd give up a chance to change the world? To fight at my side? All to protect this selfish princess who couldn't care less about you?"

"You don't know her."

"And you do?"

"I think I do."

"Then you're a fool."

"Maybe you're right."

"Of course I'm right. This is your chance to change things. To choose which side you'll fight on, now and in the future."

Jonas's hold grew tighter on me again. But I'd taken the short reprieve to focus all my attention on my dragon's tear. I knew it would help me turn to my stronger Darkling form. Weak power flowed along my arms into my hands, and I attempted to push Jonas away.

It didn't work. I wasn't even able to pop a horn. I felt the draining sensation begin again.

"Michael—," I managed. I couldn't see him. All I could see was one shadow on me and another swirling around, agitated. Then Michael's shadow attached itself to me as well.

He'd chosen sides. He was going to help Jonas drain me of my last bit of energy, wasn't he?

Hope flittered away from me.

"Stop," Jonas said, and there was no smile in his voice now. There was panic. "No, you mustn't—"

He gasped. Whatever Michael was doing to him wasn't pain free and drowse inducing. All I could see was swirling gray and black, a disembodied battle surrounding me. I couldn't even tell the two shadows apart.

A moment later I heard an ear-piercing scream. Then nothing.

I was shaking violently. I braced a hand against the glass wall of the cell next to me so I could remain standing. Kassandra rushed to my side and put her arm around my shoulders to help support me.

Michael quickly took form in front of us. His eyes glowed a brighter green than I'd ever seen before. He was filled with power. He'd destroyed Jonas to save me and had absorbed the other Shadow's energy in the process.

"You both need to leave," Kassandra said shakily. "Right now."

Despite Michael's glowing green eyes, his expression was flat. "But aren't I supposed to be your servant now, Princess Kassandra?"

I found it difficult to speak, so luckily Kassandra took over. She glared at Michael.

"What are you, stupid or something? That was just a lie so we could get you out of the dungeon. Nikki would never give you away. She's crazy about you."

His eyes lit up and he looked at me. "Is that true?"

"Of course it is," I managed, my voice raspy.

Kassandra shook her head. "So he's a hottie, but he's not too bright, is he?"

The other guard stood there, shaking in his boots, staring at us in shock. He didn't try to stop us from leaving.

Michael snatched his amulet from the floor—despite currently being incorporeal, he was able to grasp solid objects—and he put it back on as we hurriedly followed Kassandra through the two sets of doors and out of the dungeon.

"The guard managed to pardon Michael in the dungeon database," she explained. "So we won't have any trouble getting out of here."

When we got into the elevators, the alarm had already ceased blaring. It was a relief to my ears.

"I'll tell them what happened," Kassandra said. "That Jonas killed the guard and attacked Nikki, and that Michael saved everyone."

"That's exactly what did happen," I said.

"Yeah." She blinked rapidly. "Wow! That was so freaking awesome. I can't believe I ever thought this place was boring. What a rush!"

The elevator opened up to the lobby level, and we ran across the marble floor.

"You okay?" I finally asked Michael, breathlessly.

"Yeah, I think so. You?"

"I'm feeling a bit drained," I admitted. "It's been one of those days."

"Wait." He grabbed my arm.

Elizabeth stood in front of the doors with her hands on her hips, blocking our way.

"Kieran is looking for you," she said, and her eyes moved to Michael. "He wanted me to keep watch here in case you tried to escape."

Michael and I exchanged a glance. I clenched my hands at my sides. I felt exhausted and more than ready for a weeklong nap to recover my energy, but I summoned what little power I had left.

"I suggest you get out of our way," I warned.

"Or what?"

"Or you'll be sorry."

Elizabeth's lips curled at the sides. "You do remind me of myself, Nikki. There is a definite family resemblance."

"She's nothing like you," Michael growled.

Her smile grew. "Oh no? Willing to do anything for love, even if it gets her in terrible trouble?" She blinked, and pain shadowed her expression. "Real love means breaking the rules others have for us; rules we have for ourselves. I felt that way for Kieran, but . . . I don't think he loves me anymore. Even after everything I've sacrificed for him."

"He can't stand the sight of you," Kassandra confirmed. "No offense intended, of course."

Elizabeth's pained look deepened. "Is that true?"

Kassandra nodded and shrugged. "Sorry."

Elizabeth's face crumpled, and tears welled in her eyes. "I knew it."

"He's not worth it," I told her. "Even you could do better than him, and that's saying something."

She looked at me. "Because of Kieran, I've done many things I've come to regret. Things I can never take back. All to earn his love." She let out a shuddery sigh and regarded me for a long moment. "Go, Niece. I won't try to stop you. This will be one small step on the path of rebuilding our trust."

She stepped away from the door.

"I just have to ask one thing," I said. "Did you sic that hell-hound on me?"

"Hmm." She crossed her arms and pressed her lips together. "Perhaps this path of rebuilding trust will be a long one."

I glared at her. "I'll take that as a yes."

Michael grabbed my hand. He gave Elizabeth a withering glare as we passed by her toward the glass doors. "Come near the princess again at your own peril."

She staggered back a step. Whatever she'd just seen in his eyes had scared her deeply.

Kieran was going to be furious. But I had to admit, it was a nice way for Elizabeth to show him he didn't have power over her any longer. It didn't help me forgive her for what she'd done to me and my father, or for siccing the hellhound on me. Not in the slightest.

Michael was so strong and full of energy from draining the other Shadow that I felt the magic coming off his skin in waves. His hand was almost too hot to hold.

I wasn't feeling quite as perky at the moment, to say the least. But we made it to the waiting gateway a few blocks away in minutes.

Kassandra hugged me. "Nikki, it was *so* super great meeting you."

She was still clueless, even after everything that had happened. To her, it had just been an exciting experience that had all worked out okay.

To me, it had been two—no, make that *three*—close

brushes with death that had left me trembling and grateful to be alive.

"Yeah," I said, deciding it was much easier to play along. "I, uh . . . feel the same. Other than the fact your brother and his dog nearly killed me."

"My mother will be soooo mad when she hears what Kieran tried to do. Especially after she promised you'd be safe. He doesn't normally get in trouble for anything, but he'll get it for this."

"Listen, Kieran told me the prophecy was a lie. He was blackmailing the dragon oracle to get it."

She nodded. "I knew it!"

"You did?"

"Well, no, but after meeting you, I can't imagine you're ready to destroy the world. You're way too nice. I'll tell my mother that as well. She is going to be so mad at Kieran. Hooray!"

"Well, good."

Michael tugged at my hand. "I knew the prophecy was a lie."

I grinned weakly. "Even you had doubts."

"Maybe a couple."

Kassandra glanced at my wrist. "You're sure about not letting me trade you for that bracelet? I have a really gorgeous diamond tiara—"

"Sounds good," I said quickly, "but, no, thank you."

She pouted. "Fine, be that way." Her attention moved to Michael. "I did have you officially pardoned, but it would probably be best if you don't come back here for a while, just to be safe."

"Trust me, that won't be a problem."

"Now go. And take care of each other, okay?"

I gave one last nod to the only other demon princess I'd ever met, and then Michael and I went through the gateway hand in hand.

22

A few moments later we were back in the Shadowlands castle. After all the gold, silver, and glass of the Underworld, the unfriendly stone walls and dark interior were a strange relief. I turned to look at Michael.

"We made it," I said.

"We did."

Then he kissed me so passionately it took my breath away. He held his hand over his amulet so it wouldn't electrocute me, which I totally appreciated.

I smiled up at him when we parted. "What was that for?"

"Thanks for rescuing me from the dungeon."

"Well, you rescued me right back. Actually, *twice*. Will you take an IOU?"

"I . . . I can't believe that happened. The hellhound, the . . . the Shadow." He sighed. "And I really believed Kassandra when she said you were giving me to her."

"It wasn't true. Of course it wasn't true."

"I know that now." His expression grew haunted. "I've never met another Shadow before."

"And now you have." I pressed my palm against his chest,

just shy of touching the green stone amulet that blazed with power. "What you did to him—"

"Had to be done," he said, cutting me off. "He was trying to hurt you. I couldn't let that happen."

"So you weren't tempted, even a little, to join his rebellion against demons?"

"I know right from wrong, and what Jonas was doing—hurting others on his path to change—was wrong."

"He killed Rhys's parents."

"I know." Michael's eyes flashed. "He was too dangerous. I don't think change has to be achieved by hurting or killing others. Self-defense, however, is another matter."

I threaded my fingers through his dark hair. "I totally agree." I kissed him again and felt him smile against my lips. "What?"

"You do realize there's no mistletoe here."

"Yeah, well, I don't really care."

"Good answer."

I heard somebody clear his throat behind us, and I froze before moving back from Michael. I turned to see my father leaning against the doorway.

Had he seen us kissing? Then again, how could he have possibly missed it?

Instead of denying it, I reached down and grabbed Michael's hand. My father's gaze moved to the defiant gesture before coming back to my face.

"Did the meeting with the demon council go well?" he asked.

Was he really going to ignore the kiss?

::Why are you still holding my hand?:: Michael asked.

Because I want to.

::You're sure about that?::

Never been more sure about anything.

"It didn't go as well as I hoped it would," I said.

My father frowned. "What do you mean?"

"There was a problem, Your Majesty," Michael said.

"A problem?" Again he glanced at my hand holding Michael's.

"Yes." Michael took the liberty of explaining everything to my father—and he did so much more concisely than I ever could have hoped to—starting with Elizabeth meeting us at the gateway, the hellhound attack, and finally what happened in the dungeon with Jonas.

My father's expression grew darker with every word Michael spoke.

"I can't believe this," my father said quietly.

"I know I shouldn't have used my powers. It's against the rules."

"And if you hadn't broken them, my daughter would be dead." My father looked at Michael intently.

"Kieran also tried to blackmail me," I added. "He wanted my dragon's tear bracelet. When I wouldn't give it to him, he tried to kill me. Princess Kassandra saved me."

My father's eyes grew very large, anger eating away at him until he couldn't contain it. He shifted to his demon form right before our eyes.

My father's demon form was the scariest and most fearsome

of any I'd seen. His coal black skin and large curved horns were intimidating, to say the least. His body got bigger and more muscular, his talons sharp as knives. I wondered, not for the first time, what my mother would think if she saw him like this.

"I will destroy him." His demon voice was deeper, raspier, and much more ominous than his human one.

"No, you won't," I said firmly. "He'd love to get you all riled up like this. It would give him the chance to try to kill you personally."

"As if he could."

"Besides, you can't leave the castle."

"I can if I'm motivated enough." His fists clenched. "I knew you shouldn't have gone to the Underworld." His red eyes moved to Michael. "You . . ."

"Yes, Your Majesty." Michael tensed, but he stood his ground.

My father's chest heaved with a deep breath. "Thank you for protecting my daughter when I could not. I knew I had chosen well when I assigned you to her." He shot another unhappy glance at our hand holding, but seemed bound and determined to ignore it. "I just didn't know how well."

"Dad," I began, "Michael and I—"

"I'm sorry you had to deal with such adversity today." My father cut me off as he slowly changed back to human form. "If I could have done anything to prevent the distress you've experienced, I would have. Please go and take care of your mother for me. I want both of you safe."

I held back what I wanted to tell him. He was making it wordlessly clear that, despite his forgiving Michael for breaking the rules to save my life, some rules still applied. At least that was the impression I was getting. Michael could save my life, but he still couldn't be my boyfriend.

"Do you promise not to go after Kieran?" I asked.

He pressed his lips together and didn't reply.

"Promise me," I said again. "I won't leave until you do."

He finally nodded. "I promise, Nikki. I won't abandon my kingdom to seek revenge on the demon prince. However I will be speaking to Queen Sephina by gazer the moment you leave."

That was about as good a promise as I was going to get.

"Okay, good. Oh, by the way, Florencia thinks I have your wings. I think she meant it as a compliment."

He cringed. "*Florencia.* I haven't thought of her in years."

"I don't think she feels the same. She might still be available if you're interested."

He looked at me. "I will assume you're not being serious."

"Of course not." I smiled. "Because that would totally get in the way of you and my mom getting back together."

"Nikki . . . ," he began, crossing his arms. "I've told you why that's not possible, but you continue to ignore me."

"I guess I'm just a hopeless romantic. I think when you really care about somebody, rules shouldn't matter, even the ones we make for ourselves." It was similar to what Elizabeth had said before I'd left the Underworld. For a crazy evil aunt, she was surprisingly insightful.

"That is a very dangerous attitude to have." He swept my blonde hair back behind my shoulder. "You remind me so much of myself when I was your age."

I'd have taken that as a compliment if I didn't hear so much sadness and regret in his voice. I knew it hurt him to keep talking about this, about my mother, so all I did was give him a tight hug before saying good-bye.

Michael and I left the castle, passing a few servants as we went, and we walked back to the bright, grassy clearing between the Shadowlands and the forest leading into the faery realm.

The gateway to the human world shimmered, a door-size swirling kaleidoscope of color.

"So now what happens?" Michael asked.

"Now I go home. My mother is probably wondering where I am. How long ago did I leave Melinda's party?" I glanced down at my watch for the first time since our adventure began. "Don't tell me it's only been three hours. How is that even remotely possible?"

He raised an eyebrow. "Time flies when you're having fun?"

"Yeah. So much fun." I pulled him through the gateway with me, then was reminded the moment I set foot in the human world that it was a week before Christmas and freezing cold outside. "Great. I left my coat in the castle. I guess I've been kind of distracted."

"Here." He unzipped his blue sweatshirt and draped it over my shoulders. "The cold doesn't bother me."

I felt warmer already. "Thanks."

We made it back to my house. The front light was blazing. Mom was probably inside, watching a movie and waiting to hear the details about my night out.

Michael had been quiet the whole walk here. I turned to him when we reached the big oak tree at the bottom of our front yard.

"What's wrong?" I asked.

He swallowed. "I'm sorry you had to see me like that. What I . . . what I did to Jonas. To the hellhound, too."

"You mean when you stopped them from killing me? I'm very much okay with that."

He shook his head. "I don't want you to be afraid of me."

"I'm not afraid," I said. "Seriously. Do I look afraid to you?"

He searched my face. "Not really. You look . . . uh, kind of cold still."

"If I was scared, would I do this?" I grabbed his hand, put it over his amulet, then kissed him hard on his lips, going up on my tiptoes to do so.

He laughed a little. "I guess not."

"So there you go."

"Your father saw us kiss and he didn't look happy about it."

"Yeah, I know."

"But he didn't say anything."

"Not in so many words. I think he's officially in denial that, despite all the rules and warnings, his half-demon daughter is . . . um, that she really likes a Shadow."

I almost, *almost* said "falling in love with." But I'd only known Michael less than two weeks. I liked him very, very much, but was I falling in love with him? So quickly?

The thought made my heart pick up its pace big-time and, despite the cold, I felt my cheeks flush.

"I think I finally understand why you broke up with me the other day," he said. "You were doing it to protect me, weren't you?"

"You're only realizing that now?"

His lips quirked. "I guess Kassandra was right when she said I wasn't too bright."

"She also said you were a hottie."

He shook his head, amused by this. "High praise from a demon princess."

"Don't get any ideas. She almost always gets what she wants, you know. I'd prefer it didn't include you."

His smile faded at the edges. "You were right to end things with me. I see that now. And not just for my protection, for yours as well. The rules—"

I shook my head. "I don't care about the rules or what my father might think."

"Yes, you do care. And you should. We've both seen first-hand what breaking them can lead to."

"Rules can bend," I said firmly. "And they can change."

He nodded. "I never thought so before, but now I think you might be right about that. Maybe not today, but someday. Until then, though, we need to be careful."

"Agreed. Careful is the way to be. But one thing I've learned from this experience, and from Queen Sephina of all people, is that there are shades of gray for everything. Including us."

"So that means that we're not together, but . . ."

"But we're not *not* together."

"That doesn't even make any sense."

"Trust me, it totally does."

He grinned. "If you say so."

"I do."

Shades of gray. It made me think of how Michael looked in complete Shadow form, able to drain all the energy of another living creature like Jonas had. The horrible thought twisted my stomach into knots.

"Try to forget what happened today," Michael said quietly. "Tomorrow will be better."

Forget what happened? As if that was even possible.

"Promise?" I asked.

"I promise."

"Good night, Princess."

"Good night, Michael."

He smiled, then turned and began walking away. He hadn't asked for his sweatshirt back, so I kept it, pulling it tighter around me to keep out the cold night.

I'd seen what a Shadow could really do. The reason demons were forbidden to like Shadows as more than servants was the risk of getting too close and becoming an energy meal. It was the reason some demons feared them—at least, the ones who knew what Shadows were truly capable of.

If he wanted to, Michael could be more powerful than any demon. After all, how could you fight something that didn't have solid form?

I thought of the second prophecy Irena had told me about— of the darkness that followed me, that wanted to devour me—and of Chris's drawing showing that darkness beginning to obliterate me from view.

It probably had been Jonas's shadow they'd both seen. He'd almost killed me, after all.

It *wasn't* Michael.

I knew he'd never hurt me. Not in a million years.

Even though I believed that completely, I still had a really hard time getting to sleep that night. And when I did, the nightmares arrived right on schedule.

23

I took all of Sunday to recover from my trip to the Underworld, barely even getting out of bed. I woke up on Monday morning with a clear head and a new purpose.

I wouldn't hide from my problems anymore. I'd face them— all of them—head-on.

My first problem was my mom. I'd decided to tell her, once and for all, that I'd been in contact with my father.

I'd say something along the lines of, *"Dad contacted me and I'm positive he still loves you. How do you feel about that?"* rather than, *"My father's a demon and, FYI, that makes me half demon. If you're interested in seeing him again, you'll have to be supercareful because there are all these stupid rules, and I don't want you to get yourself killed."*

That might freak her out too much or cause her to enroll me in the nearest insane asylum. Therefore, baby steps.

It would be enough to see if there really was any hope there. Hope worth fighting for.

"Hey, Mom, I need to talk to you." I cautiously approached her at the kitchen table. Bright sunlight shone through the window that looked over the snow-covered front lawn and driveway.

"Nikki." She put her newspaper down. "I need to talk to you, too."

"Oh? About what?"

"Sit down."

I tensed. "What's wrong?"

She cleared her throat. "You want me to be happy, right?"

"Happy? Of course I do. Listen, if this is about what happened last week, I'm really sorry. I'm over my drama, and I won't be taking off to the mall alone anymore without telling you."

"Well . . . good. But that's not what I wanted to talk about."

I frowned. "Okay, then what is it?"

She fiddled with the edge of the newspaper. "I know it might seem like I don't have very good taste in men, but . . . well, maybe I don't. But sometimes things happen for a reason."

"What are you talking about?"

"I just don't want you to hear it from somewhere else. It's about Nathan, your biology teacher."

"What about him?"

"He wants to see me again. Regularly. But I don't want this to be awkward for you."

A lump had quickly formed in my throat. "You *like* him?"

She nodded. "Yes."

"And you're officially dating him."

"I knew you might object—with him being a teacher at your school and with it being so close to my upcoming divorce from Robert—but, I know deep down in my heart . . . that there's *someone* out there for me." She sighed. "And if I stop looking, stop hoping, then I might never find him."

My throat tightened. "Oh. And you think that's Nathan . . . er, I mean, Mr. Crane?"

"I don't know. Maybe. Maybe not." She grabbed my hands in hers. "This doesn't mean that the two of us can't still have fun together. It's not like Nathan and I are eloping or anything. We're just dating. But . . . but can you at least try to understand?"

I didn't answer, instead crossing my arms and chewing my bottom lip.

"What is it?" she asked. "If there's something you want to say, just say it."

I opened my mouth, then closed it. "No . . . I . . . it's nothing. I think you should date whoever you want without worrying what I think of it."

She smiled. "Thank you, honey. Maybe we can both have wonderful new boyfriends after our bad experiences. Me and Nathan, you and . . . what was his name? Rhys? He's a real cutie-pie."

"I need to get to school." I grabbed my backpack, disappointment thudding through me.

"What about breakfast?"

"I'll . . . I'll grab something there." I paused. "I do want you to be happy, Mom. Seriously. Whatever it takes. I love you."

"I love you, too, honey." She hugged me tightly. "Now hurry up and get to school."

Without another word I was out of there. She hadn't even

given me a chance to mention my father. Was this a big fat sign I shouldn't ever say anything to her?

Maybe I was being selfish wanting my parents to get together after all this time. Maybe it would have been wrong to tell Mom about my father today. I'd wait and see what happened with Mr. Crane.

I shuddered. I couldn't believe she was going to date one of my teachers.

"Good morning, Princess." Michael came out of nowhere and began to keep pace with me. I hadn't even seen him appear.

I looked at him with equal parts surprise and happiness. "Why are you here?"

He glanced at me sideways, giving me a half smile.

"I mean," I began again, "good morning to you, too. Uh, why are you here?"

His eyes were almost as bright green as they'd been on Saturday night. "Your father wanted me to let you know he's spoken directly with Queen Sephina, and she's promised Prince Kieran will be punished severely for what he attempted to do."

"Really? Punished how?"

"He's being sent to Hell to inspect and report on all the dungeons there. I hear there are thousands of them. He can't leave until he finishes. I'm thinking it'll take him decades."

I couldn't help but grin. Kieran would absolutely hate that. Served him right. I felt some much-needed relief at the idea that he'd be occupied for a very long time. "Not as good as putting him in a dungeon and throwing away the key, but it's a nice start. So that's why you're here? To give me that news?"

"Yes, and I also wanted to walk you to school this morning. Is that okay?"

My smile grew. "If I said yes, would that make me seem needy?"

"Not at all."

He didn't try to hold my hand. Instead we just walked side by side to the high school. It felt good to have him here without any emergency to deal with. He was someone else—other than Rhys—who I could be completely open with. Who knew my secrets and seemed to like me anyway. I could even talk to Michael about things I'd never share with Rhys.

I told him about my mom dating a teacher when I'd rather she get back together with my father, even though I knew all too well it was against the rules.

"They're very different," he said when I'd finished. "From different worlds. She's human and he's a demon."

"So what? It worked before. I know she loved him more than anyone else."

"Do you know that for sure, or are you just hoping it's true?"

I shook my head. "I don't know. It's a gut feeling."

"If it's meant to be, it'll just happen."

I turned to comment on his fate-filled outlook but noticed his attention was elsewhere now that we'd reached the school. I followed his line of sight.

Rhys was leaning against the wall of the school, watching our approach.

"The faery king is waiting for you," Michael said without enthusiasm. "I really don't like how he looks at you, Princess. When's he going back to his regular home?"

"I don't know—"

He kissed me. Right there in front of everybody, including Rhys. And it was a *really* good kiss.

"What happened to being careful?" I asked when we parted.

"From this moment forward, we'll be careful." He glanced again at Rhys and his lips thinned. "Just promise to be careful with *him*."

"Cross my heart."

"Till next time, Princess."

I wished for the thousandth time that he went to school here with me.

After another moment, I turned and started walking toward the school entrance.

"I think your Shadow is trying to tell me something," Rhys said.

"You think?"

He nodded. "But he doesn't have to worry. I'm not interested in you that way. I've already forgotten about our kiss under the mistletoe."

If he'd forgotten it, why would he bother mentioning it?

"Well . . . good." I cleared my throat. Rhys was looking at me very closely, gauging my every reaction.

"I assume everything went okay?" he said. "You're still alive."

"Okay" was not really the word I'd use for my experiences in the Underworld.

"It's over, that's the important part." I eyed him. "By the way, the prophecy was a lie created to make me look bad and possibly lead to my death. So there's no reason for you to stick around any longer."

"I had a feeling it was a false prophecy."

"You did? Why?"

He shrugged. "Because I know you now." Then he looked at the ground. "However, I'm still staying. For a while, anyway. I want to experience the human world before going back to the faery realm to be king full-time. I have to return regularly, most evenings and weekends, but I can come back to school here in the new year. Is that going to be a problem for you?"

I thought about it. Of all my problems, this one was low on the list. In fact, the thought that somebody as weird as me was going to keep attending Erin Heights High was actually comforting. "No. As long as you promise not to try to kill me."

Rhys grinned at that. "I think I'd have to get in line. You know your best friend is a demon slayer, right?"

I froze. "How did you know that?"

"Isn't it totally obvious?"

"No."

"You're right. It isn't obvious at all. But I explored her house on Saturday night after you left and found myself unable to resist a locked door." He glanced to his left and waved at a rapidly approaching Melinda. "Here she comes now. Maybe we should tell her your little secret."

I grabbed his arm and dug my fingers in hard. "Don't you dare."

He grimaced. "Ouch. You're strong."

"And don't you forget it."

Melinda stopped when she got to us. "Hey."

"Hi," I managed. After everything that had happened—and even taking into consideration my new decision to face all of my problems instead of running away from them—I was basically tongue-tied in front of my best friend.

"Can I talk to you?" she asked me, with a glance at Rhys. "Alone?"

"I can take a hint. I'll see you later, Melinda. Nikki." He held my gaze a moment longer, and I saw those now-familiar gold flecks swirl in his brown eyes. Then he entered the school, leaving me and Melinda alone outside. A cool breeze zipped past me and I shivered.

"You didn't come back to my party," she said.

"No, I'm . . . I'm sorry."

"You went somewhere with that Michael guy?"

"Yeah."

She frowned. "Isn't he the guy who was hanging around two weeks ago staring at you all the time? The one who was lurking outside your house?"

I cleared my throat. "Uh, well, yeah. That's him. But he's actually a friend. Nothing to worry about."

"He's kind of cute for a stalker."

"Trust me, he's not a stalker. Look, about what happened at your party—"

Melinda held up a hand. "Rhys already explained everything to me."

A breath caught in my throat. "He did?"

"He said he'd had too much wine—thanks to Larissa—and kissed you as a joke before you pushed him away."

"A joke?" My eyebrows went up. "He really said that?"

She nodded. "I'm so sorry I doubted you. I never should have done that. I value your friendship so much, and I don't want to put it at risk because of stupid misunderstandings. And I won't let any guy come between us again, I promise, no matter who he is."

"You had every right. That . . . I know that didn't look so good."

"It's okay." She smiled. "Besides, Rhys finally asked me out."

I blinked. "He what?"

"He has to go home over school break and visit his family, but he says he wants to see me when we get back in January. I guess he broke up with his old girlfriend after all."

"Um, wow. I didn't know that. That's . . . that's great?"

What was he doing? Why would he ask Melinda out? Was he crazy? He was a faery king. Besides, I'd never gotten the impression he'd even noticed Melinda, let alone liked her enough to date her.

But maybe he did. Maybe I'd been too blinded by my own problems to notice anything else.

I had to admit, part of me was happy that Melinda would get what she wanted, even though I knew it couldn't possibly end well. I'd have to keep a very close eye on the two of them.

I ignored the smaller part of me that felt a slight twinge of jealousy at the idea of Rhys and Melinda dating. I mean, how did *that* make sense? I wanted to be with *Michael*, not Rhys. It couldn't happen now, but I was willing to wait as long as necessary. I didn't like Rhys that way. I never had and I never would.

"Listen, Melinda," I began, ready to face another problem

head-on. "When I was at your house the other day, before the party, I overheard you and Patrick talking—"

She held up a hand. "I quit."

"What?"

"I quit my . . . my dance lessons."

I stared at her blankly. "I don't understand."

She took in a deep breath and then exhaled slowly. "It's been too much. It's been really distracting and overwhelming and I never liked it. In fact, I *hate* my lessons. Even though my parents insist . . . well, they can't make me do anything I don't want to do. So I quit. It's over." She gave me a shaky smile. "I can finally be normal again."

She'd quit her demon-slaying lessons. Just like that?

"You're sure?" I asked tentatively.

"Yes."

"So you don't want to be a . . . a dancer?"

She hesitated. "No, I don't. To be a dancer I'd have to give up too much, sacrifice almost everything else in my life for something I don't even believe in doing. I don't want that. I want to go to school, and hang out with you, and date Rhys . . ." She smiled. "That's just how it's going to be. If anyone has a problem with it, then that's just too bad."

"Well, good."

She nodded, and then her gaze moved over my shoulder and she swallowed hard. "I just wish he'd leave me alone."

"Who?"

"Patrick."

I looked over to see a black car pulled up at the curb a dozen feet away. Patrick was behind the wheel.

"Melinda," he called.

"Would you just go away, please?" she shouted back. "I told you, it's over."

"It's not over," he replied. From what I could see, his expression was tense. "I can't give up on you."

"Then you need to try harder." She turned her back to him.

"I'll give you some time to clear your head, but then I'll be back. This has only just begun, Melinda. I promise you that." After another moment, he shook his head and drove off.

"Is he gone?" she asked.

"He is."

Melinda's eyes were shiny and she sniffed hard. "He doesn't want me to quit. Says that it's in my blood. I disagree."

The entire subject made me extremely uncomfortable. "He said he'd be back. Maybe he'll be able to convince you then."

"I don't want to talk about this anymore. It's over. And I'm happy for the first time in weeks." Her expression brightened as I followed her inside the school and we went to our lockers.

I spotted Chris, sitting by himself, his back against his locker. He was scribbling away in a sketchbook he had propped against his knees.

Melinda nodded at him. "Do you have any idea what's up with Chris? He's been acting so strange lately."

I shook my head. "I guess we all can act strange now and then, can't we?"

"Good point."

Chris looked up at me and our eyes met. He frowned and looked away again.

What was he drawing? Another vision about me? Or about someone else?

It could be a lot of things.

My best friend was a demon slayer who'd just quit her training sessions despite her very persistent instructor. My biology partner was the king of the faery realm whom I was prophesied to marry some day. My sort-of boyfriend was a Shadow prince–servant with the potential to fully drain a demon's life energy as easily as if he were drinking a milkshake.

And to top it off, my mother was now dating one of my teachers.

"We're *so* going to the mall today," Melinda said after a moment. "It's a rule that all students are supposed to go to the holiday pageant in the cafeteria at noon, but let's blow it off and leave early."

I considered that. "If we break that rule, will they throw us in the dungeon?"

She blinked at me. "What?"

I forced a laugh. "Just kidding, of course. Let's do it."

Forget dungeons, demons, Shadows, faeries, slayers, or even giant talking cockroaches . . . those things could totally wait for another day.

After all, I still had some major last-minute Christmas shopping to do.

Acknowledgments

Thank you to my editor, Stacy Cantor, for being such a complete joy to work with. My eternal gratitude also goes to Deb Shapiro and the team at Walker Books for Young Readers for all their hard work with my little demon princess.

Thanks to my agent, Jim McCarthy, for general awesomeness in all that he has done and continues to do.

Thanks to Jennifer Black, who gave *Reign Check* a beta read to make sure Nikki did, in fact, sound like a teenager and not a thirty-something writer.

Shout-outs to a few of my author BFFs (you can have more than one, y'know) who make me realize that being a writer means being a part of a wonderful, giving (and sometimes hilariously snarky) community: Eve Silver, Jackie Kessler, Richelle Mead, Megan Crane, Liza Palmer, Mark Henry, Gena Showalter, Heather Brewer, Amanda Ashby, Jill Myles, Charlene Teglia, Stephanie Rowe, and Michele Lang. You all rock!

And a huge thanks to my readers, who have had such wonderful things to say about Nikki's first adventure. I very much hope you enjoy this one, too!

Want to find out how it all began?

Then don't miss *Reign or Shine*

Discover . . .

How Nikki and Michael first met,

When she realized she was a **Demon** *Princess*, and

How she kicked some serious demon butt!